Important Author

Beyond Broadhall is the
The '86 Fix story, and if you haven't read the first book, this one isn't likely to make much sense.

So, if you're in the market for a 1980s time travel adventure, pick up a copy of The '86 Fix from Amazon.

If you've already read it, I hope you enjoy the next chapter of Craig's journey, beyond Broadhall…

Beyond Broadhall:
By Keith A Pearson

For more information about the author and to receive updates on his new releases, visit…

www.keithapearson.co.uk

JUNE 2017

1

One thing I really miss is the feel of carpet under my socked feet. It's a comforting feeling you just don't get when padding across clinical-grade linoleum. But with some of the Broadhall patients defecating on the floor with alarming regularity, carpet just isn't an option in our rooms. Things don't get much more homely above the floor. The magnolia walls of the twelve-foot-square room are bare, and the scant furnishings only extend to a desk, a chair, and a small wardrobe, all in flatpack beechwood veneer. It is a utilitarian room and for the moment, it's a place I reluctantly call home.

It's been eleven months since I sat in my teenage bedroom and my mundane life was cast into madness. I suppose you could argue it was a lot longer if you include the thirty year trip back to 1986. That weekend felt like a lifetime in itself. Ironic really, in that it prematurely ended a lifetime — mine. Now, after my mandatory incarceration at Broadhall Hospital, I am nearly a free man. Actually, that's not strictly true. I'm nearly free from the hospital walls, but I'm not free from the system that put me here. Nor am I free from the conflict and the torment which take turns to keep me awake at night.

I had an idea which I hoped might ease my insomnia. I told my case officer I wanted to put my feelings down on paper, and he took that as a positive sign. I was a little surprised when he gave me a notepad and a pen, expecting either denial or a crayon. That was just one of the many incorrect assumptions I initially made about life in a hospital for the mentally ill. I've not seen a single straitjacket and I'm not sure if that's a relief or a disappointment.

The first notepad was full within six weeks. The second within eleven weeks, and the third within fifteen weeks. My words ran out before the supply of notepads although I estimate I've still written over a hundred thousand words. Plenty of words, few answers.

My fourth notepad has been on the go for the last seven months, but I've only used the first thirty pages. I've already documented every minute of my weekend in 1986, and the days either side of it, so the fourth notepad contains mainly elaborate doodles and unanswered questions. My theory is that if I keep asking, something might come, but it never does.

With nothing more to write, I read the notepads over and over again. It feels like reading one of those best-selling novels that everyone buys despite reviewers highlighting the ludicrous plot and terrible ending. I keep reading in hope of finding both, but whatever plot was playing out over that weekend in 1986, I can't see it. I know what happened, I just don't know why. Nor do I know how it ends.

Inevitably, I always return to the first page of the first notepad, and the timeline of my inexplicable journey…

Thursday 14th July 2016 - visit parents' house circa 1.00pm and set up computer. Endure hallucinogenic episode and pass out.

Saturday 17th May 1986 - wake up at midnight. Pain, lots of. Sleep. Get up circa 8.00am as sixteen-year-old me.

Sunday 18th May 1986 - leave house just before midnight and run through streets. Pain, lots of. Pass out.

Sunday 17th July 2016 - wake up in hospital early morning. Told that Craig Pelling was killed in 1986. Head fucked.

Thursday 21st July 2016 - admitted to Broadhall Hospital.

I like playing with numbers, cracking algorithms. I still hold a theory that the dates, or at least the numbers contained within the dates, hold some meaning. I've worked through them in every conceivable way, but I still can't find a connection. Maybe there isn't one. Maybe there aren't any answers to be found. Either way, I'm now approaching the point where I have no choice but to stop looking back and start looking forward. My new life outside Broadhall, as Craig Wilson, is imminent.

I swing my legs off the bed and slip my trainers on. A glance at my watch — almost time to undertake my final challenge. If this goes as I hope, I should be deemed fit to re-enter society. The challenge is snappily named, 'The Assimilation & Integration Workshop'. Thirteen syllables and an unworkable acronym.

I stroll through the corridors of Broadhall and enter another featureless room to begin the final stage of my treatment. Once seated, I barely listen to my case officer, Stephen, as I consider how much time and ink has been wasted by giving the workshop such an unwieldy name.

He interrupts my thinking. "Craig, are you listening?"

Stephen is a nice enough chap. Early thirties, good-natured, and unbelievably patient. Born in Edinburgh, he speaks with a soft Scottish accent and has features to match: pale blue eyes, tangerine hair and milky-white freckled skin. It's his responsibility to ensure I pass seamlessly from institutionalised life back into the real world. I'm probably not making that task easy.

"Sorry, Stephen, go on."

"As I was saying, this pack contains all the basic documents you need to function. You have a bank account with a modest balance for essentials, a national insurance card, and a new birth certificate. There's also a letter of reference from your doctor should you need it for an employer, or if the job centre staff ask any awkward questions."

He hands me the envelope. The sum total of my new life, encapsulated in thin brown paper.

"Okay, Craig, are you happy to move onto the next module?"

I half-heartedly confirm I am. Today, like the last few months of my stay at Broadhall, is proving to be a painstaking experience. Perhaps if I was suffering from a genuine mental illness I'd welcome being treated like a child, but there is only so much condescension a man can stomach. As well meaning as the staff are, they couldn't begin to comprehend the real issues I have to contend with. I'm grateful they've created this new life for me, I really am, but it's a life in limbo until I can start living it.

"Sure. Ready when you are," I reply, trying to portray some semblance of positivity.

For five long hours I'm pummelled with information, interspersed with questions, tests, and then a final appraisal by a shrink. At the end of the workshop, my joy at being passed fit to return to society is slightly tempered when the psychiatrist simply signs a form and places it in my file. I was kind of hoping he'd thump the front of the file with a big ink stamp, imprinted with the word 'SANE'.

The shrink leaves the room, and just as I'm about to get up and follow, Stephen gets his second wind.

"Let's just go through the plan for tomorrow, shall we?"

I inwardly groan and sit back in my chair.

"I'll drive you to the flat at 9.00am, so you need to ensure you've got everything packed by 8.30am."

That allows about eighteen hours to pack my possessions. All I own, apart from my recently acquired brown envelope and four notepads is half a wardrobe of drab clothes purloined from a charitable organisation when I first arrived. My packing will more likely take eighteen seconds.

"Once we arrive at the flat, I'll show you around, help you unpack, and we'll go through the house rules."

More fucking rules. It never ends. My entire eleven months here has been governed by rules. From the time I need to be out of my room in the morning to the time I need to be back in the room at night, and everything I do in between.

"Is there anything else you want to know, any other questions or concerns?" Stephen asks.

I rigorously shake my head.

Once I've thanked Stephen for his time, I'm out of the door before he thinks of any other trifling details he's missed. I let myself relax a little as I amble through the network of beige corridors back to the sanctuary of my room.

I close the door and slump onto the bed. Nothing to do but kill time before my final dinner at Broadhall. I lock my hands behind my head and stare at the ceiling. Now I'm in the silent confines of my room, I wait for the inevitable cascade of questions my mind will pose. These are the same questions I've asked myself a hundred times a day, and have done every day since they told me I was to be discharged. Despite the constant asking, I'm still no closer to answering any of them.

The most pressing, and significant question relates to this new life of mine.

This time tomorrow I will be sat in my own flat, having tasted the first day in the real world as Craig Wilson; a man with very little past and an uncertain future ahead. God willing, I should still have a good few years ahead of me and enough time to build a new life. I have a blank canvas on which to paint a portrait of the man I always wanted to be. It's a befitting analogy because Craig Wilson will be a two-dimensional man. It's our past that shapes us, provides depth; the light and dark of who we are. I no longer have a past, well, not one I can claim as my own. What does that make me? No friends, no family, no wife — it makes me irrelevant to virtually every person on the planet.

Whenever I think about my new life, I can't help but think about the one I lost. But that is a serious head-fucking exercise; a one-way ticket to crazy town. So why doesn't it ever go away? Why does my mind torture me by demanding answers? I think I know — closure. I need to know what happened to the people I left behind, the lives I forever changed. In particular I want to know what happened to my parents. It's a need more than a want. Some days I don't want to know because I fear it will be too horrific to bear. Other days I feel more optimistic they might have rebuilt their lives after my death.

And that's a phrase I will never be able to reconcile — my death.

No matter how many times I've tried, it's impossible to get my head around the fact I terminated my own life. I ran from my teenage bedroom and stood in the middle of the road. And in doing so, I put myself in front of the van that killed me. I was responsible for the death of sixteen year-old Craig Pelling.

Yet despite all logic and all reasoning, I continue to exist. I can only guess that I was struck by the van at the precise moment my body was between the two timelines. My teenage self was killed but I must have already been too far advanced on my journey to the future. I don't have the answer but I do know every time I think about it, I spin my mind around in an endless loop of infinite paradigms. I've got beyond the fact I did it, and the shear stupidity of my actions, but I still struggle to understand why I'm here. It's one of those questions that nobody can answer, like what lies beyond the known universe, or who voted for Honey G on X Factor.

To try and shift my mind from the question of my existence, I grab my first notepad from beneath the pillow and flick through the pages. I study the words and hope the answer will leap out at me like a bug in a line of computer code. It was Einstein who said that the definition of madness was doing the same thing over and over again but expecting different results. Reading the notes again is my madness. Still no answers but that doesn't mean I'm not without some theories. And tomorrow, I may feel inclined to explore those theories. We'll see.

I put the notepad back under my pillow and let my mind drift to the consolations I have clung to during my time at Broadhall. I'm fairly sure that the hyperacusis I once suffered is no more. I discovered it was linked to anxiety and a series of treatments helped me deal with that. I'll only know for sure if it worked when I next hear a dog bark. Then there's my weight. I arrived here the wrong side of seventeen stone but at my last medical appraisal, I tipped the scales at a shade over eleven. My body is now lithe, the subcutaneous fat gradually burnt away through the combination of a limited diet and strenuous exercise. I no longer have to avoid mirrors.

Then there is this new future I created.

Although I may have screwed up my own life immeasurably, others may have benefited. My parents were happier than they had ever been, although the sad irony is that their new-found happiness was fleeting; cut short as their son was terminated by a Ford Transit. I hope that they managed to support one another and maybe found a way past their grief. The consolation I have chosen to accept is that my grandparents should have escaped their premature deaths in 1994 as a result of my chat with Aunt Judy. Indeed, she herself was left in a better place, ready to face her own demons in the shape of the paedophile, Malcolm Duffy. I've tried to search for the case online but we are only able to access a handful of websites on the computers here. Apparently the censorship is for our own protection but it's a reminder that this is as much a prison as it is a hospital.

And what of my wife, Megan? Many a night I have lain in bed picturing her new future. At first, I couldn't escape the irrational jealousy my visions summoned but deep down I knew it was for the best. The Megan I first met at Video City deserved happiness. She didn't deserve to live a life barren, bitter and resentful. I imagine her living in a big house now. Happy, fulfilled. I see her cuddling up on the couch with a better husband than me. I see her readying children for school; a boy and a girl, handsome and pretty. I picture dinner times; the four of them sat around a table in a farmhouse-style kitchen. I see the future that I knew Megan always wanted but we never had the chance to live. It took a while but eventually the images of Megan's happy home brought contentment. I hope they're a fair portrayal of her new reality, I really do.

Beyond Megan there's Malcolm, Marcus and Geoff — three lives I tampered with to varying degrees during my weekend in 1986.

Assuming Malcolm heeded my advice, his beloved Star Wars collection should have remained in his possession, rather than that of the thieves who stole it from the back room of Video City in 1990. Whether he sold it or continued it, I hope that both possibilities kept him away from Mali Surat, his devious Thai bride. However, I can't see Malcolm still being alive if I'm honest. He wasn't exactly a health-conscious man, and I have grave doubts he would have lived much beyond his seventies whether Mali Surat had fed him to death or not. Maybe he had a more befitting end to his time on earth though. I hope he did, and at least I gave him some chance of that.

My former schoolmate and subsequent boss, Marcus Morrison, is an interesting one. I didn't confront him for his own benefit, more the benefit of everyone he treated like shit. I'd be lying if I said I wasn't a tad curious how Marcus's life panned-out after our altercation at the skate park. Did he come to terms with his sexuality sooner, or bury it deeper? Did he finally stand up to his homophobic father? And if he did either, is Marcus Morrison now a better man for it? It would be easy to hope Marcus had an awful life but it wouldn't make me feel any better. Maybe my intervention was the catalyst Marcus needed to reflect on his attitude and behaviour.

Geoff Waddock, my former colleague at RolpheTech, is a footnote. I have no idea what Apple stock is worth these days but if Geoff did follow my impromptu advice and invest in it, rather than in banking stocks, he should be a wealthy man. Maybe I should get in touch with him and see if he wants to offer a reward for my sage investment advice. He never knew me as a sixteen-year-old and therefore would have been unaware the teenager who called him in 1986 died a few hours later. Perhaps it's not such a ridiculous notion if I do get desperate for money.

And lastly, there are the two women who bookended my life — Tessa and Lucy.

I can't imagine things would have turned out differently for Tessa after my aborted seduction and warning about Marcus. I wonder if she did marry that lead singer of a semi-famous band or if perhaps life took her in another direction. It doesn't really matter if I'm honest. I have now come to terms with the fact Tessa was never going to be part of my life, this or my former. She's now just the girl who took my virginity, well, Craig Pelling's virginity.

Of all the lives that I am no longer part of, there is one, apart from my mother, which brings the greatest lament — Lucy. The ten years we worked together are gone and although I could walk back into her life tomorrow, we'd be strangers. It's not an option anyway. By now, Lucy should be enjoying her new life in Brighton. Even though RolpheTech never closed in this timeline, and I don't know why it didn't, her sister's offer would have still have materialised as before. Lucy would have still sold up and moved with her daughter. It's ironic that Lucy's departure is the one event I never instigated but it still summons the deepest regret. I miss her.

On balance, my brief trip to 1986 might not have been a complete disaster for everyone and perhaps some lives are better for my interference.

Whether I want to find out if those lives are better, is another question.

2

There are two breakfast sittings at Broadhall. I take the early sitting which is between 7.45am and 8.30am. Supposedly, this sitting is for patients who are less likely to self-harm with a butter knife or hurl their porridge around the canteen. I have never considered either, so I take my seat and dig into a bowl of municipal muesli. The word bland doesn't do it justice. However, it is a staple of the diet which has enabled me to shed almost six stones of bulk from my frame, so I put up with it. I don't even think of it as food any more; it's just fuel without fat, sugar, or flavour.

I eat quickly and leave the canteen before anyone can try to engage me in conversation. I have avoided meaningful conversation with other patients throughout my stay, and I have no desire to change that now. I hurry back to my room to find Stephen waiting for me.

"Morning, Craig. Thought this might come in handy."

He hands me a battered black holdall. "It's not exactly Louis Vuitton but it'll do the job," he adds apologetically.

I take the holdall and try to ignore the radiating whiff of sweaty trainers.

"Thanks, Stephen, appreciated."

"So, how are you feeling?" he asks, for possibly the thousandth time since we first met.

"Excited," I reply with a smile.

I know the game now, and how to play it. Even the slightest sign that I'm anything less than deliriously happy and Stephen will jump on it.

"Good, I'll leave you to pack," he says as he takes a glance at his watch. "I'll meet you at my office in, shall we say, half an hour?"

"To be honest Stephen, I really want to get out of here. Any chance we can leave sooner? I'll be packed in a few minutes."

"Um, okay," he agrees, obliging as ever. "Give me five minutes to get your release paperwork ready."

I thank him, and he darts off to reschedule his morning, closing the door behind him. I drop the holdall in the corner of the room and take a seat on the edge of the bed. This chapter of my life is nearly over. I consider Stephen's question and how I'm really feeling. Nervous, a little apprehensive maybe. Above all though, my analytical mind wants to deal with the questions that have been haunting me for the last eleven months. I know I'll never be able to ignore them. I could try to move forward and forget my life as Craig Pelling but what life would that be? Realistically I can't plan for any sort of future if I'm still tethered to the past.

I have no option but to put my mind at rest, get the answers I seek, and the closure I need. Only then can Craig Wilson begin to live his life.

I get up from the bed and grab the holdall. A quick spray of deodorant to mask the smell before I stuff the contents of the wardrobe into it. There's no thought to the haphazard packing process as I tuck the four notepads down the side and lay the brown envelope on top of the balled clothes. I then grab my limited collection of toiletries and zip them into a pocket on the side of the holdall. Packing completed within forty-five seconds.

I stand in the middle of the room and slowly survey my temporary home for the last time. I'm not sure why, it's not as though there is any sentimental attachment to it. Sometimes I forget it was never my decision to call this place home. It's a prison for broken souls and a hospital for broken minds. It has served its purpose. Time for me to move on.

I grab the holdall and leave without a backward glance.

Fifteen minutes later and I'm strolling across the staff car park, legally a free man. Stephen is at my side, fiddling with a bunch of keys as we approach a row of cars parked in front of an imposing brick wall. Another reminder of what this place really is.

Stephen points towards a pea-green Citroen 2CV parked at the end of the row.

"That's me," he says proudly.

It's an embarrassing excuse for a car but as long as it gets me out of this place, I'll take the ride.

Stephen unlocks the driver's door and drops into his seat, the thin body panels creaking their objection. He reaches across and unlocks my door. I throw my holdall onto the back seat and clamber in. We exit the car park and crawl noisily in second gear towards the main gates. A uniformed jobsworth checks Stephen's paperwork and slowly walks around the car, inspecting each side with feigned diligence. Satisfied there are no escapees clinging to the bodywork, the guard waves us on as the barrier in front of us slowly raises. All that stands between life at Broadhall Hospital and the real world is twenty yards of tarmac. I smile to myself as we swing left onto the main road. Freedom.

Our destination is my former home town of Farndale, about fifteen miles north of Broadhall. I was given the option of where to start my new life and my decision prompted an awkward conversation with

Stephen. He questioned why I wanted to live in Craig Pelling's home town — my original claim that I was the deceased teenager being the primary reason for my incarceration. I told him I had vague memories of living in the town at some point in my former life and he eventually conceded that perhaps the familiar surroundings might help me to settle.

As we navigate through the rural roads away from Broadhall, I get the opportunity to determine if my hyperacusis really has been cured. Notwithstanding Stephen cheerfully wittering away about nothing in particular, the car provides an assortment of random metallic sounds. Mile after mile of squeaking, rattling, and grinding, accompanied by the weedy engine incessantly screeching in protest at its workload. I spend most of the journey grimacing while I reminisce about the quiet interior of my shitty Mazda.

We eventually reach the outskirts of Farndale and turn into a quiet residential street that just about falls within the town's southern boundary. After a few hundred yards Stephen eases off the accelerator and the engine lowers its tone to a waspish rattle, low enough we can actually hear one another.

"It's just up here on the left," he says as he helpfully raises his hand and points towards the houses on my left.

"That's left, eh?"

"Sorry," he says as his milky-white cheeks blossom pink.

He swings the car towards the kerb and turns off the engine. The brief moment of silence is exquisite.

"Right, ready?"

"Yep."

I'm out of the car before he has the chance to analyse my three-letter reply.

I grab my holdall from the back seat and Stephen joins me on the tree-lined pavement. We stand side-by-side and look at the charmless brick building in front of us. A matching pair of detached 1930s houses stand either side; one rendered pale blue and the other a buttery yellow. My new home is the proverbial sore thumb.

"It's much nicer inside," Stephen chirps, as if he'd read my mind.

We make our way down the path towards the communal front door. Stephen informs me there are six flats in the block and my home, for the next few months at least, will be number five on the second floor. He points out the entryphone system as he unlocks the door and holds it open for me. We make our way through the drab entrance hall and up two flights of stairs to an equally drab landing, the doors to flats five and six opposite each other.

Stephen opens the door to flat five and I follow him into a tiny hallway. I release my hold on the heavy front door and it slams shut behind me, casting us into darkness. Panic ensues as we both blindly pat the walls looking for a light switch. Stephen gets lucky and a weak bulb coughs into life above our heads. We're standing uncomfortably close to one another.

"The lounge is through here, I think," Stephen stammers as he grabs the nearest door handle. It's the bathroom.

"Must be this one."

We make our escape into a room about twenty feet long by about twelve feet wide. A modern fitted kitchen with built-in appliances occupies a third of the room to my left and the rest of the space is designated as the lounge, dominated by a rust-coloured couch and armchair. It's all very clean, bright, and functional. The few sticks of furniture are the same beechwood veneer as those in my room at Broadhall. I'm disappointed to see the floor is covered with laminated wood rather than carpet.

"What do you think?" Stephen asks.

"Yeah, really nice. I like it."

It's not exactly homely but it's a step up from my previous accommodation. Stephen invites me to take a look around the rest of the flat: a small double bedroom, a bathroom, and a storage cupboard. Even taking into account the fifteen seconds I waste needlessly staring into a cupboard, it's a brief tour. I return to the lounge where Stephen has seated himself in the armchair.

"Let's just go through the house rules and then I can leave you in peace."

I grit my teeth and smile. *Nearly there Craig, keep calm.*

"I need to stress that the property is owned and managed by Social Services so if you break any of the rules, they do have the power to evict you. Understood?"

I nod and he hands me a sheet of paper containing the rules which I'm expected to abide by.

"Have a read through at your leisure, but the main rule they're really strict on is that you're not allowed guests in the property between the hours of 11.00pm and 8.00am."

Seeing as I don't know a soul, let alone anyone I'd invite for a sleepover, I can't see that being a problem for me.

"And they're also strict on anti-social behaviour, noise in particular. It's a fairly quiet street and they don't want any of the tenants upsetting the neighbours."

Also not a problem for me.

Stephen hands me a folder containing instruction manuals for the appliances and heating, a list of contact numbers, and a map of local amenities.

"There is a telephone in the bedroom but it only accepts incoming calls. You'll have to sort yourself out with a cheap mobile phone if you want to make calls."

"Great. I think I'm good to go then," I reply as I stand up, hoping Stephen gets the hint.

He does, and he gets up from the armchair and hands me the keys to the flat. I see him out the door with a handshake and a promise to call on Thursday with an update.

Once the door is closed I stand in the tiny hallway for a moment to appreciate the complete silence. How I've missed it. Even at night, Broadhall was never totally quiet as an after-hours soundtrack of closing doors, hushed voices, and footfall played on a constant loop.

I return to the couch and unzip the holdall. I pull out the most recent notepad and a pen, sit back, and take a deep breath. My new life begins with a to-do list. My new bank account has a balance of £200 which has to last until I receive my first job-seeker's allowance. I've never claimed any benefits in my life but it looks like I'm going to need some state assistance for a while. I'll nip into the job centre tomorrow. In the meantime I need to get some food in, and sort out a mobile phone.

I make another list of the basic provisions I'll need and tuck it into my pocket, along with the bank card and pin number. I consult the map for the nearest convenience store and determine it's only a half-mile walk. Then another marker on the map catches my attention — the library.

It's been a good few years since I last set foot in a library but I'm fairly sure they provide computers with free, and more importantly, unrestricted Internet access. And access to the Internet is what I need to begin my quest for answers.

I drop the notepad on the couch and clasp my hands together. I need to think about this as once I open the lid on my past, there's no putting it back. Stick or twist? Every thought and every plan I had for this moment is now a reality, and a far cry from the theoretical.

Notwithstanding the fact I'm almost certainly stuck with this life, do I really want to begin it by discovering how my actions in 1986 affected those around me? Thirty-one long years have passed since that weekend. If those actions created positive outcomes then that's great, and I can move forward with that fact as a consolation. But what if I made things worse for anyone? Can I cope with an already weighty burden of guilt?

Push forward or take a glance behind me? What to do.

If it were not for two particular people, I think, on balance, I might have chosen to remain ignorant. While I might be keen to learn the fate of Lucy, Megan, Aunt Judy, et al., I can probably live without knowing. But the need to discover how my parents fared is too strong.

I get up, reassure myself I'm doing the right thing, and leave the flat.

3

As I stroll along the road away from the flat, I keep a close eye out for anomalies in my surroundings. Call me paranoid but when you've been institutionalised for eleven months, it's hard not to let your imagination run wild. I've seen enough time-travel films to understand the potential consequences when you mess with the past. In one of the Terminator movies, mankind is almost obliterated by computers, simply because one guy developed a dubious program called Skynet. I doubt my dabbling with the timeline will have such grave consequences, but you never know.

Half a mile later, I see nothing to suggest mankind is at war with our Microsoft Overlords.

My other paranoid concern is that somebody will recognise me as Craig Pelling. I assure myself it's a ludicrous concern. It's been almost thirty-one years since the teenage version of me walked these streets. I doubt even my own mother would be able to spot any obvious similarities between that gawky kid and the man I am today. And what reason would anyone else have to remember Craig Pelling? I silently chide myself and accept the chances of being recognised are virtually nil.

The library is a good twenty minute walk from the flat and once my paranoia subsides, I savour every step. To feel the slight summer breeze and warm sun on my skin, without being hemmed-in by chainlink fencing, is a simple but sweet pleasure. I should have done this more often, and seeing as I no longer have a driving licence, I will be doing this more often. Craig Wilson has never passed a driving test — something else I have to put on my to-do list.

When I reach the front door of the library, it’s almost with disappointment that I have to swap the sun-bathed street for the gloomy interior. Maybe my reluctance to enter is also because I’m minutes from potentially unearthing some bitter truths.

I push open the door and head through a lobby into the main library. A quick scan and I spot the enquiry desk off to the right, a diminutive women with pearl-coloured hair sat behind. I approach the desk and offer a smile to the tiny woman. She looks up at me over the thick frame of her glasses.

“What can I do for you?” she asks, her voice crisp but friendly.

“I need to use a computer to check some stuff on the Internet. Is that possible?”

Despite lying to people in authority for the last eleven months, my voice says “stuff” but I’m sure my face says “porn”.

“I assume you’ve not booked a computer with us before?” she replies.

“Err, no. I’ve just moved here.”

“Okay, that would explain why you don’t know the system. You need to book a computer in advance.”

“Right. How do I do that?”

“You can do it online,” she replies without a drop of irony in her voice.

“So if I want to use a library computer to access the Internet, I need to use a computer with Internet access to book it?”

“Yes, that’s right. Or you can phone in.”

I puff my cheeks and count to ten in my head.

“To avoid having to go outside, find a phone box and call you, can I book one now please?”

She turns to her left and grabs a yellow folder which she opens and studies intently.

"We've got slots available every day this week. When were you thinking of booking?"

"Now maybe?"

"No problem. If you're not a member, we just need you to complete a form and provide some ID."

I want to throttle her for taking me around the houses, but I offer a pained smile and comply with her request. A few minutes later I take a seat in front of an archaic computer monitor with an hour of web browsing booked. This is it.

I'm about to conduct my first search, fingers hovering over the keyboard as my heart beats a little faster. Do I really want to do this? I spin the question around in my mind for the thousandth time. There is no right or wrong answer, only instinct. But can I really trust my instinct again? My mind flashes back to the time I was sat in front of the Commodore 64 in my teenage bedroom. I trusted my instinct then and look what happened. Different keyboard, same idiot calling the shots.

My fingers grow impatient and take control of the situation, almost of their own volition they type…

Farndale Borough electoral role online

Before I can make a conscious decision not to, I hit the enter key and click the first link for the council website. My eyes scan the page looking for an obvious way to search the electoral roll to determine if my parents are still living in Farndale. The page only tells me how to add my own details, remove them, or edit them. There doesn't appear to be any way to search for local residents online. However, the final line on the page informs me that I can check a physical copy of the electoral roll at my local library. That's handy, assuming I don't have to book an appointment.

I go back to the Google home page and search both my parents' names. I suffer several false-dawns as I click links to pages that either require payment to view the information or are clearly for different people with the same name. My basic bank card is only good for cash machine withdrawals so I have no way to make an online payment. It was always going to be a long shot as my parents were technophobes so I can't see them having social media accounts. Couple that with the old man's obsession about his personal information falling into the hands of marketing companies, it's no surprise there's little sign of them online.

I decide not to waste too much time searching for my parents. I'll go and take a look at the electoral roll once I've finished at the computer. Beyond my parents, there are a few other names I want to search for, before my hour expires.

I go to the Facebook home page and groan when it prompts me to join before I can do anything. My frustration mounts when I realise I don't have the necessary email address to open a Facebook account. Another five minutes are wasted as I try to set up a Gmail account with my new name, only to be repeatedly informed that virtually every suffixed version of 'Craig Wilson' is already registered. I lose patience and settle on craigwilson1686@gmail.com.

With my new email address in hand, I set up my Facebook account. Finally, and with almost half my time already used, I'm able to start searching for people.

I stop and ponder who I should start with. Maybe it would be better to begin with somebody I have the least concern for. I decide on Marcus and type his name into the search box. A list of results appears and there are scores of users with the same name. Most have profile pictures that look nothing like the Marcus Morrison I remember from RolpheTech, so I scan past them. A few cause me to stop and double-check, and there are plenty of profiles with no image at all. As the results peter out, I have to assume he's not on Facebook.

My next search bares more success and I click on the smiling profile picture of Geoff Waddock. As I'm not one of his Facebook friends, I can only access a limited amount of information on his page, but I do smile to myself when I see he's retired to Cornwall. There are several pictures of Geoff, or at least a slimmer, happier version of him compared to the miserable sod from RolpheTech. In a number of the images he's stood with an attractive middle-aged woman I assume is his wife or partner. Perhaps he did listen to my investment advice. Whatever story unfolded after my call, Geoff appears to have lived a happy ending.

The next search returns a bittersweet result — Tessa. The profile picture is of her and I assume, her new husband, taken on their wedding day. Her location is cited as London and her job role creative director at some ridiculously-named marketing agency. I am pleased her life appears to have panned-out exactly as before, and it's a welcome surprise I don't feel the disappointment I would have once felt. Perhaps the emotional turmoil I've been through has finally broken her spell, and I'm now over my obsession with Tessa. It the grand scheme of things, I've got more to worry about than my teenage crush on Tessa Lawrence. That much I do know.

With the three least consequential people on my list now checked, I sit back in the chair for a moment to reflect. Notwithstanding Marcus's absence from Facebook, I'm buoyed by what I've discovered about Geoff and Tessa. It gives me some hope that the next names I search for will return equally positive results.

I type the name 'Dave Wright' and strike the enter key. I don't see any reason why his life should have been changed as I never interacted with my best friend during my trip to 1986, but it would be comforting to confirm that. I check the first dozen profiles with no luck and then scroll down the page to see the magnitude of my task. It scrolls on, and on, and on — there are hundreds of results. With barely fifteen minutes of my session left, I decide to abandon my search for Dave for the time-being and move on.

Those fifteen minutes pass and my initial positivity is spent. There doesn't appear to be an account for either Megan or Lucy. It then dawns on me that either or both could well be married in this version of my reinvented future, and using their marital surname. If that is the case, I have no hope of finding them, least not without some serious research beyond my current resources.

I'm just about to google Harold Duffy's name, to see if the paedophile scumbag was brought to justice before his death, when a pop up appears on the screen…

SESSION EXPIRED - PLEASE BOOK A FURTHER SESSION AT RECEPTION

My curiosity for Aunt Judy's justice is greater than my contempt for the woman at the reception desk so I get up from the computer and plod back across the library.

"Hi, me again. I don't suppose I can book another session on the computer?"

She tilts her head slightly, her blank expression suggesting she's already forgotten the conversation we had only an hour ago.

"We do ask library users to go online or telephone when they want to book a computer."

Just as I'm about to lose it with her, she continues.

"But seeing as you're already here, I'm sure we can book you in. When would you like to book a session for?"

"Now?" I sigh.

She consults the yellow folder again. "I'm sorry but all six computers are booked for the rest of the afternoon. How about tomorrow?"

I'm fairly sure I could plead insanity if I kill her here and now. With my history I think I'd maybe get away with ten to fifteen years.

"Just forget it," I grumble. "Can you tell me where I can find a copy of the electoral roll?"

"It's in the reference section upstairs."

"Thank you. I assume I don't have to book online or phone in to look at it?"

"No, that would be a bit silly," she scorns.

I roll my eyes and head for the stairs without another word.

The upper floor of the library is deathly quiet, and besides an anoraked pensioner browsing the shelves, I've got the floor to myself. I wander up and down the aisles until I find the local resources section which houses the electoral roll records, alphabetically arranged in coloured binders. I pull out a blue binder marked on the spine with a large letter ‘P’ and carry it across to a table and chairs in the centre of the room.

I take a seat and open up the binder. I flick through the pages past Patterson, Pearson, and Pelkowski, until I reach a page with the name Pellham at the top. I slowly run my finger down the column of names and addresses, passing Pelligrini and Pellish — the name Pelling isn’t even listed. Shit. There can only be one of three reasons why my parents aren’t listed. Either they no longer live in the town, have chosen to have their details excluded from the records, or…

I gulp hard as panic grips me. I try to reassure myself that they could just as easily moved or decided not to be on the electoral roll. Just because their names don’t appear, it doesn’t mean they’re dead. I can’t accept that.

I get up and dart down the stairs, leaving the binder open on the table. I crash through the door back onto the street and draw deep breaths to calm the sickening feeling rising from the pit of my stomach. I bend over, my hands on my thighs as deep breaths develop into gasps. People pass by and stare, mild concern painted on their faces but nobody stops to check if I’m okay. I don’t want them to. I want to return to the sanctuary of the quiet flat to think, maybe even to grieve — my pernicious imagination again. Is it pessimism or negativity? I don’t know what to call it but my mind will only let me dwell on the most damning reason my parents aren’t listed on the electoral roll. I regain my composure and try to leave the the negative thoughts outside the library.

The walk provides some relief. By the time I reach the convenience store I’ve almost convinced myself that it’s just as likely my parents moved away. If they have, the chances of tracking them down are remote, but perhaps that's no bad thing. What is to be gained from knowing where they are? Even the thought of knowing they might be dead almost broke me. It would be reckless to investigate further; I can't fix the past so why open the door to it?

I withdraw forty quid from a cash machine within the store. I fill a basket with basic provisions, pay, and head back to the flat.

Once I've unpacked my meagre assortment of groceries, I make myself a coffee and toast a couple of slices of wholemeal bread. I've grown used to dull but nutritionally balanced food and the thought of regaining my previous bulk is a strong motivation to keep eating it. However, that doesn't stop me hankering for bacon rolls, and when I do, I think of Lucy and her lectures about my eating habits. On reflection, my inability to track her down at the library is perhaps the biggest disappointment. Wherever she is in this life, I hope she's happy.

And as for Dave and Megan, I can only hope the same. Perhaps in time I might find out but I think it might be better to leave the past behind. I tried, and came close to tipping myself over the edge once already. I take a bite of cold toast and come to the conclusion that for my new life to begin, I must draw a line under the old one. Here and now, I'm drawing that line.

Tomorrow, Craig Wilson starts his new life.

4

I forgot to set the cheap alarm clock beside the bed and wake up just before nine; an hour later than I had intended. I slept well though, and feel refreshed, invigorated. I take a shower and sit down in front of the TV in the lounge to eat a bowl of muesli. The novelty of being able to have a cup of coffee whenever I fancy is exploited and I down two more cups before heading back into the bathroom to brush my teeth.

I stare at my reflection in the mirror and frown at the t-shirt I threw on this morning. The blue fabric is faded and it's too small for me. In my former body this would have been a major issue and my bloated gut would have peeked from beneath the hem. But in this body it extenuates my broad shoulders, toned chest, and slim torso. I'm immensely proud of my new form but not so much I want to wear such a figure-hugging t-shirt. And while it didn't matter in the hospital, I'm acutely conscious I'm about to wear someone's cast-offs in public. I desperately need new clothes, and for that I need more money. That's the first thing on my agenda this morning — the job centre.

I grab the brown envelope containing all the documents that prove I am now Craig Wilson, and leave the flat.

The job centre is quite a schlep and it takes me almost half-an-hour to cross town. Even though I'm in familiar surroundings, the paranoia I put to bed yesterday re-awakens. A few times I inadvertently make eye contact with the odd person as our paths cross. I drop my head every time, hoping they don't recognise me.

I know it's illogical and I guess the feeling will wear off in time. It's disconcerting nonetheless.

With a final glance over my shoulder, I step through the front door of the job centre just before eleven. I'm slightly taken-aback to see the burly figure of a security guard stood just inside the door. He looks right through me, apparently bored or not concerned I pose any threat. I guess his function is to remove those who kick up a fuss when they don't get the handout they feel they're entitled to. I have no intention of making any fuss.

As I scan the room looking for a reception desk, a gaunt, monochrome woman approaches me.

"Morning sir. Do you have an appointment?"

Here we go again.

"No, I've never signed on before. I was hoping somebody could point me in the right direction," I reply, trying to give my best impression of a helpless child.

The woman sizes me up for a moment. I'm guessing she probably isn't much older than me and her black hair is scraped back from her forehead, tied into a ponytail. The edges of her mouth take a slight turn and a weak smile breaks on her tired face.

"Come with me," she says.

I follow her past countless desks, sombre faces sat both sides, and into a windowless office at the rear. She gestures for me to take a seat in front of a desk and she wearily falls onto the chair opposite. I squirm uncomfortably as she sifts through a drawer, eventually pulling out a form which she places on the desk. The small office is too warm, too claustrophobic.

She sits bolt upright, hands clasped on the desk. "I'm Miss Bennett. And you are?"

"Craig Pell…Wilson."

"Okay Craig, you don't mind if I call you Craig?"

Apparently I don't mind.

"You can call me Sheila."

Now on first name terms, Sheila's body language appears a little more relaxed as she sits back in her chair.

"Technically, I'm supposed to book you an appointment which would be in a few days time at the earliest."

"Oh, okay," I reply dejectedly.

"However, I might be able to squeeze you in now."

She tries to force a smile on a face that looks unaccustomed to displaying happiness.

"Thank you. That's very kind."

Sheila unclasps her hands and splays her fingers across the form on the desk. Silence hangs and my eyes dart around the room.

"Shall we get down to it then?" she says.

I nod and Sheila picks up a pen. The awkward interview commences. We go through a series of questions that I struggle to answer. Previous address? A secure hospital for the mentally ill. Work experience? A few decades of retail management in a parallel universe. Academic qualifications? Don't even go there.

Fifteen minutes in and I detect that Sheila is trying hard to mask her frustration. In the end I reluctantly pull the doctor's letter from the brown envelope and hand it to her.

"I hope you don't think I'm being difficult. If you read that, it might explain my situation a little better."

Sheila sits back in her chair and reads the letter. Essentially it says that I've been undergoing treatment for the last eleven months but I'm now fit for work. Oh, and the minor detail that I have no recollection of my life before Broadhall.

A minute passes and Sheila carefully places the letter on the desk. Her expression changes slightly, almost sympathetic.

"It sounds like you're a bit of a lost soul, Craig. You don't have any family?"

I shake my head.

"Friends?"

More shaking of the head.

"Wife? Girlfriend?"

Her final two words are delivered with a little more intonation than the first.

"No. There's nobody."

She sits forward and rests her elbows on the desk, her face cupped in her hands. She drums her fingers across her cheeks. No rings. A penny drops. Ohh, fuck — is Sheila flirting with me? I feel my cheeks redden and the already warm office gains a few more degrees of heat. It then dawns on me that many of the people staring at me outside were actually female, and their expressions weren't too dissimilar to Sheila's. Maybe they weren't seeing the reincarnated Craig Pelling as I first thought. Maybe they were checking me out.

"Are you okay, Craig?"

For most of my adult life, women have never looked at me with anything but pity or disgust. Now I'm sat in front of a woman who is dreamily staring at me. I rub my chin and the three days worth of stubble scratches under my fingernails. I forgot to buy a razor at the shop yesterday. Taking my silence as her cue to carry on, Sheila eyes me much like a vet would a nervous Labrador.

"Don't worry, I'm going to look after you," she says with a sympathetic smile.

I force a smile back at her and nod. She opens the desk drawer again and pulls out a compliment slip.

"This goes against the rules, but I'm going to give you my mobile number. You can call me any time if you need any help or just want somebody to talk to."

She hands me the slip of paper. I tentatively grasp the end between my thumb and forefinger to take it, but she keeps a grip on the other end.

"I do mean any time," she stresses before finally letting go of the slip.

"Thank you," I gulp.

Desperate to bring the subject back to more formal matters, I ask her when I'll get my first payment, emphasising my dwindling funds.

"We are able to grant emergency payments and I think your circumstances qualify. Leave it with me and I'll ensure a payment hits your bank account in the next twenty-four hours."

Keen not to dampen Sheila's helpful attitude, I stand and offer her my hand. She grasps it tightly and I allow the handshake to go on a little longer than is really necessary.

"Thank you Sheila, you've been very kind. I appreciate it."

"I hope you do. Don't lose my number."

I give her a parting smile and dart from the office. The security guard eyes me quizzically as I physically shudder my way across the room and out the door. Back on the street, I tuck the compliment slip into the pocket of my jeans and pray I never have to dial the number scrawled on it.

With my bank account about to be boosted, I meander aimlessly through the streets and turn my attention to the next task of the day. After yesterday's painstaking trip to the library, I need a more accessible method of getting online. I need a mobile phone, and I know where I can buy one, but visiting that particular store summons some seriously conflicted thoughts.

Curiosity wins, and prods me in the direction of RolpheTech.

I withdraw fifty quid from a cash machine and make my way back across town. After my encounter with Sheila, I test my theory that I'm not attracting attention for any other reason than the way I look. It's quite an epiphany. I catch the eye of several women and offer a slight smile which is reciprocated every time. For a man who has never received the admiring glance of a stranger, it feels like I've been gifted some sort of superpower. By the time I reach the edge of the retail park where RolpheTech is situated, there's a bounce in my step and a permanent grin etched on my face.

Both are gone when I turn the corner and I'm greeted with the familiar, and still depressing, concrete facade — my workplace for all those years. Is this really such a good idea? I know that neither Geoff or Lucy will be beyond those walls but there must be other members of staff I used to work with. Or will there? I was never manager of this store and logic would suggest my replacement in this timeline wouldn't have made the same recruitment decisions. Maybe he, or she, looked for something completely different when conducting interviews for new staff.

There's only one way to find out. I steel myself, push open the front door and tentatively enter the building.

For a few seconds I stand, gobsmacked. An expanse of polished wooden floor stretches out in front of me, the gum-spotted carpet no more. I look up, expecting to see the water-stained ceiling tiles and fluorescent lights. Now there's a smooth artexed ceiling dotted with warm spotlights. Everything else has changed, from the displays to the customer service desk, which isn't even in the original location. Clearly the branch has received the makeover it so desperately needed when I was manager. If I couple that with the fact the branch is actually still open, it raises a question about Marcus. Was he ever appointed Sales Director in this timeline?

Conscious I've been standing in the same place for at least a minute, I wander towards the first aisle and soak up the now unfamiliar surroundings. It soon becomes clear this is not my branch; there is nothing left of the tired store I once managed and I might as well be in a different store altogether. I scan for familiar faces but the four members of staff I spot never worked here in my original timeline.

I slowly meander through the aisles until I stumble upon a wall of mobile phones. With my limited budget I only have the choice of four phones and I spend five minutes deliberating which is the least terrible. My procrastination is interrupted when a twenty-something sales assistant approaches me. She enthusiastically asks if I need any help. I resist the urge to tell her I've probably forgotten more about the products in this store than she has ever known.

"I think I'm good, thanks."

She loiters for a moment, maybe deciding whether to deploy her sales training or seek a better prospect elsewhere. Undeterred, she tucks an errant strand of honey-blonde hair behind her ear and presses on.

"Are you after a cheap mobile phone?" she asks.

I turn and face her. The badge fixed to her unflattering RolpheTech blouse displays her name.

"Honestly, Chloe, I'm good. Besides, I don't think you're going to make much commission from my purchase I'm afraid."

"Okay, if you're sure. If you change your mind just come and find me."

Chloe gives me a smile, the brilliance of her green eyes triggering a poignant memory of Lucy in her younger days. For a moment I just stare at her as a hundred visions of Lucy flood my mind.

"Are you okay?" Chloe asks.

"Sorry, yeah. Do you mind if I ask you something?"

"Um, sure," she replies hesitantly.

Without even thinking about it, the line I had drawn under my old life is erased in a heartbeat.

"I think an old friend of mine used to work here. I've been away for a few years and I was hoping to catch up with her. I wondered if maybe you knew her. Lucy Ashman?"

Chloe ponders for a moment. "Sorry, I don't recognise the name, but I've only been here for six months."

Her reply doesn't surprise me. Judging by the lack of recognisable faces amongst the staff I've spotted, it's quite likely Lucy never worked here.

"Okay, no worries. Can I take one of these?" I say as I point to a forty-quid phone.

"Sure. I'll grab one from the stock room and meet you at the sales desk. It's just to the side of the main doors."

Chloe disappears and I saunter over to the sales desk where I pull two twenty-pound notes from my pocket. A minute passes and she returns, clutching my new phone. She hands it to a chubby, bored-looking guy behind the counter and turns to me.

"James will take your payment. Will you need as sim card for the phone?"

"Actually, yes."

She turns to James. "Can you help this chap with a sim card?"

He grunts something I don't catch. Just as she is about to disappear and leave me with her charmless colleague, Chloe stops and throws him a question.

"James, do you remember somebody called Lucy? Apparently she used to work here."

"Lucy Ashman?" he replies with no interest.

Chloe looks across to me. "Was that the surname?"

Suddenly my interest switches from the aesthetically pleasing Chloe to the sullen man behind the desk.

"Yes, yes, that's her," I squawk excitedly.

James apparently doesn't share my excitement and returns to the subject of sim cards.

"Cheapest sim card is a tenner. That do you?" he mumbles.

"Fine, whatever. You used to work with Lucy?"

"Yeah, but she left a few years ago."

"I don't suppose you know where she works now?"

"That'll be £49.99 in total with the sim card," James replies curtly.

I pull a tenner from my pocket and hand it over with the two twenties.

"She left to start her own business. She banged on about it for weeks. Something to do with helping old folks with computers."

"Do you know where the business is based? Is it local?"

James shoves the phone and sim card across the desk and shrugs his shoulders.

"Think so, not sure. Was there anything else as my lunch break started two minutes ago?"

I shake my head and James immediately slopes off. I turn to thank Chloe but she's already chatting to another customer. I grab my new phone from the desk and leave the store. Once I'm outside I stand for a moment, pondering what I'm going to do with this new information. If Lucy left RolpheTech a few years ago then it's still possible she moved to Brighton. But what if she didn't? What if Lucy is currently sat at a desk in an office here in Farndale?

It's a question I turn over as I make my way back to the town centre in search of coffee, free wi-fi, and an answer.

5

Both Starbucks and Costa are packed with suits on lunch so I retreat to a quieter independent coffee shop a little off the beaten track. I order the cheapest coffee on the menu, and, furnished with their wi-fi code, I take a seat at a table in the corner. It's only when I finally sit down I realise just how badly my feet ache; I must have covered six or seven miles this morning. There is a world of difference between the smooth miles on a treadmill in the Broadhall gym and pounding the pavements of Farndale.

While I wait for my order to be called, I quickly unpack my new phone and insert the sim card. It takes an age to wake and then I have to go through the initial set-up before I can use it. I complete the set-up just as my order is called. I dart over to the counter, grab my coffee and return to the table, eager to begin my search for Lucy. It doesn't take long to find her.

The first search result is an article from the local newspaper, dated almost three years ago…

Local Entrepreneur Helps The Elderly to Connect Online

With eight years of tech experience behind her, local mum Lucy Ashman has just launched her new service to help the elderly residents of Farndale get online. Her new venture, called Senior Connections, will provide one-to-one support to transform even the most tech-shy pensioner into a confident silver surfer.

Beside the article there is a picture of Lucy stood between two stony-faced elderly men. Both look like they'd rather be dead, and probably are now. I zoom in on the picture so Lucy's smiling face fills the phone screen. It's been a long time since I last saw that face. I feel a sudden and irrational pang of guilt for not ringing her when I left RolpheTech. Not much I can do about that now, and I have to remind myself that the woman in the picture is not the same Lucy anyway. That life never happened for either of us.

I open another browser tab and search for Senior Connections. I click through to a slick website which suggests that Lucy's venture is still in business. It only takes a few minutes of browsing the website to determine what a great concept it is. Lucy was the only one of us who had the patience to deal with our elderly customers and she's clearly found a lucrative niche. I click through to the contact page which displays a map for the company's offices, here in Farndale. That's interesting. If her business is as successful as it appears, that would be good reason for Lucy to decline her sister's offer and stay around here. It certainly appears Lucy never moved to Brighton in this timeline.

I take a sip of coffee and contemplate what I'm going to do now I've found her. Realistically, Lucy is the only connection to my former life I can rekindle. Is it a good idea though? Can we ever get back what we had before? My compulsion just to hear her voice wins out and I dial the number on the page.

"Good morning. Senior Connections."

It's just four words but enough of Lucy's voice to make my heart skip. Unfortunately my impulsive call hasn't been given much thought beyond hearing her voice.

"Oh…um, hi," I splutter.

What the hell do I say? I should hang up.

"What can I do for you?" she asks.

Hang up Craig.

"I'm calling about my uncle. He needs some help getting online."

Idiot.

"Okay. Does he have a computer?"

"No, we were thinking of getting him a tablet or a laptop."

"We might be able to help you with that. We sell a range of easy-to-use tablets and computers that your uncle might like to come and try. Would that be a good starting point for him?"

"Yeah, that's sounds a good idea. Could I drop by and take a look first?"

"Sure. Our office is on Victoria Road and we're open until five o'clock Monday to Friday. Just pop in and we'll show you some options."

"Perfect. Appreciate that."

"No problem. I'll look forward to seeing you later."

"Thanks. Bye."

I hang up.

Maybe thirty seconds of conversation with a total stranger. A friendly voice but not a friend. I take a large gulp of coffee, the ingestion of caffeine doing nothing to ease my racing pulse. This is what I hoped for, to find Lucy, so why do I feel so apprehensive, so anxious? My head says leave it but my heart says otherwise. I pick up my phone and look at the map on the website. While her office is only a five minute walk away, the Lucy I knew is a lifetime away. I empty my coffee cup and leave.

The streets are busy with lunchtime shoppers as I make my way towards Victoria Road. I don't look at anyone and have no idea if anyone looks at me. I just put one foot in front of the other, ignoring the question of whether this is a good idea or not. I reassure myself I'm not committing to anything just by walking to Victoria Road. At some point I need to make that call, but for now I'm happy to plod blindly through the streets.

Without being consciously aware of the journey there, I suddenly find myself stood outside the door of Senior Connections. Now I do have to make a decision and that's something I don't have a great track record on.

I pull my phone from my pocket and stare at the screen just to kill time but hoping some inspired reasoning suddenly hits me. It doesn't. What do I do?

I open the door and my legs carry me up the stairs to the office on the first floor. I don't recall giving them such instruction but suddenly I'm pushing open a door into a reception area. A single window lights the small space which houses just an unoccupied desk with two chairs sat in front of it, and two white panelled doors behind. Nobody around, still time to change my mind. My hesitancy is arrested when one of the panelled doors opens and a woman in a light grey trouser suit walks in.

The woman in the photo is now real, stood just eight feet away from me. I have to consciously fight the impulsion to greet her as my old friend. Over and over again I tell myself this Lucy doesn't have a clue who I am.

Once I've got past the shock of seeing her, I notice a few subtle differences from her counterpart in my timeline. Her previously long auburn hair is now cut into a shorter style that just brushes her shoulders. Her opal-green eyes sit below a long fringe that almost touches her eyebrows. Coupled with the lack of a RolpheTech uniform and it's not quite the same person I saw almost every day for a decade. It's still Lucy though, just not my Lucy.

"Can I help you?" Lucy asks.

My brain eventually connects to my mouth and I find a reply.

"I called earlier about my uncle," I croak.

"You're keen," she chuckles. "Take a seat and we'll have a quick chat about your uncle's specific needs."

Without warning, she disappears back through the door and returns a second later, holding a Starbucks coffee cup.

"You don't mind if I drink this?" she asks. "I've already had to suffer two cold coffees this morning."

"Course not."

Lucy sits behind the desk, takes a quick sip of coffee and opens a notepad. She then plucks a pen from a pot and drums it on the desk while she waits for me to take a seat. It's a habit that used to drive me potty during meetings, but seeing a recognisable flash of the Lucy I once knew almost brings a smile. I shuffle across to the desk and take a seat opposite her.

She sits forward, her elbows resting on the desk.

"Shall we start with your name?"

"It's Craig."

"Nice to meet you Craig, I'm Lucy. And what's your uncle's name?"

A thick mist suddenly forms in my head. I desperately sweep every corner of my mind for a random name but everything is cloaked in the impenetrable mist. Seconds pass and Lucy's brow furrows as if she thinks I'm either a crank or just wasting her time. Why can I not think of a single bloody name?

"Bungle," I randomly splutter. It sounds more like an outburst of Tourette's than a name. I have no idea where it came from or what in God's name possessed me to say it.

The furrow in her brow deepens as an eyebrow is raised. “Uncle Bungle?”

I smile sheepishly. “Sort of a nickname we’ve always used. I’ve can’t even remember his real name.”

“Right,” she says. “Does your…erm…Uncle Bungle have any experience with computers?”

She places the tip of the pen between her teeth and bites down on it. I catch the look in her eye, one I’ve seen a thousand times. I chew my bottom lip but it’s too late and my chest begins to slowly heave. Lucy tries to fight it but the corners of her mouth turn upward and a snort escapes from the back of her throat.

We both lose it at almost the same moment.

The sound of raucous, uncontrollable laughter fills the small room. Embarrassingly awkward yet strangely comfortable considering the circumstances. Just as I think we’ve regained control, one of us sniggers and it sets the other one off again. It takes a few minutes for us both to clear our throats and for composure to return.

“I’m so sorry. What must you think of me? That was really unprofessional,” Lucy eventually coughs, her cheeks stained with tears of laughter.

She opens a desk and pulls out a box of tissues. She plucks one herself and dabs her eyes before offering the box to me.

“No need to apologise. For what it’s worth I haven’t laughed like that in a long, long time.”

Lucy wafts her hands in front of her face. “Me neither, but this isn’t helping Uncle…your uncle.”

“Probably not. Sorry, where were we?”

“I have no idea. Shall I show you some tablets?”

Lucy gets up and I follow her through one of the doors behind the desk. She leads me into an office with a table in the centre, a dozen tablets laid-out on top.

"Shall I demonstrate a couple of these and you can decide which one might best suit your uncle?"

Lucy spends the next hour patiently explaining the functions of tablets I have no intention of buying. She knows nothing about me but I know virtually everything about her and our conversation is effortless, verging on flirtatious. I've never been one of those people who can walk into a room and strike up a conversation with a stranger but I now know how it must feel. Lucy assumes my gregarious nature is who I am but it's not. All those subtle signals humans subconsciously display; easy to miss, difficult to read — I know every one of Lucy's. In my previous life this would be no different to the thousands of conversations we had but here and now, I have an ulterior motive — I want my friend back. I shamefully exploit every bit of information I know about her to push exactly the right buttons.

As the presentation comes to an end, Lucy goes through a text-book close but I tell her I need to consult with my fictitious Uncle Bungle before I make any commitment. She nods politely and it appears our time is over. Almost reluctantly, we return to the reception area and Lucy holds her hand out for me to shake.

"Give me a call once you've had a chat with your uncle. It was a real pleasure to meet you, Craig."

I take her hand and savour the smooth feel of her skin as our handshake becomes more of a hand-holding exercise. If there was ever a perfect time to ask the question I desperately want to ask, this is it.

"Look, I'll understand if you say no, but I don't suppose you fancy a quick drink one night this week?"

"Um, yeah. I'd really like that," she giggles as her cheeks flush red.

Lucy hands me a business card with her mobile number and we agree to meet on Saturday evening at a bar down the road. The same legs that carried me up the stairs without permission are redundant as I float back down the stairs on a cloud.

I make my way along Victoria Road, aimless but pleased to have made progress with Lucy. As I contemplate what to do with the rest of the afternoon, I catch a view of myself reflected in a shop window. It serves as a reminder that I really should invest in some new clothes. That doesn't fill me with the same level of dread that it once did because mirrors are no longer a damning reminder of my obesity. However, my concern today is still for pounds; the monetary rather than weight variety.

I visit another cash machine and withdraw sixty quid. I then amble to the main shopping centre and scour the various levels in search of budget menswear. The last time I was here was just before the Heathland school reunion, but I won't be browsing the same shops and I certainly won't be visiting expensive department stores. I need to fund almost an entirely new wardrobe for the same money I spent on a single shirt that day.

My search ends as the escalator delivers me to the top floor of the shopping centre, bang outside a discount clothing store. Posters in the window tantalise with offers of clothing for less than most people spend on a decent lunch. This is the sort of store I used to scorn when I had money, and therefore choice. I have little of either today so with some reluctance, I make my way inside.

An hour later I'm stood in a long queue consisting mainly of loud women with louder offspring. The hellish queue moves forward at a ponderous pace. Eventually I reach the front and I'm beckoned towards a spotty young woman who clearly went to the same charm school as James at RolpheTech. Without a word, she tips the contents of my basket onto the counter and impassively scans the seven items: two pairs of jeans, two polo shirts, two t-shirts, and a lightweight jacket.

"That'll be fifty-eight pounds," she grunts.

I can't help myself. "*Please* is the word you're looking for."

She scrunches her face and looks at me as though I've just called her mother a whore.

"Pur—lease," she heckles.

I throw three twenty pound notes on top of the counter and shake my head. Two pound coins are slapped on the counter in their place along with a receipt.

"Next," she calls above my head.

I stare at the pile of clothes and then at the woman.

"Am I supposed to wear them out of the store? Is that how you do things here?"

"You wanna carrier bag?"

"Pur—lease."

My clothes are unceremoniously stuffed into a carrier bag which I'm required to pay an additional five pence for. I leave the store promising myself I'll never return.

With no other pressing tasks on my agenda for the day, I decide to head back to the flat and see if I can get online via a neighbour's unsecured wi-fi.

I step onto an escalator just behind a young couple who selfishly block my progress by standing next to one another, holding hands. With no other option, I stand and survey the open concourse on the ground floor from my elevated position four floors above. As I casually scan the scores of bodies moving across the floor, I catch a glimpse of a figure at the far end, bustling towards an open lift door — an elderly man with a bald dome, carrying a walking stick. I do a double-take and squint intently at the figure as I try to eek-out the full scope of my forty-something vision.

Is that…? Was that…?

The figure disappears into the lift and the door closes.

With my heart in my mouth, I barge past the young couple. They protest in vain as I charge down the escalator. I leap the final four steps and sprint past shops and bewildered onlookers. I cover the seventy yards in seconds and thump the lift call button. I look up to the panel above the door. Including the car park levels, there are twelve floors in the shopping centre. I'm now on the third floor and the lift is currently a floor below me. And it's not moving. I thump the button again, and again. The light behind the number two remains steadfastly lit.

Then it goes out.

Five or six long seconds pass until the lift eventually chimes its arrival. The door slowly opens. Empty.

I step inside and furiously press the button to send the lift back down a floor. No matter how hard, or how many times I press the button, the door stays open. Frustration mixes with anger and I'm just about to smash my forearm across the panel of buttons when the door finally closes. More seconds pass before the lift begins its tortuously slow descent. I step across the lift so I'm inches from the door. It chimes again, and slowly the door slides open. When a foot of open space is available, I squeeze myself through, stumbling past the small crowd waiting on the other side.

I scan left, then right. So many people but none of them recognisable. I break into a slight jog and circumnavigate the perimeter of the floor. Nothing. I do it again, slower this time, and glance into every shop window as I pass. Nothing. A third and more methodical loop brings greater desperation but the same result. In a final act of desperation I spend the next hour searching every floor, every store. Hopeless.

Beaten, I slump down on a bench and ask myself the question my search was unable to answer — could that old man really have been *my* old man?

6

Baked potato with tuna; nutritionally balanced and cheap. I pick at my evening meal for half-an-hour but my appetite isn't there. I get up from the couch and cross the lounge into the kitchen area. I place the plate on an empty shelf in the fridge and slam the door shut. I'm too skint to throw good food away. A few hours on from my possible sighting of the old man and it feels like I'm mentally back to square one.

The ghosts of my parents haunted me all the way home and now, within the quiet confines of my new home, their spirits continue to invade my every thought. Notwithstanding the fact the old man I saw might not have been my old man, what could I have done about it? It's not as though I could have bowled up to him and said hello. It would have been proof he was still alive I guess, but nothing more.

Whether the elderly man I saw was the old man or not, the thought alone prods an already raw wound. I need to deal with this, one way or another. I can't spend the rest of my life chasing down every elderly resident in Farndale who bears a passing resemblance to either of my parents. I can cope without knowing a lot of things but I have to accept that the fate of my parents isn't one of them. It's going to hurt whatever I learn, but I've got to do it. Short-term pain, long-term sane — a mantra I repeat to myself as I slump back down on the couch.

I try to distract myself with thoughts of spending Saturday evening with Lucy but even that isn't enough to kick my negative thoughts into touch. I need to find something positive to balance me out; one of the many coping mechanisms I was taught at Broadhall.

I grab my phone and search for wi-fi networks.

Within a few seconds the phone locates eight signals. I scan the list one by one, each of them displaying a small padlock icon next to the signal indicator. I'm good with a computer but not skilled enough to hack a password-protected wi-fi network. The sixth signal on the list has no padlock — bingo. I move around the flat to enhance the single-bar signal and secure two further bars while stood near the bedroom window. One tap of the screen and I'm online.

For the next twenty minutes I sit on the edge of my bed and scour a national newspaper archive for articles about Harold Duffy. I have to go back to September 1988 to find what I'm looking for. The front page displays a police mugshot of Duffy next to the headline, 'TAKE HIM DOWN: PAEDOPHILE CARETAKER GETS LIFE'. I squint at the tiny text which continues inside the virtual paper with a double-page spread. There is a graphic in the centre of the page, showing the timeline of events from Duffy's earliest crimes through to his initial arrest in January 1987. With twenty-nine victims eventually coming forward over many months, all of whom took to the witness stand, the thirteen jurors delivered a swift and unanimous verdict — guilty on all charges. Delivering his sentence, the judge made it clear that Harold Duffy would spend the rest of his days in prison.

The article ends with a photo of the first victim to come forward, and the woman heralded as the bravest — Judy Sullivan. The photo appears to have been taken on the steps outside the court and even with the low quality reproduction, there is no mistaking Aunt Judy wearing a lurid orange headscarf and mustard-yellow jacket. She looks as world-weary as I remember but the fear has gone, replaced with a defiant expression. It appears the demons I awoke on that afternoon in 1986 have finally been put to rest once and for all.

I allow myself to bask in a self-satisfied glow. Now all I need to do is check if Aunt Judy kept her end of our deal.

John Williamson's error of judgement hit the national headlines back in 1994. While there were the seeds of an Internet service in the UK back then, it was far from mainstream and there were very few news websites. However, I can't imagine that the devastating crash which killed both my grandparents and claimed three other victims isn't referenced anywhere online. If Aunt Judy did as she promised and somehow convinced my mum to keep my grandparents off the road that day, there should have only been three victims.

I google 'John Williamson lorry crash'. The search engine does its job and spits out a blog article from a road safety charity at the top of the search results. The title reads, 'Death by Distraction: The Legacy of John Williamson'.

I let my finger hover over the link. I think about the twenty-nine victims of Harold Duffy who found justice because I convinced Aunt Judy to face her fears. Twenty-nine women who, had it not been for my interference in 1986, would never have found peace. Surely their victory is worth more than whatever lies beyond the single line of blue text I'm about to press. I should take that victory and savour the fact I did something worthwhile for all those women. Why push my luck? I don't *need* to know if my grandparents avoided the accident, do I?

I nervously tap my finger on the side of the phone. Seconds pass and the tapping becomes more intense. The whole point of this exercise was to balance the spiralling negativity surrounding my parents. I've achieved that, so why dig deeper? I feel like a gambling addict; one more hand, one last bet. Why walk away from the table at break-even when I can leave with a win? Stick or twist?

I can't help myself and press the link.

I read the first two paragraphs of the article. As the words sink in, bile rises in my throat and suddenly the few mouthfuls of baked potato I consumed earlier try to make the return journey. I swallow hard to keep the contents of my stomach in situ but the bile continues to burn my throat. Scarcely able to believe my own eyes, I read the article again. Some words drift through my mind, others smash their way through. The second paragraph in particular sets the room into a spin…

"The lorry ploughed into the rear of the coach at almost forty miles-per-hour, instantly killing thirteen of the passengers. The driver of the lorry, John Williamson, was also killed in the crash. Four further passengers later died in hospital as a result of their injuries. In total, the crash claimed the lives of eighteen people including four children."

I read the article over and over again but the details are just background noise compared to the five words which continue to scream from the page — *eighteen people, four children, killed.* I drop the phone onto the bed and pace up and down the twelve feet of space at the end of the bed, like a zoo tiger in a pen too small.

My mind analyses the damning results of my handywork.

Without my grandparents' Ford Orion to act as a buffer, the rear of the coach would have taken the full impact from the lorry. I may have afforded my grandparents a few more years of life, but the absence of their car caused the death of far more people on the coach than the three who died in the original timeline. Almost subconsciously my brain does the maths. Notwithstanding the demise of John Williamson, who I couldn't give a shit about, and taking my grandparents out of the equation, the net death toll was an additional twelve people. And four of them were just kids.

My actions inadvertently caused the death of twelve people who should still be alive today. I've just traded almost five hundred years of combined life so my grandparents could enjoy what? Another ten years between them maybe?

What the fuck have I done?

I inexplicably yearn for my room at Broadhall. I want to hear Stephen's soft Scottish voice, telling me it wasn't really my fault. I wasn't the one driving the lorry that careered into the back of the coach so how can I take the blame? How could I have known what would happen? All I wanted to do was keep my grandparents safe, and who wouldn't do the same thing given the chance? Every question is rhetorical because nobody is ever going to give me an answer. Nobody has, or is ever likely to have answers to such improbable questions.

Both the bedroom and my mind become increasingly claustrophobic. I need to get outside to clear my head, to regain some control. Much like the time I first arrived at Broadhall, I can feel myself sliding down a mountain of questions towards an abyss. I can't go there again.

I leave the flat and trudge through the streets of Farndale. No plan, no route, and no real purpose other than to quieten my mind. I put one foot in front of another, staring blankly at the few feet of pavement in front of me and focusing on nothing other than the next step. I stop once, outside an off licence. I haven't touched a drop of alcohol in almost a year and haven't missed it as much as I would have once expected. But now? Can a ten quid bottle of vodka wash away the guilt? Will I feel any better tomorrow?

I walk on.

I have no idea how far or for how long I walk but when I eventually return to the flat, evening has become night. I clamber up the stairs, physically and emotionally exhausted. I head straight to the bedroom and without undressing, crash onto the bed. As I lie in the dark waiting for sleep to come, I repeat my new found mantra — s*hort-term pain, long-term sane*. I can dissect the results of my actions in 1986 a million ways but the conclusions will remain the same. No matter how I have changed things, for the better or worse, there isn't a damn thing I can do about it now even if I wanted to.

The final face I see before I fall asleep is Aunt Judy's. Twelve people dead, twenty-nine able to live again. I need to cling to the latter.

7

I awake to a pounding head and stomach cramps. Coupled with tiredness after a fitful night's sleep, I feel lousy. My mind immediately starts to replay the events of last night but I don't give it the chance to gain traction. Still wearing the ill-fitting charity clothes I wore yesterday, I crawl from my bed to the bathroom. I stand and empty my bladder, grateful there is no mirror above the toilet. I suspect my headache is down to dehydration and my stomach cramps because I've barely eaten anything in the last twenty-four hours.

I strip off and stand under the shower for ten minutes, nudging the temperature higher and higher until my skin tingles and glows pink.

With a towel around my waist, I pad back to the bedroom and grab the bag of budget clothes from inside the wardrobe. I slip into a pair of jeans and a black polo shirt. I return to the bathroom and stand in front of the mirror, cursing under my breath. With so many thoughts pinging around my head yesterday, I forgot to buy a razor. This isn't good because today I start my new job and I was hoping to make a positive impression. Four days worth of stubble does not convey 'reliable and upstanding citizen'.

I check the time on my phone while I brush my teeth; just past eight. Out of habit, I'm about to check my email inbox and Facebook page before I remind myself that no friends will be emailing unfunny jokes or posting pictures of their breakfast. On reflection, my previous life was no better for either. I head into the kitchen. I force myself to eat a bowl of muesli and down a mug of strong coffee. Both prove to be a remedy and I leave the flat just before eight-thirty, feeling vaguely human again.

The timing of my first day at the charity shop couldn't have been better planned. I need something to act as a distraction from the past, and to add some semblance of normality to my life. Granted, two days work a week in a charity shop wouldn't be my first career choice but it's better than moping around the flat and tormenting myself. And if nothing else, at least it will prove to Stephen I can function back in society.

I arrive outside the local branch of MISSO just before nine. It's an acronym that makes it sound like a Thai restaurant but apparently it stands for Miscarriage Support Organisation. I was offered the choice of working here or at another shop run by a charity that re-homes dogs. Too many memories of wishing ill-will on barking dogs quickly discounted that option. Besides, I've experienced the trauma of a miscarriage first hand. Megan might be a stranger in this life but the pain we endured together as teenagers will always stay with me.

I push open the door to the shop and step inside. There is a counter sat centrally against the rear wall with a closed door behind. Every inch of wall space is shelved and laden with random items of junk that I can't imagine anyone ever buying. Four freestanding rails occupy the floor space and are jammed with items of clothing. Statistically speaking, at least a dozen of the garments were probably worn when their occupant died.

I cautiously move through the shop towards the counter. I get half way across the floor when I hear laughter and the door behind the counter swings open. A rotund woman with white hair fills the doorway and abruptly gasps when she spots me. Startled by her reaction, I instinctively raise my hands in surrender. We reach a stand-off. She eyes me with panic while frantically waving her flabby right arm to beckon whoever is on the other side of the door. It dawns on me that I probably look like a vagrant or shoplifter, although why anyone would want to steal a ceramic shire horse or a Barry Manilow CD isn't clear. I try to calm the situation.

"I'm Craig. I'm supposed to start work here today. Aren't you expecting me?"

The rotund woman eyes me suspiciously as another aged face appears behind her shoulder. The second face belongs to a thin woman with a pronounced nose and silver hair tied into a bun. Now I have two sets of eyes assessing me but no reply to my question.

"I don't know anything about a man working here," the thin woman at the rear whispers.

Her rotund colleague concurs with a nod.

"We don't know anything about a man working here," she parrots in a thick west country accent, clearly the spokeswoman of the two.

"Okay, there's obviously been some miscommunication here. You're not expecting somebody to start work today?"

The two women confer in hushed whispers. The spokeswoman eventually shares their prognosis of the situation.

"We're expecting a woman, Carol Wilson."

"Ahh, my surname is Wilson, first name Craig. Perhaps there's been a mix-up with the names? I can show you some identification if you like."

More hushed whispers.

"Wait here. We'll check with head office."

Both women disappear, closing the door behind them. With little else to do I browse the inventory of tat on the shelves, most of which should be in a skip. I spend five minutes sifting through boxes of worn shoes, mismatched china, obscure cooking utensils, dog-eared books, and a ridiculous amount of VHS cassettes. It's a depressing journey through the lofts and garages of people too lazy to go to the local tip. Just as I toy with the idea of withdrawing my offer of unpaid labour, the door behind the counter opens and the rotund women waddles towards me.

"I'm sorry my love, there was indeed a mix up. We don't get many men volunteering here so I was a bit taken aback when I saw you. I'm Brenda by the way, branch manager" she says, her accent and demeanour conjuring up images of a Cornish farmer's wife.

I offer Brenda a smile while trying to hide my shock that she is almost spherical. There must be a raised platform behind the counter as Brenda looks barely five foot tall stood in front of me. A puff of white hair covers the top of her head like a cumulus cloud. Her grey slacks and peach-coloured blouse make no attempt to hide her odd shape. Still, she appears friendly enough, almost maternal.

"No problem, Brenda," I reply.

"Shall we start off with a cup of tea, then I'll show you around?"

I nod and follow Brenda through the door into a small lobby with four further doors leading off it. The silver-haired woman seems less sociable and disappears beyond one of the other doors without a second glance in my direction.

"Stockroom, toilets, kitchen and the office," Brenda says while pointing to the various doors.

We take the door into a small kitchen that immediately reminds me of the tatty staffroom at

RolpheTech. Brenda flicks the kettle on and pulls a mug from a cupboard.

"Tea okay?"

"Please. Milk, no sugar."

"We don't get told much about the people who volunteer here so maybe you'd like to tell me a bit about yourself?"

I decide that showing her my letter from the shrink is preferable to an awkward conversation.

"Might be easier for you to read this," I say as I hand her the letter.

She takes a pair of glasses from a case in her pocket, puts them on and studies the letter. A minute passes before she silently hands me back the letter and returns the glasses to her pocket. The silence is broken as the thin woman joins us.

Brenda makes the introductions. "Emily, this is Craig, our new volunteer. Craig, this is Emily, my assistant manager."

Emily holds out a bony hand attached to a stick-thin arm. Judging by her featherweight frame, it's clear who has first option on the custard creams.

"Nice to meet you young man," she says politely.

I gently shake her hand, trying not to crush her brittle fingers.

"Craig here has been in hospital for best part of a year," chirps Brenda.

"Oh, nothing too serious I hope?" Emily asks.

Brenda interjects. "He's had some sort of trauma. Can't remember fuck-all about his life, can you love?" her west country accent softening the edges of her 'fuck' to an almost socially acceptable level.

"You don't have any memories?" Emily asks with some concern.

Still somewhat taken-aback by Brenda's language, I shake my head.

"If he doesn't remember anything," Brenda helpfully adds. "He might be one of those sex monsters you read about."

A look of horror descends on Emily's lined face.

"You're not a sex monster are you?" she splutters.

"Jesus. No, I'm not," I protest. "I just can't remember much about my life before I was admitted to hospital."

Brenda starts to chuckle away to herself.

"I'm pulling your leg, Emily," she laughs. "We should be so lucky."

Emily glares at me suspiciously and mumbles something before she turns and leaves.

"Sorry about Emily," Brenda says. "She's a lovely woman but a bit uptight if you know what I mean."

"Right, I'll bear that in mind."

"So you really can't remember anything?" Brenda asks, changing the subject while she makes the tea.

"Very little," I lie. "But I used to work in a shop though. That much I do remember."

"Good. Some of the fucking idiots they send us don't have the sense they were born with," she says casually.

She turns to hand me a mug of tea, apparently unabashed and unapologetic for her language.

"Drink that and I'll show you around. Then we can find something useful for you to do. See if you can put whatever is left in your head to good use."

With a warning that she'll be back in five minutes and not to nick anything, Brenda waddles out of the kitchen. I stand and sip my tea in silence, glad that on first impressions, my quirky colleagues should be a welcome distraction from more troubling matters.

Almost ten minutes pass before Brenda returns. She gives me a quick tour of the shop and then leads me into the stockroom. I can't quite place the smell but it's somewhere between sweaty armpits and a dank cellar. The space is about twelve hundred square feet with no natural light. Half of the back wall is taken up with a wide roller shutter that gives access to a delivery area at the rear of the building, Brenda informs me. Tall shelving units run all around the other walls with two further units stood back-to-back in the centre. Every shelf is crammed with bags, boxes and assorted bric-a-brac.

"I call this room hell's toilet," Brenda says. "Cos' the little devils like to deposit their shit here."

Noting my puzzled expression, she expands her analogy.

"People seem to think that because we're a charity, we'll take every piece of crap they no longer want. You name it, we've had it: everything from soiled underwear through to used sex toys. Seen it all I have."

I squirm at her words. Brenda notices, and delights in embarrassing me further.

"Emily once opened a carrier bag and amongst all the clothes she found a huge black dildo. Gave her quite a fright it did."

I remain speechless.

"Funny thing was, I don't know what happened to it. Maybe Emily snuck it into her handbag but I never saw it again. Shame, we could have used it to display watches on the counter."

Brenda lets that image sit for a moment before she turns and looks up at me, her expression stern.

"And just so you know Craig, if I catch you stealing sex toys, soiled underwear, or anything else, I will call the police. We clear on that?"

I offer a weak smile and nod, not entirely sure if she's serious.

"Good lad. Let's get you to work shall we?"

For the next three hours I learn first-hand why Brenda gave the stockroom its nickname. My task is to sort through the shelves and put aside anything that might be saleable, while everything else has to be dumped into a skip in the delivery area. Even with the roller door fully open, it's as hot as hell and the smell is horrendous. I sort countless bags of unwashed clothes, boxes of tired bric-a-brac, and scores of unsafe electrical products. It doesn't take long to realise that the crap in the shop is actually better than ninety percent of what I've unearthed. By the time I've half-filled the skip, I've gained a new respect for those who volunteer to work in shops like this. It's a shitty, thankless job.

Brenda eventually rescues me and I'm sent on my lunch break. I spend several minutes scrubbing my hands with soap and hot water but the smell of the stockroom lingers on my budget clothing. Despite the pungent smell that follows me down the road as I go in search of a sandwich, I appreciate the positive feeling born from doing something worthwhile with my time. It may be a nasty, unpaid job but I do welcome the sense of purpose it brings.

I treat myself to a crayfish and rocket sandwich which I eat on a bench in the cool confines of the shopping centre. I sit and watch the people passing by for twenty minutes, maybe with the faint hope I might spot the old man again. No such luck. I make my way back to the shop to find Brenda waiting for me.

"Good news. You've got a second pair of hands to help you out this afternoon," she grins.

"Oh, okay. Who's that then?"

"Me. Ready to re-enter hell's toilet?"

I doubt her offer is negotiable so I reluctantly follow Brenda back to the storeroom.

As we open the door we're hit with a stinking wave of humid air. Brenda snaps her hand to her mouth as I turn my head in disgust.

"Best get that shutter open," she mumbles from beneath her hand.

I dart to the end of the room and wait while the painfully slow mechanism raises the shutter. Sunlight slowly creeps into the room until we're both bathed in the sun's rays. On a beach in the Mediterranean it would be blissful. Here, stood amongst bags and boxes of trash, not so much.

"Right, I'll sort and you shift. Okay?" Brenda orders rather than asks.

For the next two hours we work like dogs. Despite her advanced years and over-sized frame, Brenda whirls around the room like a small moon orbiting a planet. I start to warm to her boundless energy and affable nature. Her broad use of industrial-grade language, delivered with a Cornish twang, is as amusing as it is inappropriate. I think I quite like Brenda.

We eventually stop for a breather.

"Right, my love. I think we both deserve a cold glass of squash."

She bustles off to the kitchen and I arrange a couple of plastic crates as makeshift seats. Brenda returns holding two large glasses of orange squash.

"Here, get this down you," she says as she passes one of the glasses to me.

We plonk down on the plastic crates and both take large gulps of ice-cold squash.

"That hit the spot. We'll take five minutes and get cracking again," Brenda says, her enthusiasm relentless.

We sit in silence for a minute. I'm hopeless when it comes to making small talk and scrabble for something to say. Thankfully Brenda beats me to it.

"This memory problem of yours. Does it mean you can't remember your family either?"

This is not a topic of conversation I'd want to discuss with anyone, let alone a virtual stranger.

"My parents think I'm dead," I reply, hoping the brutal answer will quash any further questions on the subject.

Brenda takes a sip of her squash and seems unfazed by my frank statement.

"When did you last see them?"

"A long time ago," I sigh. "I don't even know if they're still alive."

"And you're not just a little bit curious?"

"Truth is Brenda, even if they are still alive, I'm fairly sure they wouldn't take my reappearance well."

Brenda turns and puts a hand on my knee. "Don't you want to know if they're still around?"

All I know is that I don't know. Yesterday's damning revelations suggest I might be better-off not knowing anything further about this new timeline I created. This cat can't afford to be curious.

"I don't know Brenda. It's complicated."

She looks at me, a sympathetic smile creasing her already heavily-lined face.

"Ever heard the term war baby?" she asks.

"A baby born during the war, fathered by a serviceman?"

"More or less. There were other names back then, far less polite, but they all meant the same thing. Anyway, you're looking at a genuine war baby."

I don't know what I'm supposed to say in response to this revelation. I try a curious expression.

"I never knew my father. All Mum ever told me was his name and that he was a Canadian soldier. She died when I was nineteen so suddenly I was in the same boat as you are now, more or less. I had one remaining parent but he didn't know I even existed."

Brenda appears to be going somewhere with this so I sit and listen patiently.

"I got married a year later and had kids of my own. It was hard, not having parents to share my life with but you just get on with it. Then before I knew it, the kids are grown up and leaving home. Then my husband died, poor sod was only fifty-two. Suddenly I was nineteen again — alone, just a helluva lot fatter."

She pauses for a moment, her smile fading a little.

"It got to 1998 and I finally plucked up the courage to look for my dad. I managed to track him down with some help from the Canadian Veterans Society."

"Did you meet him?" I ask with genuine interest, hoping for a happy ending to Brenda's tale.

"I was too late, my love. He died in 1996 — I missed him by just under two years. My son bought us tickets and we flew over there to visit his grave. I got to meet his family though and my three new step-brothers. Funny thing was, they told me their dad always wanted a daughter. Maybe if I'd got off my fat arse a few years earlier he'd have discovered he already had one. But I was too worried about the consequences, and I suppose I was scared of being rejected. That fear cost me the chance of meeting my dad."

I feel a lump bob in my throat. "I honestly don't know what to say Brenda."

"Nothing to say, but you should know it taught me a valuable lesson; it's better to regret doing something than to regret doing nothing. Whatever you're worried about, don't let it fester too long. If you have even the slightest inkling your parents are still around, find them sooner rather than later. Trust me, regret hangs around a damned sight longer than any worries you might be having."

Brenda clambers to her feet and necks the remainder of her squash. I remain seated, letting her words sink in.

"Come on then, time to get back to it you lazy sod," she chuckles, any latent sadness from our conversation well masked.

I get to my feet and step towards my stumpy colleague.

"Thanks, Brenda."

"You're welcome, my love. I'm not as daft as I look you know."

Despite having received eleven months of professional therapy, a five-minute conversation with the manager of a charity shop finally changes my mindset. My task over the coming days is to find out what happened to my parents. I've got to face my fears or spend a lifetime living in blind regret.

Short term pain — long term sane.

8

As if Mother Nature has decided to set an appropriate backdrop to my first task of the day, I walk briskly down the street under sombre grey skies. My destination is the local council offices, or more specifically, The Department For Births, Deaths, and Marriages. I'm fairly certain I'll be their first visitor who has experienced all three first hand.

I can't say I'm relishing this task but my chat with Brenda, and a ten-minute call to Stephen last night, has fuelled my resolve. This is now a process of elimination. It doesn't appear my parents are living in Farndale any longer so the next, and most perturbing possibility is that they're no longer alive. It's not a possibility I want to explore but I have to discount it if I'm to move forward. I'm praying I won't find a record for either of my parents, but even if my worst fears are realised, a definitive answer has to be better than this tortuous limbo.

I arrive at the council offices just after ten and enter a bright foyer with a vast maple reception desk in the centre. Enormous framed prints of local landmarks hang on the smooth white walls that abut polished granite floor tiles. It all feels a little too decadent, too corporate for a municipal building. I wonder how many council-funded services were sacrificed to pay for all of this.

I approach the desk and ask a faceless woman for direction to The Department For Births, Deaths, and Marriages. She flashes me a plastic smile and points me towards the lifts in the far corner with instructions to go to the fourth floor. I return an equally insincere smile and squeak across the polished floor to the lifts. The lift is just as indulgently designed as the foyer with lots of chrome and mirrors, but it makes for a pleasant, albeit brief ascent.

I arrive on the fourth floor and follow the wall-mounted signs down a corridor and through a door to an anteroom. A row of six chairs are lined up against one of the walls, sat opposite a small table laden with various pamphlets. The nondescript space could as easily be a waiting room for a doctor, dentist, or optician. But this is a waiting room for people to register one of three significant life events; two joyful, one grave. I'm here for the latter.

I approach a service window at the rear. Beyond the glass is an office with four desks, three of which are occupied by council minions, all staring blankly at computer monitors, oblivious to my presence. As I wait for somebody to assist, I try to calm my growing anxiety by taking deep breaths. Three seconds to inhale, three seconds to exhale. I manage twenty-seven breaths and calculate a wait of one hundred and sixty-two seconds before somebody finally approaches the glass.

"Can I help?" says a plump, middle-aged man. His hair is almost gone, and judging by his expression, so has his will to live.

"I was hoping to check the death records of a couple of people if I can?"

"I need names and the death dates," he replies dryly.

"I don't know the death dates I'm afraid."

The man sighs and is about to say something I suspect won't be helpful.

"It's my parents. I've been in hospital for nearly a year and lost touch with them. I just need to know," I plead.

His expression softens slightly.

"Janet and Colin Pelling. Please."

A few seconds pass while the man contemplates his next move. He eventually grabs a piece of paper and a pen which he slips under the window.

"Write their names and dates of birth. I'll take a look. I assume they were both residents of Farndale?"

I nod and scrawl my parents' names on the paper. I know both their birthdays but I can only provide an estimate of the year they were born. I jot the info down and slip the paper back under the window. He snatches it up and plods over to an empty desk where he collapses onto a chair and grasps a mouse. I watch him as he switches his focus from the paper to the keyboard, then to the screen. My anxiety returns with a vengeance.

Get the fuck out of here Craig. You don't need this.

The anxiety develops into panic as my trusted breathing technique proves futile. The man continues to jab away at the keyboard, frowning several times in the process as he squints at the screen. There surely can't be more than seconds remaining before he delivers the news I might not want to hear. I turn away and my eyes focus on the door I entered a few minutes ago.

Do it Craig. Run.

I take a step forward. From nowhere, a reminder of the last time I ran away pings into my mind. The very reason I'm stood here is because I tried to outrun fate minutes before I left 1986. I turn back to the window and the now-empty desk where the man was sat. I lean forward slightly to improve my line of sight and my head thumps against the glass. Three faces turn in my direction as I clamp my hand to my forehead and curse under my breath. Stifled laughter, then they turn back to their screens. A door to the side of the window opens and the plump man appears holding the piece of paper.

"You alright? You'd be surprised how many people do that."

I give him an embarrassed smile as a dull ache spreads across my cranium.

"Do you want to take a seat?" he asks, a hint of sympathy in his voice.

"No, thanks. I'm okay I think."

He shuffles forward a few steps.

"Maybe we should take a seat."

It's more of an instruction than a question. His tone is definitely sympathetic but I detect it's not towards my impending headache. This does not bode well — being instructed to take a seat is rarely a precursor to good news. My stomach flips and the look in his eyes suggest I'm right to be concerned. My legs tremble and I fall onto one of the chairs lined up against the wall. He takes a seat next to me and shuffles awkwardly.

"Can I ask your name?" he says in a low voice.

"Craig," I reply, my mouth now bone dry.

"I'm Jim."

Judging by his body language, it's clear that Jim's training hasn't covered this particular scenario. It seems he wants to be sat here even less than I do and dives right in.

"I searched both names but couldn't find a record for Colin Pelling."

"Which means?"

"He never died in this borough. I can only search our records and you'd need to search the national archive online if you wanted to search other boroughs."

"Right. And Janet Pelling?"

His eyes look everywhere but at me. He eventually fixes his attention to the floor at my feet.

"There is one record for a Janet Pelling. The date of birth is a year out, but the day and month are the same as those you gave me."

I stop breathing momentarily, my brain stunned and incapable of sending instructions to my lungs. A sudden rush of adrenalin-fuelled panic rectifies the situation and I gasp for air. I feel like I'm going to die. Jim looks like he'd take death over being sat with me as I draw loud raggedy breaths.

"Are you okay?"

I want to tell my perceptive friend I am obviously far from okay but words are hard to come by. I manage two.

"When? How?"

Jim pauses for a moment. "1996," he eventually says softly.

Twenty-two years. My poor Mum has been dead for twenty-two years. How can that be?

"How?" I repeat.

"Do you want me to call someone, Craig? This is a lot to take in on your own."

"How did she die?" I snap.

He runs a hand across his bald scalp and lets out a resigned sigh.

"Suicide."

The urge to run is so overwhelming I can't resist. Without any thought I get to my feet and stagger towards the door. Jim's final word repeats in my head, over and over until I start to question if it's an actual word. Nothing makes sense, nothing seems real.

I bypass the lift and crash through a door to a utilitarian stairwell. I stop for a moment to try and calm myself, conscious that a fall down the stairs won't help my situation. I take deep breaths and slowly descend down the stairs, keeping a firm grip on the handrail. The thick fog in my mind begins to clear, and by the time I reach the door at the bottom I have pulled myself back from the brink of a complete breakdown.

I stagger across the polished granite floor and out the main doors. I scan the area and spot a bench. I make my way through the expensively landscaped gardens that front the council building. Only when I'm safely sat down do I dare think about what I just learnt — my mother took her own life, twenty-two years ago.

It doesn't make any sense.

In my former life I never understood suicide. I couldn't comprehend the existence of a place so dark, so void of hope. A place where death is a compelling alternative to living. However, in my early days at Broadhall I skirted past that place once or twice. I somehow found the resolve to push past it, but for some reason it appears my mum couldn't find that same resolve.

Beyond trying to make any sense of Mum taking her own life, why 1996? It was ten years after I was killed so surely that couldn't have been the catalyst. It's stone-cold comfort. Maybe it was the old man who drove her to it. Did he revert to type after my death? That makes no sense either as without me in their lives, there was nothing keeping her shackled to him. Why kill yourself when you can get a divorce?

Far from finding closure, I've opened Pandora's box. I get up from the bench and trudge in the vague direction of the flat.

Half-an-hour later I'm sat in the lounge in complete silence, if you exclude the noise in my head. I had prepared myself for the worst, knowing that one or both of my parents could be dead. I could never have prepared for this eventuality. People die, I get that, but people rarely take their own life. The fact I will never see my mum's face again is hard enough to take, but the fact she made a conscious decision to kill herself is heartbreaking. I can't see past it.

Hours pass and I remain seated on the couch. I cry, I shout and I pummel the upholstery with my fists. More than at any point in my life I need someone to talk to. My need is irrelevant — there's nobody to tell, much less anyone whom I can unburden the truth to. This fucked-up world and every broken life within it is of my creation. It is now my hell and I must endure it alone.

I get up and leave the flat. I stride purposely down the street towards my destination.

The last moments of this day I'll remember will be a trip to a convenience store and opening a bottle of vodka in the kitchen. Anything beyond that, alcohol will take care of.

A drunken coma will be my sanctuary for the rest of the day.

9

Twilight and early-morning birdsong wake me just after five in the morning. The couch is not as comfortable as it looks and every bit of me aches. I stumble to the kitchen and down two painkillers with a pint of water. I set the alarm on my phone to go off in two hours and climb into bed. Sleep promptly returns.

The two hours pass in a heartbeat, and before I know it, my phone trills away on my bedside table. I turn it off and lie in silence, my mouth dry and my head thick. Fragments of yesterday start to piece together, regret being the glue holding them in place. Inevitably, I begin to question my actions and conclude the bottle of vodka wasn't a great idea. I've got work today, and I'm due to meet Lucy this evening so a hangover is the last thing I need. I clamber out of bed and head to the kitchen in dire need of strong coffee.

With coffee made, I return to the couch and the empty vodka bottle sat on the table, next to a pack of cheap disposable razors. Even in my most reckless of moments I still managed to remember my shopping list. It almost raises a wry smile.

I sip my coffee and stare at the bottle. Did that really help? I could argue that it took me away from the constant heckling of questions I am in no position to answer. They're still there though. I need to push on, keep wading through the pain until I find all of my questions are answered. I tell myself this is like having toothache and being afraid of the dentist. You can put off the appointment but the pain won't go away. At some point you've got to enter the surgery, sit in that chair and open your mouth. I've entered the surgery but there's still more pain to face before I move on.

I take a shower, have a long overdue shave, and check the weather forecast on my phone. It's sods law that after yesterday's cooler weather, it's going to hit thirty degrees today. Not ideal if I'm to spend another day languishing in hell's toilet at the shop. Assuming it's going to be another dirty, sweaty day, it makes sense to wear the charity clothes that came with me from Broadhall. As cheap and nasty as my new clothes might be, I can't afford to ruin them.

I get dressed and watch the morning news while I eat a bowl of muesli. The TV provides a distraction, the food doesn't. I leave the flat earlier than I really need to but I fancy a slow saunter into town this morning. I've got a lot to consider and I'm hoping the blue skies and early morning sunshine will spark some positivity in my thinking.

Half-an-hour later I'm a little sweaty but devoid of any inspiration. In reality, what can I do with the damning information I learnt yesterday? My mother is dead, and has been for a long time. Notwithstanding the fact I have no idea where he now lives, or even if he's alive, the old man is the only person who can provide answers. But I suspect he won't be too forthcoming if his dead son turns up to talk about his dead wife. While it's all well and good having the stomach to find the answers, realistically, where do I find them?

Pushing the same questions around my head is a fruitless exercise so I try to focus on more positive matters, and my date with Lucy tonight. Thinking about it, is 'date' the right word? I'd say our relationship has always been more like that of close friends. Obviously Lucy is an attractive woman but I've never felt there was any romantic connection between us, certainly not from Lucy's perspective anyway. I was married and she was a colleague, a good friend, simple as that.

I stop dead in my tracks as if I'd walked into a brick wall. What the hell am I thinking?

I have to remind myself that Lucy and I don't have a relationship of any kind. Apart from the hour or so we spent together in her office the other day, we're as good as strangers. If I'm even to class her as a friend, I have to start from scratch, rebuild everything. Tonight won't be a date in the traditional sense; it will be a chance for me to lay the foundations of our friendship. And with everything else going on in my head at the moment, I need to take things one step at a time.

I arrive at the MISSO shop twenty minutes before opening time. Brenda is already behind the counter, trying in vain to make a pile of cheap jewellery look enticing. She's traded in her slacks and blouse for a bright blue dress. She looks a bit like a hot air balloon. After telling me in no uncertain terms that I look like shit, she suggests I grab a cup of tea. I head into the kitchen and do exactly that. As I take my first sip, Brenda joins me.

"Heavy night was it?" she chirps.

"That obvious?"

"You don't get to my age without experiencing your own fair share of hangovers. Was it purging or pleasure?"

"Purging. Definitely."

"Oh dear. Would I be right in guessing it had something to do with our chat on Thursday?"

I take another sip of my tea. Brenda eyes me with a look that is probably instinctive, maternal. A woman I barely know is offering me a chance to offload, to talk.

It's a sad indictment of my life that she is really the only person offering me that chance. I take it before I analyse the reasons not to.

"It's my mum. I found out she's dead," I croak.

Brenda steps towards me and places her hand on my shoulder. She looks up at me, her expression empathetic.

"I'm so sorry, my love. Do you want to talk about it?"

"If I'm honest, I'm struggling to get my head around it. It doesn't seem real," I sigh.

"Something like that can be a shock and the mind tries to block it out I reckon. Probably easier to cope with it that way. I know there's not much I can say that'll make it any easier, but I can listen. If you want to get anything off your chest, it's better than keeping it bottled up, that I promise you."

She keeps her hand fixed on my shoulder but doesn't say anything else, leaving the door open for me to step through should I choose. I feel the muscles in my chest tighten and a lump dances in my throat. I place my cup on the kitchen counter and press my fingers into my temples. I do everything within me to fight the overwhelming urge to cry.

Brenda takes the initiative.

"Come here, my love, let's hug it out. You'll feel better, I promise."

Without waiting for my approval, Brenda wraps her arms around me and gently pats my back. The last time anyone showed me any affection was back in 1986 when Mum hugged me in the kitchen the night I left. She used to say that a hug gave more comfort than a thousand words ever could. Maybe this is as close as I'm ever going to get to that comfort again. I'll take it.

A silent moment passes before Brenda breaks away. She takes my hands and grips them tightly.

"I might not know you very well, but I know that pain too well. Whenever you feel like you need to talk, you come and see me."

The kindness of strangers — a simple hug and a few compassionate words but it means so much, almost too much. I feel my eyes misting as I smile back at Brenda.

"Sorry, that wasn't very professional and I shouldn't bring my problems to work," I sniffle.

"Oh, bollocks to that. You work here for bugger-all so the least I can do is give you a hug when you need one. I know you might think I'm a daft old cow but I do understand how you must be feeling. Just you remember that."

"I will. And I certainly don't think you're daft."

"Just an old cow then?" she laughs.

She pats me gently on the arm and waddles out of the kitchen. Just as she gets to the doorway, she turns back to face me.

"I meant every word of what I just said, my love. You're only on your own if you want to be."

And with that she turns and leaves.

I pull myself together and finish my tea. I've barely known her more than a few days but Brenda has already filled a friend-shaped hole in my life. I could do with a few more Brendas in this barren life.

I take a moment to pull myself together and head out to the shop to get my instructions for the day. Emily is stood on the opposite side of the counter, trying to de-tangle a nest of cheap jewellery.

"Morning Emily," I say as cheerfully as I can.

"Morning," she replies curtly. Odd woman.

Brenda asks if I mind returning to the stockroom for a few hours as the shelves in the shop need replenishing. I was kind of hoping not to be working on my own and Brenda detects my hesitancy.

"Sally works on Saturdays so I can send her in to give you a hand. She'll be here in about half-an-hour."

I give Brenda a knowing smile and make my way out to the stockroom. The unventilated room still holds a pungent odour but at least it's fairly cool. I know that won't last as the sun works its way around the building so I immediately open the shutter. I puff out my cheeks and delve into the first bag of god-only-knows what.

As nasty as the job is, it's easy to get lost in it and a mindless half-an-hour passes quickly. I'm so focused I almost soil myself when the stockroom door suddenly swings open. I glance up from a box of kitchen utensils, and do a double-take.

"Hi, you must be Craig. Nice to meet you. I'm Sally."

I know — you were my mother-in-law for twenty-five years.

I stand, open-mouthed and stare at Megan's mother. What hideous twist of fate has dropped us into this room together?

I run through a mental checklist to ensure I'm not mistaken: late sixties, average height, thin frame, long hair dyed blonde, and amber eyes. Even the jeans and checked shirt she's wearing seem familiar. There's no mistaking Sally Franklin.

"Sally?" I splutter.

The faint lines on her forehead deepen as she squints at me.

"Sorry, have we met before?"

Somewhere in my shocked mind, a lever is thrown and I switch from the Craig who knows Sally to the one who has never met her.

"No…sorry, my mistake."

Sally approaches me and holds out a hand.

"Thought not. I'd definitely remember you," she purrs.

I shake her hand while I inwardly cringe at her blatant flirtation.

"So, where do you want me?" she asks with a slight raise of her left eyebrow.

"Um, we need to sort through that pile of bags."

"Let's get down to it then shall we?"

The next hour is beyond excruciating. Notwithstanding Sally's cougar-like behaviour, questions about Megan burn but can't be asked. I try several times to swing our conversation around to the subject of children and family, but Sally sweeps my questions aside every time. In the end I just ask her outright if she has kids. Again, she changes the subject without an answer. I can only assume she doesn't want to admit having a daughter the same age as me.

One thing I do learn, and Sally emphasises several times, is that she divorced six years ago. It's a fact that surprises me, not least because Sally and Trevor celebrated their fiftieth wedding anniversary in my previous life. As Sally chatters away, I barely listen as I try to work out how my actions in 1986 could possibly have caused their divorce. Nothing comes of it.

As the temperature in the stockroom slowly increases, Sally decides to remove her shirt. She deliberately stands in my line of sight and slowly undoes the buttons. She peels herself out of the sweat-soaked shirt, and for one horrific moment I panic she might not be wearing anything underneath. I breathe a sigh of relief when I see her white vest top. Despite her age, her body isn't too dissimilar to that of Megan's in middle-age and that familiarity prompts me to stare for just a few seconds too long. Sally notices.

"Like what you see?" she says with a wicked grin. "A lot of hours in the beauty salon and the gym."

As my face reddens, my mind decides to conjure up the image of me and my former mother-in-law, going at in the stockroom like sweaty rabbits. So very wrong on so many levels. While I may not have had sex in a long, long time, that's one line I will not cross. I need an escape plan before I do something monumentally stupid.

"I need a cold drink. Can I get you one, Sally?"

"Gin and tonic, with ice. Please," she replies with a wink.

"Oh, I think there's only orange squash."

I dart out of the stockroom, wincing at my parting statement.

As I pass the open door to the office on my way to the kitchen, Brenda calls my name. I backtrack and stand in the doorway.

Brenda is sat at a desk with a mug of coffee and a laptop computer in front of her. She looks up from the screen, an agitated expression on her face.

"Twatter," she says abruptly.

"Sorry?"

"Twatter. Do you know anything about it?"

I glance at the screen where the web browser displays the Twitter home page.

"You mean Twitter?"

"Twitter, Twatter, makes no bloody odds. I can't work this damn thing," she groans.

"What are you trying to do?"

"The idiots at head office say we need to have a page for the shop on social thingamabobs. I don't have the first clue about this Internet stuff and I'm just about to throw this fecking thing across the room."

I can't help but chuckle. Then I realise this is a chance to extract myself from Sally's clutches.

"Would you like me to set it up for you?"

"If you could, my love, you'll be saving me from a potential coronary."

I drag a chair from the front of the desk and position it next to Brenda. She nudges the laptop towards me like it's emitting a bad smell.

"I don't know how people have the patience to deal with these bloody things."

I consider referring her to Lucy's service but I suspect Brenda will always be an unwilling adopter of this new-fangled technology.

"Don't worry. We'll have this sorted in no time."

Brenda hands me a memo from head office with basic instructions for setting up pages on Twitter and Facebook. I quickly scan and discard them. Brenda is right — whoever wrote the instructions is clearly an idiot. I show her how to set up an email account and then I create the Twitter page, explaining the steps as I go. Quite what they're expected to tweet about is anyone's guess. I move over to Facebook but Brenda doesn't appear interested in listening to any more of my condescending commentary and changes the subject.

"How are you getting on with Sally?" she asks with a wry smile.

"She's…friendly."

Brenda lets out a huge belly laugh. "That's one word for her. Predatory might be another."

I've been set up.

"Right, I get it," I groan. "You knew she was some sort of man-eater when you stuck her in there with me."

Brenda's laughing becomes almost hysterical. I sit with an indignant look on my face until she eventually calms down.

"Sorry, my love, I thought it might help take your mind off things."

"Yes, well, it certainly did that."

Brenda dries her eyes on her sleeve and finds some composure.

"Sally is harmless really. Poor woman has had a tough time of things and is just trying to eek out whatever joy she can from life. Don't take it personally."

"I see. What tough times has she been through?"

Her smile quickly subsides and she pauses for a moment, perhaps uncomfortable with the direction our conversation has taken.

"Sally's daughter had a miscarriage," she replies, her voice low. "Must have been seven or eight years ago now. That's why she volunteers here."

"What's her daughter's name?" I ask, knowing the answer but I need to hear it.

"Megan. Least it was, poor soul."

A small word with huge implications. "What do you mean, *was*?" I gulp.

Brenda sits back in her chair and appears to drift off in her own thoughts for a moment.

"Brenda," I say gently, nudging her back to reality. She stares blankly at the desk but eventually replies in a hushed voice.

"Every woman who works here has been touched by miscarriage at some point in their lives. I lost a baby myself, long time ago. Sally took the hardest hit though.

She lost a grandson and a daughter because of a miscarriage."

"What? How?"

"She was five months in, her first child. Megan was a career woman and left it late to have kids, late-thirties I think. Anyway, she suffered a catastrophic miscarriage in the bathroom at home and collapsed unconscious. She lost so much blood. By the time her husband came home she was already gone. Poor girl, God rest her soul."

Brenda slips back into her own world which is just as well because I'm lost for words. I feel like I've been kicked in the gut by a horse. I had imagined a hundred different lives that Megan could have lived without me. The possibility of such a tragic ending never crossed my mind.

The now-familiar feeling returns. I feel faint, dizzy, sick.

"I need to take an early lunch," I croak.

Brenda continues to gaze into space but nods.

I stagger out of the office and through the shop onto the street. I stand dazed, trying to get my head around the fact Megan is dead. I have to repeat that fact over and over again because the words make no sense on any level. Megan is dead. She can't be. Jesus, she can't be. It's beyond unreal, beyond any nightmare.

A deep panic ensues. I grapple with my breathing as lungs and mind lose connection. Shards of light flicker in the corner of my eyes as my blood pressure soars and my heart hammers like a piston. I have to sit down before gravity puts me down.

I stagger across the pavement and fall to my backside, propped up against a brick wall. A hundred anxious questions clamour for attention. My mind is too fragile and I can't bear to face any of them, except one

— what have I done to deserve this? Every time I think I've turned a corner, found some stable ground, fate unleashes another seismic blow in my direction. How many more hits before I fall, never to get up again? How much more grief can one man take?

I wait for my breathing to settle down. When I'm sure my legs can support me, I clamber to my feet and stagger away.

I walk aimlessly with no thought to time or place. Mental images of my life with Megan rotate in a slideshow as I walk. Most poignant of all is the picture of Megan in a hospital bed after we lost Jessica. Clearly Megan had an undiagnosed condition that lay dormant, ready to strike once she fell pregnant. This life, that life; it didn't matter. I remember the depth of her grief when she was first told about the hysterectomy, and that she would never be a mother. Obviously we never knew it at the time but when they removed her womb, they removed a death sentence. All those years we thought fate had played us the cruellest of hands when, in reality, it had saved Megan's life. Fate wasn't so forgiving this time.

From nowhere, my train of thought arrives at a damning conclusion — this is life teaching me a lesson.

Rather than accepting what I had and making the most of it, I used an improbable opportunity to apply a lazy fix. I spent most of my adult life wishing things were better but never considered how they could have been worse, much worse. I grasped negativity and clung to it while the positives drifted by unnoticed. I could have changed any part of my life without a thirty-year trip to the past, but I didn't. I sat and complained, felt sorry for myself, but did nothing to change it. I wasted my opportunities and now I'm being punished for it — my own personal purgatory.

My wife is dead. My mother is dead. Those twelve people on the coach are dead. Christ, even I'm dead.

There is no way to spin any positivity from this. My selfish, misguided plan for a better life has royally fucked everything.

10

I take a slow walk back to the shop, burdened by a crushing guilt. My analytical mind searches for even the most tenuous strand of positivity but there's nothing there. It feels like I'm stood on the edge of a cliff with the spectre of my past urging me to jump. Perhaps I should. Who would care? Perhaps all that is stopping me is the realisation that it would, once again, be the easy option. The very reason I'm suffering this life is because I've always sought the easy option. If I take it again, it would prove I have learnt nothing,

But I do wonder how many more times I can skirt that dark place before I'm tempted to enter.

I arrive back at the shop ten minutes late and apologise to Brenda. She reminds me that I'm an unpaid volunteer and therefore my wages won't be docked. I head back to the stockroom, actually hoping Sally is there. She is.

"There you are. I was beginning to think I'd scared you off," she grins mischievously.

"Sorry Sally. I was helping Brenda with something from head office."

"Never mind. I've got you to myself again now."

I don't need this. What I actually need is to talk to the only person who can begin to understand my grief. I get straight to the point.

"Brenda told me what happened to your daughter."

Her head slowly drops as her shoulders slump. She suddenly looks more like the mother-in-law I once knew.

"Brenda had no right to tell you," she scowls.

I ignore her protest and try the empathy angle.

"My girlfriend miscarried, years ago. It was touch and go at one point but she lost our baby and they had to conduct an emergency hysterectomy. It's why I volunteered here."

She doesn't say anything but slowly sits down on a crate and puts her head in her hands.

"I didn't mean to upset you Sally. If you don't want to talk about it, I understand."

She lifts her head and looks up at me.

"Her name was Megan, my daughter. She was only thirty-eight. No offence, Craig, but I've talked about it a thousand times to a thousand people. Makes no odds. I lost my daughter and my unborn grandson on the same day. There are some things people can never understand. Some things you never come back from."

Sally doesn't know it, but I understand exactly how she feels. I let the silence hang in the room for a moment.

"What was she like, Megan?"

Her face brightens a little and a faint smile appears.

"She was an amazing woman. She worked so hard and didn't take shit from the people who tried to hold her back. She worked her way up from PA to director of a financial services company in London. She had it all: big house, doting husband, incredible career. But the one thing she always wanted was kids. Maybe she left it too late. Maybe if she'd tried earlier, rather than working all hours, things might have turned out differently."

Her smile fades. "That's all I have now. A whole heap of maybes."

"I've got plenty of those myself," I reply gently. "Along with a ton of what ifs."

She looks at me quizzically. “I probably should have asked before I made a spectacle of myself. Are you married?”

“I was, in another life.”

“But not now?”

“Technically not. I was, err, estranged from my wife but I found out recently I’m actually now a widower.”

By recently, I mean just over an hour ago.

“Oh, God, I’m sorry. You seem so young, you know, to be a widower.”

I drop my head and ignore her question. Discussing the same woman in a different context is too surreal. I switch the conversation back to Sally.

“What about you, Sally? What happened to your marriage, if you don’t mind me asking?”

“No. It’s okay,” she murmurs. “We never really got over losing Megan. Then Trevor’s brother died and he went off the rails. He started drinking too much and losing his temper over stupid things. I just couldn’t live with him.”

Trevor had two brothers, one of which was Malcolm Franklin, my old boss at Video City. I try to think of a way of establishing which brother died.

“Probably little consolation but at least Megan and her uncle are together now.”

Such a crass, clichéd thing to say but it was the best I could do on the spur of the moment.

Thankfully Sally smiles. “That’s a sweet thing to say. Megan was really close to her Uncle Malcolm so maybe you’re right.”

Having got away with such a puke-inducing statement, I do some quick calculations in my head. Malcolm would have been in his mid-seventies when he died so he clearly never married Mali Surat or moved to

Thailand, both of which he did in his late-fifties in the original timeline. A tiny consolation I guess.

"What did Megan's husband do for a living?"

"Graham? He worked for the same company as Megan. Still does I guess, but I haven't spoken to him in a long while. They'd only been married for three years so I didn't know him that well. Don't get me wrong, he was a lovely guy but he was only in her life for a relatively short time. I'd imagine he's moved on now."

I think back to the day Sally and Trevor arrived at the hospital when we lost our baby. They cut me out of their grief on that occasion and I wonder if they did the same to Graham. Only natural I suppose, but it still hurt to be excluded.

"Anyway, isn't it about time we got on?" Sally huffs. "This conversation probably isn't doing either of us any good."

She gets up from the crate and sets about sorting through another bag of clothes. I guess it is time to get on.

Despite the subdued atmosphere in the stockroom, the afternoon passes quickly. Sally's overt flirting doesn't resurface and we only talk about matters relevant to the job in hand. I'm not sure if she's embarrassed, or scared I'll quiz her about Megan again, but she appears keen to avoid any meaningful conversation. It helped to be in her company though. I doubt I could have coped without Sally. Even though she didn't know it, just talking about Megan probably stopped me falling over the edge.

Before I leave, Brenda takes me aside and slips a piece of paper into my hand. Her home phone number. She makes me promise to call her if I feel down or just need somebody to talk to. I gratefully agree.

As I start on the long walk back to the flat, my mind wanders to tonight and drinks with Lucy. I'm minded to postpone. As much as I want to spend the evening in her company, I'm not in the right frame of mind. Then again, maybe I need a release. I can't carry on taking hit after hit without blowing off some steam. Maybe a few drinks and some frivolous conversation will balance me out, take my mind off things.

I'm still undecided when I walk through the front door of the flat.

Dinner is a concoction of wholemeal pasta with mozzarella, tomatoes, and pesto sauce. If nothing else, it's filling. After eating, I decide to take a bath. The tub takes an age to fill but I'm rewarded for my patience as I finally ease myself into the steaming water.

I lie there for a while, content to do nothing and think about nothing. It's only when the water begins to cool that I hurriedly shampoo my hair before ducking my head beneath the water to rinse. The absolute silence and opaque light beneath the surface prompts a question — what would it be like to drown? It's hard to imagine this calmness descending so quickly into unimaginable panic. The thrashing of arms and legs as your lungs balloon with water and you desperately gasp for air that isn't there. Thinking about it makes me shudder and I force my head back above the surface and inhale a deep breath. No, drowning is not for me. I think I'd much rather swallow a handful of sleeping tablets and drift away from my woes, never to come back. Painless, peaceful. It's an almost enticing prospect.

As both the bathwater and my thoughts lose clarity, I get out and check the time; forty-five minutes until I'm supposed to meet Lucy. Too late to cancel? Do I want to cancel? As I get dressed in the best of my budget clothing, I'm still undecided. Maybe I can just go along, have a drink or two and then make my excuses if I don't feel sociable. I agree with myself that it's a workable plan, and head into the bathroom to make myself look vaguely presentable.

Half-an-hour later I enter Bar Mirage. This used to be a traditional spit and sawdust pub before some faceless public company acquired it and ripped out the soul. Now it's all muted colours, mirrors, and minimalism. It's achingly trendy. On the plus side, it's surprisingly quiet for a Saturday evening, or maybe I'm just unfashionably early. I'm served with an overpriced pint of lager within a minute, and find refuge at a table in a darkened corner.

I sit and watch my fellow patrons as I nurse my pint. Young, happy, and spirited. Everything I'm not. I feel a million years old and a million miles from my comfort zone. Maybe this wasn't such a good idea, least the venue wasn't. I stare at my pint and try to ignore the feeling that everyone is looking at me, judging me. I focus on the beat of an obnoxious track playing from a speaker above my head. I've never heard it before and wouldn't be disappointed if I never heard it again. Still, I close my eyes and let the rhythmic bassline lull me away.

The track ends just as I sense somebody stood nearby. I open my eyes and look up.

"Keeping you up?" Lucy chuckles.

I snap back to reality and hurriedly stand, bashing my shin on the table leg in the process. It's an innocuous knock but hurts like hell.

"Fuck! Bastard! Sorry," I wail.

Lucy fights hard to hold back laughter as I hop towards her and plant a kiss on her cheek. Assuming I'll adhere to the correct social etiquette, she moves her head to present her other cheek. I stand motionless for a moment before I realise she was also expecting a kiss on both cheeks. I move in but Lucy turns back to face me. I catch her puzzled expression a split second before our foreheads thump together.

Great start.

I retreat a few steps and apologise profusely while Lucy nurses her forehead. Any preconceived ideas she may have had about my coolness have just been shattered.

"I'm so sorry. Are you okay?" I fumble.

"Um, I think so. Never been head-butted on a date before, but I'm sure I'll live."

"Drink?" I ask. "Or shall I just book a taxi?"

"Wow, you don't mess around. We've only just got here."

"Christ, no…that's not what I meant," I splutter.

She keeps a poker face for a few seconds before a smile breaks.

"I'm kidding. I know what you meant and I'll have a white wine, large please. I've got a feeling I'm going to need it."

I return an embarrassed smile and head to the bar.

As I wait to be served I take the opportunity to study Lucy's attire, reflected in the mirror behind the bar. This version of Lucy appears a little more confident, her outfit more revealing than anything I ever saw the old Lucy wear. Her brick-red skirt hangs a good few inches above the knee, contrasting with her luminous, tanned legs. Her top is some sort of cream-coloured lace number, cut short at the shoulders to reveal her tanned arms. If I didn't know her, which I sort of don't, I'd say she was well out of my league, or at least Craig Pelling's league. I may be physically different now but the lack of confidence and hang ups are the same.

The barman cuts my lecherous thoughts short as he asks what I want. He disappears briefly and returns with Lucy's drink. I turn away with little change from a fiver and limp back to the table.

"Sorry about the wait."

"I'm just glad you made it back in one piece," Lucy giggles before she takes a large gulp of her wine.

"Yeah, sorry. Not my finest five minutes. You probably weren't expecting drinks with Mr Bean."

"I happen to like Mr Bean."

"Really?" I reply with surprise, although I know full well she's a massive Rowan Atkinson fan.

"I preferred Blackadder. Pure comedy gold," I add.

"Oh my god, I absolutely love Blackadder," she shrieks.

For the next two hours it's like shooting fish in a barrel. Lucy must think she's met her soul-mate because I happen to like everything she likes and share the exact same views on so many subjects, all of which I bring up in conversation. As the time flies, so do my troubles. My original plan to perhaps leave after a few drinks isn't given a second thought.

Only two aspects of our evening dampen my good mood. Firstly, the bar is rammed with the type of people who wouldn't be seen dead in what I'm wearing, and they're noisy. Secondly, the cost of the drinks is a significant drain on my meagre bank balance.

Thankfully, I happen to know that Lucy prefers a particular, more traditional drinking establishment down the road. It's certainly not the type of place you'd go on a first date but it's far more our scene so I suggest we head there.

"Have you been stalking me?" she playfully replies to my suggestion.

"No. Why?"

"The Rose & Anchor is my favourite pub."

"Well, let's get out of here then."

We exit Bar Mirage onto the quiet street.

As we walk side by side, I put my hands in my pockets and Lucy links her arm into mine. For a second I feel awkward but it soon passes and by the time we reach The Rose & Anchor, it feels right. Almost too right. Maybe it's the alcohol clouding my mind but as I hold the door open for her, I'm suddenly struck by how effortlessly beautiful Lucy looks this evening. It's the same woman I worked with for almost ten years, but I can't see her now. And I'm stirred by feelings that don't quite fit with the dynamics of our relationship, least the one we had. It's an odd feeling. Wonderfully odd, but odd nonetheless.

The main bar in the Rose & Anchor is gloriously olde worlde. An inviting oak bar spans one side of the room, opposite a huge inglenook fireplace. The walls are all oak-panelled and the beamed ceiling sits low enough that any patrons over six foot need to mind their heads. The only nod to modernity is a juke box affixed to a brick pillar at the rear, the volume set to an unobtrusive level.

Beyond the aesthetics, the customers are significantly lower in number and much older in years than in Bar Mirage. When I managed RolpheTech, we had post-work drinks in The Rose & Anchor hundreds of times over the years. Being in here again sparks a warm feeling of familiarity.

Lucy offers to buy the drinks and I offer the bare minimum of chivalrous protest in return. It doesn't work, thankfully. We take our drinks over to an empty table and Lucy tells me how she and her workmates used to occasionally drink here after work. She regales me with stories of drunken antics but the names of her colleagues are meaningless to me. I smile and laugh anyway.

As time slips by, another round of drinks are acquired and Lucy suggests we check-out the juke box. Apart from the coin shoot, there are no mechanical parts. A touchscreen offers the choice of thousands of tracks, sorted by genre, artist or album. Lucy steps forward and prods away at the screen.

"Anything in particular you want to listen to?"

This could be a watershed moment. Do I say it? There are many good reasons not to offer the answer which immediately comes to mind. However, the alcohol in my bloodstream and the overwhelming need to feel close to someone trump them all.

"How about, 'Truly Madly Deeply' by Savage Garden?" I casually reply.

Lucy spins around and stares up at me, her eyes wide, mouth slightly agape.

"Are you kidding me? Why would you choose that particular song?"

"I just love the words. Why do you ask?" I reply innocently.

"You're not real, you can't be. Of all the songs you could have chosen, you chose *that* one."

I stand motionless and pretend to look confused. "Sorry, you've lost me."

"First dance at my wedding," she sighs.

"What? You're married?"

She shakes her head. "No, sadly not. But I've always had a vision in my head of that song playing for the first dance at my wedding. Unfortunately that wedding hasn't happened on the account of there being no fiance, or even a suitable boyfriend."

"Fancy practicing that dance?" I ask.

Lucy beams and turns to face the juke box. She quickly prods the screen a few times before the opening chords to 'Truly Madly Deeply' gently chime across the room. I know it's her favourite song, and just for a moment I feel a little guilty for playing this card. As Lucy wraps her arms around my waist, that guilt drifts away.

In fact, so much drifts away in that moment I almost forget about Craig Wilson's problems.

Almost.

11

For four minutes and ten seconds we hold one another and rotate slowly. It would have been perfect had it not been punctuated by thoughts of Megan, swirling through my mind like the Ghost of Christmas Past. For a second I'm not in a pub with Lucy. I'm stood in the middle of a dance floor in a village hall, holding my new bride as we prepare for our first dance as husband and wife. Cameras flash and the song begins — Richard Marx, 'Right Here Waiting'. Megan looks up at me and pouts a photograph album smile. It doesn't hide the wistful sadness in her eyes.

I try to shake the vision from my mind. That life never happened and maybe Megan was better off for it. So many years together and so little happiness. Did I actually do her a favour by sending her down a different path? Thirty-eight years is too short a life, but it was a good life, a better life. Perhaps less is more, and that has to be the way I look beyond Megan's fate in this timeline. It helps to quash the irrational guilt currently stifling my feelings towards Lucy.

I return to reality just as 'Truly Madly Deeply' ends.

Lucy looks up at me, just as Megan once did. Different woman, different life. Her opal green eyes surreptitiously share her thoughts, if you know how to read them. I'd wager that Lucy can't quite believe she's in the midst of a romantic embrace with a guy she only met once before tonight. It's out of character. She knows it and so do I.

"Can we talk for a moment?" she whispers.

"Sure."

"Look Craig, there's something you should know. I have a teenage daughter."

"Right."

"So, we're like a package deal. I know most guys seem to have a problem with sharing so I thought I better mention it."

"Right."

She releases her arms from around my waist and folds them across her chest.

"Is that all you can say?" she huffs.

Lucy has always had a slight tendency to over-dramatise. I've met her daughter dozens of times and we got on okay, at least as well as a middle-aged man can get on with a teenage girl.

"I didn't mean to sound uninterested. It's just a non-issue for me."

She closes her eyes for a second and nibbles her bottom lip.

"Oh god, I'm messing this up aren't I?" she says apologetically. "I didn't mean to sound so defensive."

"Lucy, it's not a problem. I assume you are who you are because you're a parent?"

She nods and looks around the room.

"So I get it. Nothing has changed. It doesn't bother me in the slightest. Okay?"

For a second it feels like I'm her manager again. Chiding her for being a drama queen over some petty issue.

"You're going to think I'm mad, but I've never felt this type of connection with anyone before," she says. "Don't panic though. I'm not hoping to get you up the aisle next week, but I think we could be good together."

"So do I."

"It's like, um…Tetris," she says.

"Eh?"

"You've played Tetris before?"

"The video game? The one where you have to fit different shapes into a solid wall?"

"Yep. That's the one."

"Okay," I reply hesitantly. "Yes I have."

"Well, more often than not, the pieces don't fit together properly. You drop them down and your wall ends up with gaps everywhere. That's a bit like my previous relationships — gaps everywhere. But with you, all the pieces seem to fit perfectly. "

"It's an interesting analogy."

"My point is, I really like you, Craig. There are no gaps, but I don't want to invest myself emotionally if you're only looking for something casual."

"I'm not."

"Good."

What happens next is as surreal as it is wonderful. Lucy Ashman, my great friend from a previous life, steps towards me. For a moment there is nobody else in the pub. We're in our own little bubble, oblivious to everything apart from each other. She lifts her hand and places it on the back of my head before gently pulling me towards her. I don't resist. I close my eyes a split-second before our lips meet.

It is not a kiss of frantic passion but a tender, lingering kiss. The tip of her tongue dances delicately just inside my mouth. Slowly, measured. I savour the sensation, the intimacy. The fact I am enthusiastically kissing my friend is somehow lost in the moment. I'm not sure I even care any more.

I couldn't even begin to estimate how long our faces are locked together. Time, like everything else around us, just dissolves away. Truth be told, I could live in our bubble forever. Suddenly I have a connection, a lifeline to grasp. Something of my previous life that isn't tarnished, broken. One woman, two lives, but there is enough overlap between the two for me to seek haven.

Ultimately the moment has to end and we withdraw in unison. Lucy takes my hands in hers while we hold one another's gaze.

"See what I mean? Every piece fits perfectly," she coos.

I look into her eyes, losing myself as an indistinct feeling suddenly engulfs me. There's a hint of familiarity to it but it feels out of kilter with the situation. On further introspection I realise I have felt it before — the moment Tessa kissed me in her bedroom when we were teenagers. That was the moment I knew, at least I thought I knew, I was in love.

This time it doesn't compute. Lucy is my friend. No, Lucy *was* my friend. But what is she now? And why has that feeling suddenly resurfaced, seemingly from nowhere?

It must be the alcohol, or the need to rekindle our friendship, any friendship for that matter. It must be that, surely. But if that's all it is, why is my heart doing cartwheels in my chest? Why is my skin tingling? And why do I feel the overwhelming urge to say something profoundly stupid?

Now I think about it, maybe it's something Craig Pelling could, and should have said to Lucy before his life was turned inside-out. I know why he didn't. He was too scared it would destroy what they had. Too afraid of the potential for rejection, for humiliation. Instead, he clutched a teenage crush in one hand while clinging to the frayed strands of his marriage in the other.

On reflection, it's no great surprise Craig Pelling resorted to type — an idiot who buried his head in the sand.

But now, standing here as Craig Wilson, I can see clearly. Now I've reached a point where there is little left to lose, it's time to finally accept this feeling for what I think it is, what I hope it is.

"You seem miles away. Having second thoughts already?" Lucy asks.

"No," I chuckle. "Just enjoying the moment. I've been waiting a long time for that kiss."

"There's plenty more where that one came from."

And on cue, Lucy moves in and we engage in our second kiss.

We return to our table and sit with our hands clasped together. We talk more and despite my best efforts, Lucy swings the subject away from the general chit-chat of earlier. Questions become more probing, more personal. Where did I grow up? What do I do for a living? Are my family local? I try to bat them away with humorous answers or by turning the question back at her. It doesn't take long for Lucy to spot my deflection and I fear our bubble is about to be burst.

"Are you always this guarded?" she asks, a deep line creasing her forehead.

What do I say to her? Do I lie or do I tell her something approaching the truth? The letter from the Broadhall doctor won't help me here.

"My life is a bit complicated."

Her body language changes in a flash. The Lucy who hates being pissed around withdraws her hand from mine.

"I thought you were too good to be true," she groans. "What is it? You're married? On the run from prison? About to join the circus?"

"Calm down, it's nothing like that."

"Please don't tell me to calm down, Craig."

"Sorry."

An uncomfortable silence hangs over the table. We both grab our glasses and neck our drinks, for differing reasons I suspect.

"I've been in hospital for the best part of a year," I eventually confess.

Lucy's expression softens slightly and she waits for me to expand on my statement.

"I had some sort of amnesic breakdown which left me with no memory of my life before I was admitted to hospital."

I slump back in my chair and stare at my empty glass on the table.

"How long have you been out of hospital?" Lucy asks, her voice low.

"Six days."

The silence returns momentarily.

"So you could be married, but just don't remember?"

"I'm definitely not married, Lucy. There would be a record of it somewhere, but there isn't."

"Do you remember anything?"

"Bits, but not much. It's like trying to remember a dream. When you focus on the detail there's nothing there."

I look up and try to determine her feelings. Her face displays sympathy but her eyes show a wariness.

"That's why you evaded my questions about your family and where you grew up?"

"Primarily. As I said, it's complicated."

"Right," she sighs. "Too complicated to explain?"

"You know those Tetris pieces that all fitted nicely together? Well, I think I'm about to scatter them."

Lucy rolls her eyes and stands up. "I need another drink."

I watch her move across the room to the bar. I figure I've now reached the point of no return. The moment where I snatch defeat from the jaws of victory. It's taken me a decade to finally get to this point with Lucy and now I'm about to blow it. How much do I tell her? What do I tell her? Patently I can't tell her the truth but I need to assure her than I'm worthy of her emotional investment.

She returns and places two glasses on the table. I take a sip of lager and pat the seat next to me.

"Sit down and I'll try to tell you everything."

"Okay, as long as it is everything. I'm too old and too weary to be dating men with baggage."

Lucy takes a seat and I begin my hastily prepared defence.

"The reason I was a bit vague about my family is because I've only just discovered that my mum is dead. I have no idea where my dad is, or even if he's still alive. Apart from my parents, I don't have any other family."

"Gosh, that's awful. Sorry…I didn't mean to pry."

"It's okay, but you see why I wasn't so keen to discuss my family?"

"Of course…hold on a minute. What about your Uncle Bungle?"

Fuck. The problem with telling lies is remembering them. Christ, what do I say now?

"Um, he doesn't actually exist."

Moron.

Her eyes widen and she pulls back from the table. “You’re freaking me out now, Craig. Why did you come to my office then?”

I reckon I have about five seconds to come up with a plausible explanation why I wandered into Lucy’s office and made up some bullshit story about a fictitious uncle.

Lucy takes a nervous gulp of wine. It spikes a memory of her sat at her desk sipping coffee.

“I saw you in Starbucks,” I splutter.

“I’m not with you.”

“Please don’t think I’m some sort of stalker but I spotted you in Starbucks and followed you back to your office. That’s when I decided to call you.”

“You followed me? Don’t you think that’s just a bit creepy?”

“Ordinarily, yes. But I’ve never done anything like that before in my life, I promise you.”

“So why did you?”

“Because the moment I saw you I was blown away. Can’t put my finger on it but there was just something about you. I didn’t think about it, just acted on impulse.”

“So let me get this straight. You saw me in Starbucks and thought I was ‘the one’, and decided to follow me?”

“Yeah, that’s about the strength of it. I understand it seems bit weird but I knew I’d kick myself if I didn’t try to find out who you were.”

She sips her drink and begins to chuckle.

“So, there’s no Uncle Bungle?”

“Afraid not.”

“Well, if nothing else, you gave me a laugh. And I guess I should be flattered you went to so much trouble for a date.”

Well saved, Craig.

"But promise me something will you?"

"Anything."

"No more lies."

"Scouts honour."

She nods and her defensive stance eases a little. "Is everything else you told me true?"

"Everything else I've told you is the absolute, gods-honest truth," I reply, trying my best to look earnest. "I genuinely don't remember much about my life before being admitted to hospital. But clearly I'm no threat to either myself or anyone else, as otherwise they wouldn't have let me out. I've got a job working part-time in a charity shop, although I think I used to work as a manager in retail. There is no Mrs Wilson, nor has there ever been one. I live in a one-bedroom flat courtesy of Social Services and I own assets that value the sum total of nothing."

I draw breath and take another sip of my lager. I pause a moment for effect, then look her straight in the eye.

"So, you see Lucy, I'm quite the catch. What woman hasn't dreamt of dating a man with no money, no real job, oh, and no memory?"

I spot the tell-tale sign in her eyes that she's trying hard not to smile.

"But, on the upside I've got no baggage, no history and no hang ups either. What you see is quite literally what you get."

I sit back in my chair. Nothing else I can say or do now.

Lucy doesn't fight the smile any longer. "Thank you," she says softly.

"What for?"

"Just for being honest. I couldn't care less if you're skint or what you do for a living. All I want is somebody who is honest, somebody who is genuine. The fact you seem able to read my mind, make me laugh, and like Blackadder is a bonus though."

"So, we're good then?"

She leans across the table and plants a kiss on my cheek. "The pieces are all back in order."

But just when I think I've put all the personal stuff to bed, Lucy decides to press me a little further, subduing the atmosphere once again.

"I hope you don't mind me asking, but were you unaware your mum had died, or was the memory lost with everything else?"

"She died over twenty years ago. I get to grieve all over again, not that I remember the first time."

The lie falls effortlessly from my mouth. I feel uncomfortable enough just talking about Mum's death, let alone lying about it. Seems I have little choice though and Lucy presses me further.

"So you only found out a few days ago?"

"Yesterday."

"Oh god, Craig. And you've been dealing with that on your own?"

"Sort of. I told a woman at work and she's been great. But there's nobody who knew my mum that I can talk to."

"Have you been to her grave?"

A question so obvious but I hadn't even entertained the thought.

"Not yet."

"You should. It'll help."

"You think?"

"Grief is a strange thing, Craig. Everyone deals with it differently, but being physically close to the person you lost can help. My granddad used to religiously visit my nan's grave every Sunday morning. He'd chat away to the gravestone like she was stood next to him. He said it kept her memory alive and helped him deal with his loss."

Lucy could be right. Perhaps visiting Mum's grave will help me come to terms with her death. At least she won't be shocked to see me.

I give Lucy a nod and try to steer the conversation elsewhere.

"So when are we going to do this again?"

"Do you fancy coming over to my place, for dinner?"

"I'd like that. When?"

"How does Tuesday night work for you? Grace is away on a school trip next week so you won't have to suffer an inquisition from a moody teenager."

"It's a date."

As we finish our drink the barman rings the bell for last orders. Having both already consumed a little too much alcohol for a first date, we agree it would be sensible to leave while we can both stand. Holding hands, we take a slow walk to the taxi rank under dark skies.

Ten minutes, and several lingering kisses later, I'm waving goodbye to Lucy as she waves back from the rear seat of a taxi. The thrum of the diesel engine eventually fades into the distance and I turn to make my way back to the flat.

I can scarcely believe, after all the pain of the last few days, that a single ray of hope is finally breaking through the murk. I can also scarcely believe just how very pissed I am.

Again.

12

I'm too old for this shit. I have a double-whammy hangover from two consecutive nights of excessive alcohol consumption. The only consolation is a text that greets me when I dare open my eyes.

Thanx for a great time. Really looking forward 2 Tuesday nite. Lucy xx

Twelve words and two kisses. I read the text again, basking in the fuzzy glow like a lovesick teenager, and searching for some hidden meaning that probably doesn't exist. Unfortunately, it doesn't take long for guilt to temper my happiness. My mind see-saws with conflicted feelings. I now have the chance of a future with Lucy, something I could never have envisaged in my previous life. But at what cost? Everyone else I ever cared for is either dead or unaware of my existence. Some price to pay.

I get up and stagger into the kitchen to make myself a coffee. I swallow a couple of painkillers and stand in the kitchen waiting for the wooziness in my head to clear. Memories of last night fade in. Some good, some bad. The lies I told Lucy about my life fall into the latter category but what choice did I have? The only saving grace is this version of Lucy doesn't know me well enough to spot the tell tale signs I'm fibbing. The old Lucy would have seen through my bullshit with ease. I suppose of all the things I should feel guilty about, telling a few white lies to Lucy is the lightest burden.

I finish my coffee and slump down on the couch. For the first time since I left Broadhall six days ago, I have nothing to do, nowhere to be and no one to see. This is far from ideal because I know my idle mind will torment me all day if I don't find something to distract it. One major stumbling block is my lack of funds. I spent close to fifty quid last night so whatever I do today, it needs to be dirt cheap, or better still, free.

I eat a bowl of muesli, watch the news and go through my morning ablutions. Another hour spent — just another twelve hours to kill. I flop back down in front of the TV and flick through the channels. I know I'm distracting myself from the one thing I could, and should do today, but I don't want to think about it. I know Lucy was right and it probably will help, but I'm not sure I have the fortitude to visit my mother's grave.

An hour of watching Sunday morning TV changes my mind.

Having resigned myself to the inevitable quest, the practical aspects present my next challenge. There are three cemeteries in Farndale alone, with god-only-knows how many graves. As time-rich as I might be, I dread to think what an entire day spent trudging around cemeteries would do to my already fragile state of mind.

I head back to the bedroom and the half-decent wi-fi signal. I sit on the edge of the bed, open a web browser on my phone and search for cemetery records. The first two websites I visit require payment to access their data. Not an option. The third website apparently doesn't and I'm able to click through to a search form. I tentatively enter my mother's full name and the year she died, 1996. I press the search button and a spinning disc signifies my search is underway. Seconds pass and I wonder if the site has crashed, or if I'll be prompted to enter my credit card details to view the results. Five seconds later, I have my answer.

1 RECORD(S) FOUND: Janet Georgetta Pelling (nee Wilson)

DOD: 12th October 1996

CEMETERY: St Mary's Churchyard, Farndale

My heart sinks to my stomach. The almost infinitesimal slither of hope that Jim at the council made a mistake, is gone. The information on my screen is too specific to be anyone else other than my mum. She died, of that there is no doubt now, and the gut-wrenching pain returns for a second sitting.

I stare at the screen for too long and repeat the search, hoping that somehow the result will be different. It's not, nor is it on the third or fourth search. Now I have my answer, I absolutely have to heed Lucy's advice. The alternative is to sit here and listen to that spectre, beckoning me to a place I really don't want to go.

I check the location of St Mary's Church on Google Maps and leave the flat.

The only pleasant aspect of my morning thus far is the weather. The temperature is probably somewhere in the early twenties and the few cotton-wool clouds in the sky drift lazily on a gentle breeze. My destination is just over four miles away to the north of the town centre. Such is my reluctance to complete the journey, it could be forty miles away for all I care.

As I plod through the streets I try to keep my spirits up by thinking about Lucy. In truth, she is the one thing in this life to be optimistic about. I daydream about Tuesday evening and our dinner date. The fact she chose her home as the venue, and made a point about her daughter being away, suggests there might be more than just paella on the menu. Maybe I'm being presumptuous but even so, the thought makes me a little nervous and butterflies begin to flutter.

I plod on through the town centre and beyond. Every step closer to my destination exhausts my optimistic thoughts and trepidation builds. Several times I stop as the raging battle in my mind becomes too raucous. One side wants me to turn around while the other insists I keep moving. The legion urging me to keep moving just about win out but each victory becomes increasingly narrow.

It's just after midday when I reach the northern fringes of Farndale. I'm sweaty, tense, and nauseous. Some of my symptoms could be attributed to my hangover but they worsen as I close in on my destination so I can only conclude otherwise. I stop, engage my breathing technique, and consult the map on my phone — just a few more streets to cover.

I slow my pace further as I turn into a leafy residential street. A church spire looms above the rooftops on my right. A tortuous hundred yards later I turn into a narrow lane, bordered by high hedgerows on both sides. The church lychgates are maybe forty yards ahead of me, the weathered timbers supporting a roof drooped with age. Considering it's a Sunday I half-expected the place to be a hive of activity, but all I can hear is birdsong from the broad oak trees fronting the churchyard, and my pounding heart.

I pass through the lychgates and follow a short path beyond the canopy of the trees. I'm greeted by the sight of a handsome church, constructed with blocks of grey stone. I have no idea how old the building is, but it looks like the elements have been at work on the stone for several centuries. The path on which I'm stood leads all the way up to the main door of the church, with two further paths splitting off left and right about thirty feet ahead. The path to my left disappears behind the church while the path on the right runs parallel to the front elevation.

I follow the path to the right. The grounds host about thirty headstones, all mottled with patchy moss and lichen. They look impossibly old and a cursory glance reveals names and dates from the 1800s through to the early 1900s. There are no floral tributes on any of the graves, the occupants now forgotten ancestors rather than beloved family members. I guess this is where the church graveyard was originally established and would have been at full occupancy long before my mother passed away.

The path comes to an abrupt end at the far boundary. I pause for a moment, next to the final resting place of one Frederick Royston Cox; 1835 to 1854. Nineteen years old. Just below poor Frederick's name is a single line of faint text engraved on the headstone, 'Godspeed Our Brave Son'. I wonder if he was a soldier, sent to fight in a foreign land for Queen and Country. Whatever fate befell young Cox, I suspect I'm the first person to contemplate his life, and his death, in many a year. It's a sad thought, but also my mind's way of subconsciously distracting me from the reason I'm here.

I offer a silent prayer for Frederick Royston Cox and walk back along the path.

As I mindlessly gaze across the graves to my left, my peripheral vision suddenly captures the movement of a black smudge. My head snaps back to the path, and a man stood twenty feet in front of me.

"Splendid afternoon isn't it?" he chirps.

Dressed top-to-toe in black and donning a white dog-collar, it doesn't take Sherlock Holmes to deduce I'm looking at the Parish Vicar.

"Lovely," I reply.

The vicar moves along the path towards me, closing the distance between us to a few feet. I'd wager he's a good few years beyond middle-age, his hair more grey than brown. He holds out his hand and introduces himself.

"Father David. Pleased to meet you."

I shake his hand and return his smile.

"Craig Wilson."

"So what brings you to our churchyard this afternoon, Craig?"

His intelligent blue eyes don't offer any clue as to whether his question is accusatory or if he's just being friendly.

"I'm looking for a grave. I know it's here, not sure where though," I cautiously reply.

"In which case, I can probably help. What's the name?"

"Pelling. Janet Pelling."

He ponders the name for a few seconds while scratching his head.

"Janet Pelling you say?"

I nod.

"Do you know when she was buried?"

"1996."

"I've only been priest here for about ten years so I wouldn't have conducted her funeral. I can check the records in the vestry though, if you'd like me to?"

"Honestly, I don't want to put you to any trouble. If you just point me in the right direction, I'm sure I'll be able to find it."

"Oh, it's no trouble at all," he declares, a little too enthusiastically. "If you follow this path to the rear of the church, that's where the main cemetery is located. Go and start your search and I'll check the records. Give me twenty minutes."

Before I can argue, Father David spins around and scurries back into the church without another word.

I inwardly sigh and traipse along the path towards the left flank wall of the church. When I turn the corner I'm met with enormity of my task.

The cemetery spreads across a huge area, maybe four or five acres dotted with hundreds of graves. As I stare out over the depressing sea of granite and stone memorials, the option to abort returns. This is a stupid idea on so many levels. Barely a week has passed since I left Broadhall and death has been a constant shadow. Yet, despite the overwhelming grief I've suffered, here I am, stood in a huge fucking cemetery. It's one thing to confront your fears but lunacy to encourage them.

I'm caught between the need to flee and the need to talk to my mum, or at least her grave. Neither option is particularly rational, but what is rational about my life now?

Caught in two minds, I postpone any decision and slowly trudge along the path which snakes up towards a clump of beech trees at the far boundary, some two hundred yards away. The silence is wonderful, the view less so.

I amble slowly past rows of headstones positioned a few yards beyond the path edge and I fight the urge to read the inscriptions. I pass a grave with an arrangement of bright yellow flowers leant against the polished granite headstone. On closer inspection I realise the tribute is shaped like a teddy bear. From nowhere, it triggers a reminder of those four children killed on the coach; killed in lieu of my elderly grandparents.

I quickly move on before my mind has the chance to torment me further, or my legs buckle. Both are a given if I stare at the child's grave any longer.

With no desire to view any other harrowing tributes, I keep my focus on the right of the path where a wide expanse of lawn slopes down to a holly hedge about sixty yards away. From my elevated position I can see a twee cottage, presumably the vicarage, sited in the middle of a well kept garden beyond the hedge. Of more interest is a bench, positioned next to an open archway leading through to the vicarage garden.

I plod down the slope and take a seat on the bench.

From my position, the graves are hidden beyond the brow of the slope. For that I'm grateful. With my weight removed, my feet begin to throb gently. The not-unpleasant sensation proves a timely distraction from the throbbing in my head. I close my eyes and take a moment to enjoy the silence. I tilt my head back and let the sun's rays warm my face, the light breeze taking the edge off the heat. Notwithstanding the constant reminder of my mortality, this would be a wonderful place to sit and while away a few peaceful hours.

I decide it would be sensible to stay where I am and wait for Father David to find me once he's established the location of Mum's grave. Without his guidance the task would likely consume half the afternoon and what remains of my fortitude. It's not a tough decision.

Despite the stillness of my surroundings, a knot of anxiety in my chest continues to tighten with every passing minute. I employ a relaxation technique Stephen taught me. I imagine a warm, thick, orange liquid slowly filling every part of my body. It starts in my toes and creeps up through my feet into my calves, like sap rising in a tree. It fills my legs and lower torso before creeping up to my chest, the anxiety being absorbed into the viscous orange liquid. It passes my neck and fills my head, soaking up every negative thought. My body feels heavy, numb.

The final stage is to imagine a tap in my ankle. I mentally open the tap and the orange liquid oozes out, taking with it my anxiety and stress. My mind becomes so free it begins to float away.

It is as perfect a state any man in my situation could wish for, but for one minor flaw — the overwhelming urge to sleep. I can't resist and fall into a gentle doze somewhere between sleep and consciousness. I remain vaguely aware of the faint birdsong and the sun on my face, but nothing else. As I relax I can feel myself slipping further away from time, from reality, from everything.

Whatever time passes, I am oblivious. I am sat in possibly the only outside space in town where there is nothing within my environs to disturb me. No passing traffic, no chattering people, no screaming kids, no barking dogs. My mind can wander aimlessly without the prospect of a sudden noise spiking anxiety.

Until there is a noise, that is.

My ears capture it immediately and relay their discovery to my brain, which reacts by flooding my body with the stress hormone, cortisol. This is how I used to start most mornings back in my former life, due in part to my hyperacusis. But there is no dog barking, nor is there thumping music from a car stereo.

There are three sharp knocks. Wood on wood.

My heart rate quickens and I open my eyes for a fraction of a second before the harsh sunlight stings my fully dilated pupils. I instinctively screw them shut again. I attempt to sit upright too quickly and my neck cricks, drawing a sharp intake of breath through gritted teeth.

"Fuck," I mumble under my breath.

"You alright, Craig?" a thin voice asks.

Like the opening chord to a favourite song, there is enough of the voice to be instantly recognisable. My mind almost caves in on itself as I raise a hand to shield my eyes before I open them again. Even with my hand to my brow, I keep my gaze low and squint to keep the sunlight out. The first thing I see is a pair of brown suede shoes and the end of a walking stick, which I assume was the wood being knocked against the bench to wake me.

Slowly my eyes adjust and I'm able to raise my head. A face comes into focus. It can't be, I must still be asleep.

The face smiles at me.

"Welcome back, son."

"Dad?"

13

My mind likes to compartmentalise things. It has systems and procedures that bring order to my thinking, most of the time. But the one thing my mind doesn't like is excessive emotional input. Logic and emotions don't play well together and it throws everything out of sync. The way my mind is wired is great for problem solving but not so great when dealing with highly emotive situations.

The cogs grind to a halt and my mind shuts down.

The last thing I remember is the look of concern on the old man's face, just before my vision fades to black.

I don't think I've ever fainted before, least not that I remember. Having now experienced it I'm surprised there isn't a moment, just before the fall from consciousness, when you realise you're fainting. It just seems to happen. One second you're conscious, the next you're gone.

From beyond the blackness I'm suddenly aware of a hand gently patting my cheek.

"Craig. Craig. Can you hear me?"

I come around, slumped on my side, lying awkwardly on the bench. I recognise the voice but it doesn't compute.

"Well, bugger me. It really is you," the old man says.

As I open my eyes, my mind reboots and three questions spew out.

How the hell does the old man know who I am?

How did he know where to find me?

Why is he seemingly unperturbed at finding a middle-aged version of his dead son sat on a cemetery bench?

"I know what you must be thinking, son," he adds.

I doubt that very much.

I gingerly sit up and squint at the man who looks and sounds like my old man, but can't possibly be my old man.

He stands straight and takes a few steps back from the bench."1986. I know what happened," he says, the excitement in his voice obvious.

It's all I can do to sit and stare at him, open mouthed, frozen. Noting my temporary paralysis, he looks around for a moment as if he's a spy about to divulge state secrets. He then slowly drops his hand into the pocket of his beige jacket and pulls out a plain white envelope. He holds it out towards me.

"Believe me, I never thought this moment would happen but this might explain why I hoped it might."

I tentatively take the envelope from him, still too stunned to vocalise my unanswered questions. I peel the flap open to reveal what looks like folded, heavily creased pages from a lined notebook.

"The police gave those to me, after I identified…," his voice tails off.

I pull the pages from the envelope and unfold them. I study the first few lines of handwritten notes and slowly a realisation dawns. Somehow words form in my mouth.

"These are my notes from that night. 1986, before I left the house."

"The very ones. They were in the pocket of your jeans."

"But…how?"

"I've spent the last thirty years studying every word on those pages. I know them all, back to front. There's stuff there that made no sense unless you understood the context you wrote them."

"And you understand?"

"You left a lot of clues behind, son. Remember that afternoon when you came to visit me in my shed?"

I nod. That visit might have been over thirty years ago for him, but it wasn't that long ago for me.

"I knew there was something not right about you that day. The way you acted, the things you said. Don't get me wrong, you were right to say what you did, but there is no way the sixteen year-old Craig would have said any of it."

He looks at me, trying to ascertain if I've understood him. I still don't think I do.

"Turn to the last page and read it," he says.

I delicately peel back the pages and read the lines of scrawled handwriting on the final page.

I've learnt a lot here but I don't know how much of it will filter through to the future. I don't even know if these notes will return with me. Thirty years is a long time but in twenty minutes I'll make that journey back, to what I don't know. Whatever I've achieved in 1986, I can only hope I made the right decisions. Too late now anyway. For once in my life I hope I got things right. Good luck future Craig — say hello to 2016 for me.

My scrambled thoughts just before I fled my bedroom in 1986. I look up at the old man.

"These notes could have been meaningless. Why would you think otherwise?"

"At first I thought they were part of, I don't know, some English project you were working on at school. But you mentioned things in those notes that nobody could have known, and only came to light after you left us."

"Such as?"

"That stuff about your Aunt Judy and Harold Duffy. The lorry crash with that Williamson fellow and your grandparents. The line about investing in Apple shares. All that stuff came true. How would you have known any of those things?"

I put the notes back in the envelope and place it on the bench. To say this situation is surreal would be an understatement and I can't quite believe the old man is taking it all in such a casual stride. I also can't quite believe his demeanour. Why is he being so calm, so benevolent?

"So, at some point you came to the conclusion that I had actually travelled back in time and lived a weekend in my sixteen year-old body?" I ask incredulously.

"Mind if I sit down?" he asks, ignoring my question.

He doesn't wait for a reply and moves across to the bench, lowering himself down a few feet from me. His movements are more fluid than the old man I originally left behind in my former life.

"Do you know how many people knew I wasn't your biological father?" he asks.

"No."

"I can tell you with absolute certainty that only two people ever knew — me and your mother. Now, I know she definitely never told you, and obviously I didn't, so how could you have possibly known?"

This is not a subject I'm keen to revisit and remain silent.

"I'd say that unless you had psychic abilities as a teenager, it would have been impossible for you to know. But nowadays you can buy those kits to test DNA like they use on The Jeremy Kyle show. But you know that already, don't you? You mention it in your notes."

Rumbled.

The old man continues. "Have you ever heard that famous quote by Arthur Conan Doyle?"

I shrug my shoulders.

"He said that once you have eliminated the impossible, whatever remains, however improbable, must be the truth. Even taking into account the information in your notes, I never really believed such a thing could be possible. But hope is a strong motivator, son, it clouds the rational. You'd be surprised what a man is prepared to believe when all he has left is hope."

I turn and eye the old man. Its been nearly a year since I last saw him, well, the previous version of him. His face is fuller now, the stern edges gone and the lines not so deep. I can only remember the face permanently etched with a frown. This man feels like a stranger to me.

"Let's say for a minute you're not too far from the truth about what happened to me, how did you know I'd be here?" I ask, still deeply dubious about this ridiculous turn of events.

"I've been tending the garden at the vicarage for about six or seven years now. I asked Father David to give me a call if anyone ever turned up and asked about your mother's grave. I figured that if you were ever going to reappear, it would be here."

The final piece of a preposterous jigsaw falls into place.

"I can't get my head around this, around you," I sigh.

"I know. It's a lot to take in, but here I am, and so are you."

"But not Mum."

The colour drains from his face. "No," he whispers. "Not your mum."

"What happened?"

He closes his eyes and draws in a deep breath. Clearly Mum's death is a raw subject and he deflects my question.

"Have you been to her grave yet?" he asks.

"No. Don't know where it is."

"Shall we wander over to see her? I'll try to explain on the way."

I nod and slowly get up from the bench, my body still stiff from my nap. The old man steels himself and follows suit.

We move slowly back up the slope and despite the walking stick, the old man appears fairly nimble on his feet. As I watch him, the shear absurdity of the situation strikes me. A reinvented father and his long-dead son, taking a casual stroll through a cemetery on a summer afternoon. Such has been my life in the last year, very little now surprises me.

"What's with the walking stick?" I ask.

"I had a hip operation a few months back. I probably don't need the stick now but I've grown quite fond of it. Every man of my years should own a sturdy walking stick."

"Right. No arthritis then?"

"No," he chuckles. "Ever since you told me I'd get arthritis in my knees, I've been taking omega-3 and glucosamine supplements. Touch wood, my knees are good for a few years yet."

We cross the brow of the slope and return to the path. The old man raises his walking stick, as if to demonstrate its versatility, and points at a position off at two o'clock.

"She's over that way. It's a nice spot near the trees."

I follow the old man along the path, still waiting for my explanation about Mum. My patience quickly wears.

"So, Mum?"

He stops and turns to face me.

"Look, son, are you sure you want to know the details? Some things are best left unknown."

"It's not up for negotiation. I need to know."

He mindlessly taps the end of his walking stick against his shoe and appears lost in his thoughts for a moment.

"Very well, if you're sure," he eventually puffs. "I'm afraid she…she committed suicide, back in '96."

I already know the *when* and the *how*. What I don't know is the *why*. I don't even try to feign shock at his revelation.

"Why did she take her own life?"

He turns back to the path and walks on. I let him move a few strides ahead before I follow. I catch up but he continues to look straight ahead as he delivers his answer.

"After what happened to you, she was fragile, emotionally close to the edge. I lost count how many times I came home from work to find her crying. I tried my best, son, I really did, but there was nothing I could say to ease her pain. In time, she seemed to gain a little strength but then within the space of about twelve months your gran had a massive stroke and your granddad suffered a heart attack. Neither of them survived. Losing both her parents so suddenly like that, well, it was enough to push her over that edge."

I put my hand on the old man's shoulder, halting his stride, and stand facing him.

"Wait. Gran and Granddad. They both died before Mum? Earlier than '96?" I confirm.

"I'm afraid so, son. Your gran went in June '95, and your granddad about nine months later."

It's my turn to close my eyes as the blood drains from my face. My meddling didn't prolong my grandparents lives for years as I hoped.

"I know from your notes that your grandparents originally died in that road accident. 1994 wasn't it?" he asks. "I couldn't quite believe it when I saw John Williamson's name in the paper. It was at that point I realised your notes were more than just an English project."

"I changed the future so they never got in their car on that day. I wasn't to know they'd both die within a few years regardless. I thought I was giving them the chance to live for years," I sombrely reply.

"You did what you did for the right reasons. They were old, don't blame yourself."

I don't blame myself for my grandparent's fate, as much as that stings. I blame myself for removing them from the road on that day, and the additional deaths their absence caused. It's not a fact I wish to share with the old man.

"Why do you think Mum did it, took her own life? I know it must have been hard, but I don't understand why she'd resort to that."

"I don't know. If I had to hazard a guess, I'd say it was your Aunt Judy putting ideas in her head. She was always in the house, harping on about the afterlife, spirits, and other such nonsense. Maybe she convinced your mother that you and her parents were waiting for her, on the other side. I tried to talk to Judy about it but she said I wouldn't understand, that she knew things I'd never accept. Your mum seemed happy to believe it though."

Shit. The information I gave to Aunt Judy might have been the reason Mum was so quick to believe her. If she warned Mum about John Williamson's rampaging truck, and then it actually happened, all of her other crazy notions must have seemed plausible.

"I told Aunt Judy."

"Sorry?"

"I asked her to warn Mum about Williamson's truck crashing on that day, so she could ensure Gran and Granddad weren't on the road. I thought Mum wouldn't believe me so I asked Aunt Judy to convince her."

"Oh, crikey, son. I assumed you'd warned your grandparents somehow. I wanted to ask them, but how do you even start that conversation? Why did you tell Judy, of all people?"

"I didn't think. I knew she was into all that paranormal stuff so I told her I had a dream. I might have also said a few things about that stuff that happened to her at school, so she'd believe me. I never thought that Mum would swallow all her other crap."

"Well, it appears she did," he says flatly.

"Fuck. I don't know what to say, Dad."

He stares off into the distance, his face unreadable. I want to say something but the weight of guilt is so debilitating I can barely breathe.

He pulls a hanky from his pocket and blows his nose. It seems to pull him back to reality.

"As remarkable as your little foray into the past may have been, I'm assuming it didn't come with the power of prediction?"

I shake my head.

"So you weren't to know how any of this would turn out. I don't blame you, son. Hell, if I was given the chance to go back, damn sure I'd change a few things, right a few wrongs. None of us can predict the future, even if we were afforded the chance to change the past."

"Thank you," I mumble quietly.

"One thing is for sure though, son," he adds. "This whole thing is pretty bloody ridiculous don't you think?"

If only he knew the half of it.

"To be honest, Dad, it feels like a curse. I didn't ask for it and wish it had never happened."

"Do you know why, or how?"

"Not the first clue. One minute I'm sat in my old bedroom in 2016 and the next thing I know, I'm lying in bed in 1986."

"Right. One thing I don't understand though, is how you ended up in the middle of the road that night you left. I remember poking my head around the door and saying goodnight. Next thing I know, the police are banging on the door in the middle of the night to say you'd been hit by a van. What happened?"

"I decided at the last minute I wanted to stay in 1986. So I left my bedroom and ran, hoping I could avoid being sent back. I got as far as Eton Drive and suddenly the world seemed to stop. Next thing I know, I'm lying in a hospital bed, back in 2016."

"Worst night of my life," he says, more to himself.

It never crossed my mind the old man would grieve for me. In all of this, his feelings have been given the least consideration.

"I'm sorry, Dad."

"No, son, I'm sorry," he says.

He stops in his tracks again and slowly turns to me. "I'm sorry that I was such a terrible father. I'm sorry I never got the chance to make everything right. Not a day has passed in the last thirty-one years that I haven't thought about you. Not a day when I haven't felt regret, felt shame."

Of all the unbelievable, impossible twists in my life over the last eleven months, what happens next almost trumps them all. The old man drops his walking stick and takes two steps towards me. I instinctively flinch, knowing he only ever gets so close when he's about to start yelling. Not this time. He throws his arms around me and buries his head in my shoulder. I hesitantly place my arms on his back and reciprocate the embrace. Thirty-one years and against all hope, he gets the chance to say sorry. All that pent up remorse proves too much and he begins to sob.

At least a minute passes before he withdraws from our embrace and pulls a hanky from his pocket. He dabs his eyes and clears his throat.

"That *miserable old bastard* you referred to in your notes; that's not me. I can only imagine how I'd have turned out if we had never had our chat in the shed that afternoon, but we did, and you need to know I'm not that man."

That much is already crystal clear.

"It's okay, Dad. There's no need to apologise for what might have been. Different person, different life. I'm just glad you're here, I really am."

In truth, it's relief I'm currently feeling. Relief that I've finally got someone to talk to. Someone who knows what actually happened to me.

We swap wan smiles, suggesting we both understand one another, and walk on.

Sixty seconds later we're stood side-by-side in front of a black granite headstone. Two virtual strangers, inextricably linked by the occupant of the grave — Janet Georgetta Pelling. Now I can see her name, engraved in two-inch high gold letters, the stark reality of her death bites hard. I'm grateful not to be here alone.

So many questions still burn, but silence seems more appropriate and neither of us utters a word as we stare at the block of granite. The old man has doubtless stood here a thousand times and offered a thousand prayers. He clearly remembers the first time though, and places a reassuring hand on my shoulder.

"I'll never be able to replace her but I hope you'll let me be part of your life. All we've got is each other and I'd like to be the father you deserved."

I can't speak for fear of breaking down. It's all I can do to give him a slight nod, once I've wiped the tears from my cheeks. I say a silent prayer for my mum, more an apology really, and walk away.

Once I reach the main path I stand for a moment to let the old man catch up. My mind conjures up a picture of Mum, sat in her wing-backed chair in their living room. She's old, and not in great health, but she's alive. Her eyes still sparkle and her smile still lights up the room. She can still make a Battenburg and she can still tell me off when I swear. The old man never got the chance to grow old with that woman. He'll have questions, I'm sure, but I need to tread carefully with what I tell him. I've had time to come to terms with our lost future and I know how destructive it is to dissect what might have been. Far from sharing my pain, I need to protect my old man from it.

"You alright, son," he puffs when he finally reaches the path.

"Yeah, I'm okay," I assure him.

"So where do we go from here? Do you want to come back to my place and we can talk?"

I honestly don't know where we go from here. This is not an eventuality I could have ever predicted and I'm still struggling to get my head around it. I guess all I can do is accept the old man's invitation and see where it leads us.

"Sure. That would be good."

"Great. The car is parked over the way. Shall we?"

We walk silently back through the cemetery, past the church, and out through a gate into a small car park. Beyond my surprise that the old man is still driving in this life, it's with some relief I find he's traded in his Vauxhall Cavalier, and its puke-inducing suspension. He uses a remote control to beep open the central locking of a small, modern hatchback, and opens the door for me. We both clamber in, and after the old man flashes me a reassuring smile, we drive out of the church car park.

I don't know our destination, in any sense.

14

Within the first minute of our journey, two of my questions are answered. The old man informs me he now lives in a village called Hale, just a mile beyond the northern border of Farndale. That would explain why his name never appeared on the electoral role, as Hale sits in a different borough from Farndale.

"I couldn't live in that house after your mum went," the old man says mournfully. "It was too quiet, too many ghosts."

"I'm guessing it wasn't a happy home after, you know, I…left?"

"Honestly? That one weekend we had together in 1986 after our chat, best two days I ever had in that house. I was ashamed of what went before and distraught by what came after. For me, it was never a happy home."

He doesn't expand on his damning statement and concentrates a little more intently on the road ahead.

"You mind if I ask you a question?" I say.

"Sure."

"My notes. Why didn't you show them to Mum?"

"Believe me, son, I thought about it dozens of times."

"But you didn't actually show them to her?"

"You have to understand how fragile she was, son. Yes, your notes might have given her a slither of hope, but they could just have easily pushed her over the edge. She spent a long time grieving and I couldn't risk sending her back to square one."

"Suppose not."

"If I'd had the faintest inkling your mother was willing to take her own life then I would have shown her your notes in a heartbeat. I'd have done anything to stop her. I didn't have a clue though, son, so I did what I thought was best. I tried to protect her."

I can't judge him. I wasn't there. In such a fragile state, would she have really believed there was anything behind the scrawled notes? If she'd read my rambling thoughts, would it have given her comfort or torn at her already raw wounds? I doubt I'd have taken that risk either.

With the silence in the car starting to feel a little uncomfortable, I'm relieved when we pass a road sign advising us we've reached the village of Hale. A few more narrow streets are navigated before we pull into a horseshoe cul-de-sac with five squat bungalows sat in a semi-circle. Number three is directly ahead, and the old man slows the car to a stop on the tarmac driveway. He removes the key from the ignition and we sit silently for a few seconds, just the ticking of the cooling engine to focus on.

"Well, here we are, this is home now," the old man eventually chirps.

"Right," I reply, still wondering if this is all some fucked up dream and my body is still lying on a bench in a graveyard.

We get out of the car and I survey the cul-de-sac. It's quiet, peaceful even. The five homes all look impeccably kept with manicured lawns and moss-free driveways. I can only guess the other residents are also retired. It's a stark contrast to the noisy neighbourhood in which our former family home was situated.

I follow the old man across the driveway and he unlocks the front door. He leads me into a hallway and through to a spacious lounge with patio doors overlooking a small, but impeccably kept rear garden. The room is sparsely furnished, lacking any semblance of homeliness. The only personal effects are two framed pictures sat on a window sill; one of Mum and one of me, taken around my fourteenth birthday, I think. One sound from my past is present though — the carriage clock, still ticking away on a small table in the corner.

"It's nice," I say with little conviction.

"It's four walls and a roof, nothing more" he replies ruefully.

The old man offers to make tea and disappears into the kitchen. I take a seat in one of the two armchairs which are angled to face an archaic television. The lack of seating suggests the old man doesn't receive too many visitors.

"I think this is probably only the second cup of tea I've ever made you" he says as he enters the lounge, holding two mugs.

"Probably," I reply with a smile.

The old man settles into the other armchair and we swap small talk while sipping tea. We both try to ignore the time-travelling elephant in the room but the need to know is too great for the old man.

"What was she like, your mum, when she was older?"

"Do you really want to go there, Dad?"

"I'll grab any crumb of comfort I can. To know she lived a happy life in some parallel universe would be something."

Do I tell him she was never really happy? Do I tell him his counterpart made her life a misery?

"She had a few health problems, but she was…content."

He takes a sip of his tea and slowly shakes his head.

"I appreciate you trying to save my feelings, but I'd rather know the truth."

"No. You wouldn't."

"Right," he sighs. "I can probably guess. Without your intervention that afternoon, would it be safe to say I didn't make her happy?"

I don't answer him, which is an answer in itself.

"Thought as much," he says.

"Look, Dad, I've spent the last eleven months torturing myself with all of this. God only knows how I clung to my sanity through it all. And all I can say for sure is there are no answers, there is no closure. I've had to accept the life we had, for better and for worse, is gone. There is nothing to be gained by looking back. We are where we are, better to accept it and forget the past, every version of it."

The silence returns. Maybe I could have handled that better, been a little more sympathetic. The trouble is, I'm still talking to the old man from my past, the cantankerous old git who provoked conflict, and always spoilt for an argument. This old man is not the same old man.

"Sorry. I shouldn't have been so blunt. Sometimes it all gets too much."

"No, son," he whispers. "You have every right to tell it as it is. I deserve nothing less."

Now I really feel guilty.

"It's just, well, so fucked up, so ridiculous, all of it."

"You can say that again," he snorts. "Maybe you should write a book about it, it'd probably be a best seller."

"As a work of fiction, maybe."

He shoots me a half-hearted smile and changes the subject.

"Anyway, how long have you been…um, back? When 2016 came and went, and there was no sign of you, I assumed my theories were as wrong as they were ridiculous."

For the next hour I try to explain as much as I can about my new life as Craig Wilson, including my stay at Broadhall. Many questions are asked. Some I can answer, most I can't. I conclude by telling him about my job in the charity shop and my humble accommodation in Farndale.

"This flat they put you in, how long are you able to stay there for?"

"A few months. Why?"

"I don't want to put you on the spot, and you can say no, but why don't you move in here? I've got the space and to be honest, I could do with the company."

In my previous life I'd rather have stapled my scrotum to the floor in preference to living with the old man. But the prospect of sharing a house with *this* old man isn't quite so daunting.

"You've got a spare bedroom?"

"I have, and it's yours if you want it. I don't want any money, any commitment, and there are no catches. You can come and go as you please."

"Right."

"Actually, saying that, there is just one small catch," he adds.

"And that is?"

"Come with me and I'll show you."

We get up and I follow him back into the hallway. He opens a door and we step inside a double bedroom. There's no bed, no furniture.

"This is the catch," he says, pointing to a mountain of packing boxes, stacked six-feet high against the back wall.

He answers my question before I even ask it.

"Stuff from the old house. The removal men packed it up for me, and dropped it in here."

"Bloody hell, Dad, there's a ton of it. Why did you keep it all?"

"Couldn't bring myself to get rid of it but I've never had the stomach to sort through it either."

"Okay, we can deal with that. But there's no bed, no nothing."

"Tell you what, if you're not doing anything tomorrow, why don't I pick you up and we can pay a visit to a furniture shop, get you kitted out. Then we can come back here and go through this lot, together."

He looks at me, his face expectant like a kid asking if he can stay up late on a school night.

"I'm skint, Dad. I can't afford a pillow, let alone a bed to put it on."

"Money is about the only thing I haven't had to worry about in recent years," he sighs. "Your grandparents left everything they owned to your mum. When she left, all of that passed to me, along with the payout from her life insurance policy. I've got my pension to live on, which is more than enough for a man on his own, so the rest of the cash has sat in the bank doing bugger all. It's your money as much as it is mine, son."

"How much are we talking about, roughly?"

"About three hundred," he replies nonchalantly.

"Three hundred quid?"

"Grand."

"Shit. Right. In that case, you have yourself a new lodger."

The old man rigorously shakes my hand, his smile as broad as it's probably been in a long while.

We return to the lounge and chat about the mundane for another hour. Football, cars, and politics — the usual fare for two men who don't know each other that well. The conversation eventually dries up and we move onto our plans for tomorrow. Then, with some reluctance, the old man drives me back to the flat and we say our goodbyes on the street, accompanied by an excruciatingly awkward man hug.

I stand and watch him drive away. Once his car has turned out of my road and out of sight, I exhale a deep breath and amble up the stairs to the flat.

I kick my trainers off and collapse on the couch. Seven days since I began life outside of Broadhall and the craziness beyond the hospital walls is greater than anything I experienced within them. Today caps off a week-long rollercoaster ride. I just want to get off now, I really do. I want some stability, some normality. Christ, I just want the mundane life I left behind. What I wouldn't give for another day at RolpheTech, or a pint with Dave, or even to hear Megan's guttural breathing again.

None of it will ever be part of my life again.

I suppose I should try and grasp the positives. I've got Lucy, or a version of her. I've got a friend in Brenda, and as unlikely as it ever seemed, I've got the old man. So many people lost but my saving grace is that I'm not entirely alone here now. But if I want sanctuary from my past, I'll have to build it. Thick walls to keep the harrowing memories at bay. A door I can choose to slam shut whenever I feel vulnerable. It will need to be impenetrable to the past, solid. It will need to serve as my bolt-hole for the rest of my days.

Tomorrow, I'll lay the first bricks.

15

Bang-on ten o'clock, the old man pulls up to the kerb outside the flat. I climb into the car and we make our way to the same trading estate I worked on for all those years. Not an ideal start to my day but the old man's enthusiastic chatter proves a welcome distraction. We enter the furniture store next door to RolpheTech and I can't help but feel like a teenager again, kitting out his bedroom under the supervision of a father who has an opinion on every item I show an interest in.

"Buy cheap, buy twice," he sagely advises as I test the springs on a hundred quid bed.

Compared to his tightwad tendencies in my former life, I guess I shouldn't complain.

"Here, this divan looks like a good, solid bed," he calls across the aisle, a little too loudly.

A few other customers turn and inspect us. It dawns on me we probably look like an odd gay couple, bed hunting together. I'm not concerned about people thinking I'm gay, more that they might think I'm shacking up with a geriatric partner bedecked in brown corduroy.

"Okay, Dad," I reply, my voice loud enough so it's clear to everyone in the store I'm not into necrophilia.

After an hour of bouncing on beds, inspecting dovetail joints, and swinging wardrobe doors to and fro, we leave the store. I am the new owner of a double bed, a wardrobe, a chest of drawers and a bedside table, all to be delivered to the old man's bungalow on Wednesday. He is the owner of a two grand store receipt but seems happy enough with our shopping trip.

We clamber back into the car and set off towards Hale. Barely a mile into the journey and the old man suddenly suggests we go and look at cars so I'm not reliant on him for transport. I point out I don't have a driving licence.

"It must be weird, having to start again," he says.

"That's one word for it."

"Some people might see it as a blessing."

"You think?" I snort.

"Would you change things back to how they were, if you could?"

"In a heartbeat."

The old man ponders my answer for a few seconds.

"So why all that angst then, in your notes? They sure didn't read like the words of a man who was happy with his lot in life."

My turn to ponder.

"I was an idiot, Dad. I was so busy focusing on all the negativity that I didn't see what I had, or what I could have had. I spent most of my life analysing where I'd gone wrong rather than where I was. You don't realise how much you have until it's all taken away from you."

"Not so different then, were we?"

"Eh?"

"You weren't the only one who had his head stuck in the past. The way I behaved towards you and your mum, I was so angry that life hadn't delivered what I expected that I never stopped to consider what it had given me. Maybe we were both idiots, son."

They say the apple never falls far from the tree. Just like the old man, I had spent most of my life taking umbrage rather than taking stock. We may have reacted differently to our circumstances but we both wallowed in our self-inflicted, myopic misery. It probably wasn't the mutual bond either of us wanted, but we had earned it.

We spend the rest of the journey in contemplative silence until we pull up on the driveway outside the old man's bungalow.

"You ready for this, son?"

"As I'll ever be. What's the plan?"

"If we sort through everything and put all the stuff we don't want in the garage, I can arrange for a charity to come and collect it later in the week."

"Or we could take it to the tip?"

"Really? Seems a shame to throw away stuff that might be of value to somebody."

"Trust me, Dad, they won't want our crap."

"Fair enough. You're the expert," he says with a smile.

I follow the old man through the front door and into the bedroom. We stand next to one another in front of the wall of boxes, and the task neither of us are relishing. He takes the initiative and pulls a box from the top.

"Two hours from now, it'll be done. Finished. That's the way to think about it," he says cheerfully as he places the box on the floor.

I offer him a weak smile and peel the tape from the top of the box. It contains dozens of small items, all individually wrapped in packing paper.

"You might want to revise that estimate," I reply.

By the time we reach the sixth box, it's clear just how little of the contents from our old home never made it beyond this room.

"Did you actually unpack anything when you moved here?" I ask.

"Not really. Just the kitchen stuff and my clothes. I was planning to do a box a day, to lessen the load, but the first one was painful enough."

I can't say I blame him. Perhaps some people find comfort in surrounding themselves with mementos of loved ones who've passed, but not me, nor the old man it would seem. Safer to keep the memories hidden away in boxes; sometimes cardboard, sometimes psychological.

By the time we reach box twelve, I'm about to suggest we simply leave the boxes as they are and move them to the garage. If the old man has lived without the contents for over twenty years, it's unlikely he really needs any of it.

"Nice idea, but we haven't got to the personal effects yet. There should be photo albums, your mum's jewellery, and other things too precious to throw away."

I'm not sure I'll ever want to look through those photo albums, but concede the old man's request. Box twelve is pulled from the pile and dropped to the floor.

I rip open the tape and pull the cardboard flaps open. I'm greeted by a picture of a smiling woman with permed, blonde hair. Her hair is not her most striking feature though. That would be her ample breasts which are on full display.

"More than a handful there, son," the old man remarks over my shoulder.

I cringe as I stare down at the copy of Escort, sat proudly on top of my teenage collection of porn magazines. As embarrassing as the discovery is, the old man tortures me further by grabbing the magazine and casually thumbing through the tatty pages.

"If I'd have known these were in here," he laughs.

"Dad, please."

"Don't make 'em like this anymore, eh?" he says as he holds aloft a full-page picture of Julie from Liverpool, sprawled naked across the bonnet of a Ford Capri.

"Christ, Dad. She's young enough to be your granddaughter."

"I meant the car," he replies with a wink.

I snatch the magazine from him and grab the rest from the box. I drop them into a black sack before the old man can peruse the rest. I doubt his heart is up to seeing images of Lars and Sabine from the pages of Blue Climax.

"Looking at pictures of scantily clad ladies has given me quite a thirst," the old man remarks. "Fancy a brew?"

Clearly box twelve was filled with the contents of my teenage bedroom and it might be better if the old man isn't present when I empty it.

"Please."

He leaves the bedroom and pads across the hallway to the kitchen. The sound of cupboard doors being opened and closed is accompanied by whistling. For a moment I stand and listen, an involuntary smile breaking on my face. This is the man I always wanted as a father: kind, good-humoured, wise, and considerate.

"Where have you been, Dad" I whisper to myself as I turn my attention back to unpacking the box at my feet.

It soon becomes obvious that box twelve is full of the tat from my teenage years. I put everything back and stack it with a pile of boxes destined for the tip.

Box thirteen is huge, and fortunately sat at the bottom of the pile. I drag it across the floor and peel back the tape.

"Tea's up," the old man calls as he enters the bedroom holding two mugs.

I thank him and take one of the mugs. I decide to take a breather and perch myself on the window ledge, mug in hand.

"Found anything interesting?" he asks.

"Not unless you consider a batch of blank cassettes and some old text books interesting?"

"Not really," he replies. "What have we got in here then?" he says to himself while pulling open the flaps on box thirteen.

I take a sip of my tea while I watch the old man inspect the contents. The hot tea scalds my top lip and I curse under my breath. I turn and place the mug on the window ledge.

"Well, well, well," the old man says quietly.

I turn back to face him and can scarcely believe what he's holding.

"No, it can't be…"

"Yours, I believe?" he says.

He places the box for my Commodore 64 on the floor and stands back, his hands on his hips. Before he can utter another word I scoot across the floor and kneel down next to the box.

"It can't be," I mutter.

"What is it?"

I slowly run my hand over the colourful graphics on the cardboard box. The box which contains the catalyst for my fucked up life. I never thought I'd ever see it again and my heart hammers away in my chest at the very sight of it.

The potential of my discovery starts to blossom in my mind. Dare I consider the possibility that I might be able to undo the damage I've caused? My thoughts take on a life of their own and start visualising the blue screen and the commands which sent me back to 1986. All I have to do is set the computer up, enter the same details as before, and I can relive that weekend again. Most crucially though, I can ensure I'm sat in my bedroom when the counter reaches zero. Craig Pelling will not be hit by a van and I can return to the new life I had originally envisaged. Craig Wilson will be just a bad memory.

"This is it. It was the computer…that sent me back," I stammer excitedly.

The old man's face contorts, his expression puzzled.

"But, son…"

I almost tear the edges of the box lid open in my haste to get at the contents. With trembling hands I withdraw the polystyrene inner packaging — the empty inner packaging.

I look up at the old man. "Where is it, Dad? Where is the computer?" I gasp.

His shoulders slump and he draws a deep breath.

"Your mum, she gave it to that mate of yours, not long after you left us," he sighs.

"What mate?"

"I dunno…it was a long time ago."

"Think," I plead.

Every passing second increases the frustration for both of us. I want to grab the old man and shake him until the name falls from his mouth.

"Come on, Dad, it's important," I bark.

His face is so twisted with concentration it looks like a post-Christmas walnut.

"God, what's his name…Dan?"

"Dan? I never had a mate called Dan."

"It was something like that. I can't recall, sorry."

"Wait. Was it Dave?"

"Yes! That's it, Dave."

"Mum gave the computer to Dave? Are you absolutely sure?"

"Yes. He was your best friend wasn't he? I think he took your death badly and your mum wanted to give him something of yours, to remember you."

For one fleeting moment I had the key to a door which might have led to some answers, maybe even to my previous life. I feel like a starving man with a fork hovering over his first meal in weeks, only for the plate to be cruelly pulled away at the last moment.

I kick the empty box across the floor and lean against the wall.

"Why the fuck did they have to pack an empty box? Morons."

The old man takes a tentative step towards me. "What did you mean when you said it was the computer that sent you back?"

"Exactly that," I murmur. "Don't ask me how but it was the computer that connected the past and the future."

The old man wisely decides against pressing me further on the mechanics of my inexplicable journey.

"You thought it was your chance to go back, didn't you?" he says quietly.

I nod.

"Is that what you want, to go back and undo the changes you made?"

"It doesn't matter now does it? Maybe it can't be undone. Maybe I had my chance and I blew it. All that matters is the computer isn't here."

"So, that's it then? You're just going to give up at the first hurdle?"

"What?"

His face reddens, and for a moment I catch a glimpse of the old man from my previous life.

"Have your learnt nothing from your past? Are you just going to whine about the situation and stand there feeling sorry for yourself?" he barks. "Or are you going to roll up your sleeves and do something about it?"

The face might be displaying anger but his eyes say something else. They're almost pleading with me.

"I get what you're saying, Dad, but what can I do?"

"Find this Dave character and get the bloody computer back."

"I appreciate your positivity, but come on. Are you suggesting I track him down, breeze up to his front door and say hello? *'Hi Dave. Remember me, Craig, your dead mate from school? Oh, and can I have the computer back? You know, the one my mum gave you over thirty years ago?'*"

The old man remains silent for a few seconds.

"Why not?" he asks.

"Are you kidding me? For starters, we don't even know if he's still got it. And then there's the small matter of convincing him I'm not actually dead. I assume he went to my funeral?"

"I think so."

"Right. Can you not see a minor flaw in your plan then?"

"You could, you know, tell him thc truth."

"For crying out loud, Dad," I groan. "I've just spent eleven months in a mental institution for telling the truth. For some strange reason people don't tend to believe me when I say I'm the reincarnation of a sixteen-year-old kid who died in 1986."

Seemingly unable to let his ridiculous suggestion go, the old man presses his point.

"But he was your best friend. Surely there are things you know about him that nobody else knows? You could convince him."

"I couldn't, Dad, honestly."

"You could, if I came with you."

"What?"

"I could come with you. We could take your notes with us and I'm sure that between us, we could convince him. But even if he's not a hundred percent sure, maybe he'll be persuaded enough to at least give us the computer back. That's all we need isn't it?"

He stares at me expectantly, the utter foolishness of his plan seemingly moot. I return his stare and feel my defences shift a little.

"You'd do that?"

"Of course, if it's what you want. I owe you, son, more than I'll ever be able to repay."

I pause for a moment, my analytical mind instinctively processing the myriad ways this plan could fail. It is as simple as it is ludicrous, and the previous version of me wouldn't even give it the time of day. But perhaps there is something to be said about going on gut instinct alone. Besides, what do I actually have to lose?

"Do you think he might listen?" I ask cautiously.

"You haven't changed so much you look like an entirely different person. And some of your mannerisms are still there. I think you could convince him, yes."

There are plenty of reasons not to entertain this ludicrous plan but the fact the Commodore is out there, maybe only a few miles away from where we're stood, is a compelling reason to ignore them all. And I don't think I can I live with the thought there might be a chance of undoing this mess, no matter how small, and doing nothing about it.

“Alright, Dad. You’re on.”

16

For a few minutes the excitement in the bedroom is palpable. We're like two football players celebrating after a goal is scored, just before we realise the goal has been disallowed by the referee.

The practicalities of our ridiculous quest calm our celebration.

"Where does he live?" the old man asks.

"A few streets away from where we used to live."

"Even now?"

It's a good question. We were inseparable as teenagers and did so much together. But without me in his life, is it realistic to assume it would have gone in the exact same direction?

A troubling thought suddenly crosses my mind.

Dave met his future wife, Suzy, during a night out in town. Megan and I were celebrating our fifth wedding anniversary and she invited a few of her colleagues along, including Suzy.

Shit.

In this life I never married Megan so there wouldn't have been a night out, therefore Dave and Suzy would never have met, never have started dating, and never have married. It therefore seems highly unlikely Dave would have ended up living in their marital home.

"Um, thinking about it, I'm not so sure where he lives now," I reply, still trying to get my head around the fact I terminated Dave's marriage before he even met his wife.

The one consolation is that Dave and Suzy had a pretty volatile marriage. They both had affairs and I listened to Dave complain about his relationship enough times. Maybe he's married somebody a little more suitable this time. I'll run with that theory and assume I've done him a favour. And Suzy. Probably.

"So how do we find him then?" the old man asks.

We need the Internet.

"I'm guessing you don't have a computer with an Internet connection?"

"No, but the TV has Ceefax, although I haven't used it in a while. Would that work?"

"Dad, they turned Ceefax off about five years ago and no, it wouldn't help us even if we could still use it."

"Sorry," he mumbles. "I'm a bit behind the times with all this technological nonsense."

"Yeah, just a bit."

I pull my phone from my pocket and search for wi-fi networks. There are just two, both of them locked. I try to connect to the mobile network but our semi-rural location has a piss-poor signal, barely adequate for phone calls let alone Internet use.

"Do you know your neighbours well enough they might let us use their Internet connection for an hour?"

"I think Miriam next door has it. She chats to her son in New Zealand all the time on her computer."

"Right. Let's go pay Miriam a visit then."

With a real sense of purpose, we stride out onto the cul-de-sac and across the driveway to number two. We ring the bell and wait for Miriam to answer the door.

A long moment passes before a tweedy looking woman with white hair opens the door.

"Good afternoon Colin," she blusters with all the warmth of a Dickensian schoolmistress.

"Afternoon Miriam."

She eyes me up and down before returning her stern gaze to the old man. “And who do we have here?” she asks brusquely.

“This is my son, Craig.”

“Good afternoon Miriam,” I squeak.

“It’s Mrs Johnston to you young man, but good afternoon nonetheless.”

“Sorry Mrs Johnston,” I mumble.

“Miriam, we were wondering if we could perhaps connect to your computer thingamabob for an hour?” the old man asks.

“What?” she snaps.

I interject and expand on the old man’s woeful explanation. “Um, we were hoping we might be able to borrow your wi-fi connection if we could?”

“Borrow my what?”

“Wi-fi. It’s a signal that allows a device to connect to the Internet through a router.”

“Good Lord, speak in plain English will you,” she barks.

I glance across at the old man just in time to see him shake his head.

“Miriam. Can we use your computer for an hour? Please,” he sighs.

“Well, why didn’t you say that in the first place? Come in.”

Miriam spins around and marches back into the hallway. We stand and stare at one another, both hoping the other will enter first. The old man frowns and takes the lead. I follow him in to a hallway identical to the one in the old man’s bungalow, but far more lavishly decorated.

“Shoes. Off.”

We comply without question and kick our shoes into the corner of the hallway.

"In here."

We follow Miriam into what is to become my bedroom in the old man's bungalow. In Miriam's home it's a scaled-down version of the local library. Rows of oak bookshelves stretch across three of the walls, each one crammed floor-to-ceiling with books. There's an antique desk positioned next to the window with a leather-bound office chair sat in front. I breathe a sigh of relief when I spot an iMac sat on the desk.

"Help yourselves," Miriam says as she waves a hand towards the computer. "I've got some things to do in the garden so come and find me when you're done."

We both smile politely and Miriam heads off to the garden, probably to chastise some errant crocuses.

"She's a bit…fierce," I whisper.

"She's alright when you get to know her," the old man replies apologetically.

Getting to know Miriam is not exactly top of my priorities. I pull back the leather office chair and take a seat at the desk.

"What can I do?" the old man asks.

"You could ask our charming hostess to rustle up some tea, and maybe a few sandwiches?"

The old man looks at me, a horrified expression plastered across his face.

"I'm kidding, Dad. Just find a book and keep yourself occupied for the moment."

"Right. Phew."

I chuckle away to myself as I open a web browser.

The devil in me is tempted to check Miriam's browsing history to see if she's as straight-laced as she appears. My fingers hover over the keyboard for a moment until I decide against it. Whatever floats her boat, in hindsight I really don't want to know.

I enter Dave's full name, suffixed by the word 'Farndale' into the search box and hit the enter key. The same familiar website which requires payment appears at the top of the results. I could probably use the old man's credit card but that would mean setting up an account. I'll leave it for the moment and come back to it if there's nothing else.

The second and third results both also require payment to view the information. However, the fourth result sparks a virtual face-palm. I click the blue link and shake my head at the information on the screen.

COMPANY: Farndale Graphic Design - DIRECTOR: David Alan Wright

REGISTERED ADDRESS: 29 Conniston Drive, Farndale

Back in the late nineties, Dave was made redundant from his job at a graphic design studio. He decided he'd had enough of being an employee and set up business on his own, working from home. It never dawned on me to search for his company name rather than his actual name.

I pull my phone out, open the notes app and type Dave's address into a new note. It's not the marital address he lived at in my previous timeline so the theory about his marriage never happening looks a little more like fact now. Oh well.

"Got it, Dad."

"That was quick. I'll go thank Miriam and we can get out of here."

The old man heads out to find our hostess while I put my trainers back on. He returns a minute later and slips his suede loafers back on.

"You went out into the garden without your shoes?" I ask.

"Miriam doesn't like people wearing shoes on her lawn."

I don't need to say a word for him to understand what I'm thinking. We beat a hasty retreat to the old man's bungalow and the armchairs in his lounge.

"How do you want to play this then, son?"

At no point in my life have I ever considered the correct protocol for telling my best friend I've risen from the dead. Clearly this isn't something we can do over the phone. The only practical option is to pay Dave a visit and hope we can get a foot in the door before he punches me in the face.

"Okay. I think it would be better if you led this," I say. "We'll go to his house and you can introduce yourself and then give him the notes. Explain what they are and what happened that night. We can then broach the subject that your companion is actually his dead friend. How hard can it be?"

The old man scratches his chin and considers my excuse for a plan.

"It's a bit flimsy but I can't think of any other way to handle it," he eventually says. "At least your notes should add some credibility to my explanation."

"Right. We set then?"

We sit and look at one another for a moment, both expecting the other to do something.

"Well," the old man says. "Hand them over then."

"What?"

"Your notes."

"You've got them."

"No, son. I gave them to you at the cemetery."

My mind quickly replays the minutes of our first meeting in the cemetery. I read the notes and put them down on the bench. And that's where they stayed after we walked over to Mum's grave.

"Fuck."

"What?"

"I left them on the bench."

"I kept those notes safe for over thirty years and you've managed to lose them within thirty seconds?"

"Sorry," I mumble. "Maybe they're still there."

He shakes his head. "I suppose we'd better go and look then."

Thirty minutes later we're sat in the church car park — empty handed. I searched high and low around the bench but to no avail. The notes, like the teenager who wrote them, long gone.

"Well, son. That's your plan well and truly scuppered isn't it?"

"Somewhat," I sigh. "Looks like we'll have to go with plan-B."

"Plan-A wasn't great so I dread to think what plan-B might involve. Care to enlighten me?"

"I haven't the foggiest. Take a slow drive and I'll work on it."

I enter Dave's address into the navigation app on my phone and frown when it informs me our destination is only twelve minutes away.

"Make that a *very* slow drive."

With a shake of his head, the old man slips the car into gear and makes his way out of the car park.

17

Despite the old man driving like James May on a Sunday, we reach Conniston Drive within nineteen minutes. He pulls up fifty yards beyond the junction so we can discuss my cunning plan out of sight of Dave's house. He turns the ignition key and once again, we sit in silence listening to the ticking of the cooling engine.

"Well, son. I'm all ears."

"Shock and awe."

"Sorry?"

"Look, if this Dave is anything like the Dave I knew, he won't invite us in for tea and small talk. He was never a man who appreciated subtlety so I'll have to get straight to the point and pummel him with information he can't refute."

"And if he pummels you back, with his fists?"

"Don't worry, I'll be away on my toes if I think he's about to get physical."

"Good for you. And I'll stand there and take a beating on your behalf shall I?"

"You've got your walking stick to fend him off. You'll be okay."

An incredulous scowl falls across his face.

"I'm joking, Dad. I think it might be better if you wait in the car. Without the notes your presence isn't going to make any difference. He'll either believe me within the first few minutes, or he'll lose his shit. If it's the latter I don't want you in harm's way. Dave always had a tendency to punch first and ask questions later."

I expected the old man to offer some resistance but he bravely agrees to stay in the car. In fairness, I'd rather stay in the car too.

"Just think about the end game, son. We just need the computer back. Anything else is inconsequential."

He then reaches into his jacket and pulls out a black leather wallet. He extracts a wad of notes and hands them to me.

"What's that?" I ask.

"Plan C."

"I'm not with you."

"If all else fails, there's three hundred quid. If he isn't gullible enough to believe your story, let's hope he's skint enough to sell the computer."

"I can't take that, Dad."

"Shut up and take the money."

I comply and offer a weak smile in return. There's no need for further discussion or deferral. I get out of the car and close the door behind me. I stand on the pavement for a second to gain my composure as the old man gives me a thumbs up from behind the windscreen. I nod back, and turn to face the street ahead of me.

"Commodore 64, I'm coming for you," I whisper to myself.

I slowly amble along Conniston Drive towards number twenty-nine. I take time to assess the neighbourhood for clues about this version of Dave. The houses are all semi-detached or terraced, with ugly, pebble-dashed facades. The lack of architectural merit suggests these homes were built by the local council, probably back in the fifties or sixties. The front gardens are small and unkempt, many littered with discarded children's toys and the occasional kitchen appliance. It doesn't feel like the kind of street a successful graphic designer would choose to live in.

I scold myself for being judgemental. It's the people who make a community, not the buildings. Perhaps Dave likes living here and I'm certainly in no position to sneer at those who actually have their own home. I walk on.

I pass number nineteen and the road takes a ninety degree turn to the left. I round the corner and the street view changes from houses to small terraced bungalows. They appear to have been built at the same time as the houses in the street, and probably designed by the same lazy architect. I pass by numbers twenty-one through twenty-seven and stop about ten yards from number twenty-nine.

Even with a determined effort to keep my preconceptions at bay, I have to conclude Dave's home is an utter shit-hole.

The small from lawn is overgrown, clumps of brambles and other weeds flourishing around the barely distinguishable borders. The paint on the front door and window frames is flaking and blistered, with more wood visible than actual paint. The front gutter is hanging loose at one end and the roof is dotted with mounds of moss. Many of the clay tiles are chipped, and just as many are missing altogether. It's a forlorn looking structure that is in desperate need of some urgent maintenance.

Before I have chance to change my mind, I make my way up the weed-ridden path to the front door. I lift my hand to press the doorbell, only to notice the wire trailing from beneath it has been cut. This doesn't suggest Dave is keen on visitors. I ignore the voice in my head, screaming that this is a bad idea, and rap my knuckles on the frosted glass pane.

A minute passes and there's no response, no sounds from within the bungalow. I rap the glass again and turn to face the street. There are about a dozen cars lined up at intervals along the kerb. I examine each one to see if I can determine which is Dave's, but it's ultimately a pointless exercise. I turn back to the door. Still nothing to indicate Dave is at home. I'm just about to knock for a third, and final time, when I hear a muffled voice from somewhere inside.

I knock again. This time I definitely hear a voice, muttering a string of expletives. Its owner appears to be nearing the door and the voice is just about distinguishable as Dave's. I move back a few feet and stand with my legs akimbo, stretching my muscles in preparation to run. Judging by the foul language now clearly audible through the door, it's safe to say Dave definitely doesn't welcome unsolicited visitors.

The door suddenly swings open and bangs against the adjacent wall, the glass pane rattling in its frame.

I was half-expecting to be punched by a fist but the first blow is delivered to my senses, primarily my sense of smell. A waft of tepid air engulfs me, carrying the scent of age-old sweat, cigarette smoke, stale alcohol and piss. I fight my gag reflex and stare at the raging face of somebody who might be Dave but looks nothing like the version from my previous timeline.

"The fuck you want?" he grunts.

The voice is Dave's, without question. Little else is. The man before me has long hair, greasy and lank, and a fierce beard covering most of his face. And then there's his body — there's a huge amount of it, probably twenty stones at least, all fat and no muscle.

As damn awful as my friend looks, it pales into insignificance at the sight of his seated position with two large wheels either side of him.

"You're…in a wheelchair," I inadvertently vocalise.

"No shit, Sherlock. I didn't need you banging on my fucking door to tell me that."

I let my muscles relax a little. Despite the shock of seeing my old friend sat in a wheelchair, I can take comfort that there's little chance of Dave punching me, let alone chasing me down the street. Nevertheless, I'll keep my distance as he's sat at the perfect height to deliver a potent jab to the balls.

"Dave?" I confirm, unsettled by the radically different appearance of the man before me.

"Who's asking?"

I ignore his question. "I need to talk to you. It's important."

A spark of recognition appears to ignite in his head, but not enough to flame his memory.

"Who the fuck are you, and how do you know my name?" he spits.

"Let me come in for five minutes and I'll explain."

"Are you shitting me? I don't make a habit of letting people I know into my home, let alone mystery dickheads who turn up unannounced."

This isn't going well. I need to throw him a bone, offer him something to spike his interest.

"Are you a betting man, Dave?"

If this version of Dave is anything like his predecessor, I know he won't be able to resist a bet.

"Might be. What's it gotta do with you?"

"I've got a bet you can't lose, well, you can't lose any money."

"If there's no money involved, I'm not interested."

"No, wait, there is. I said you can't *lose* any money."

"You're starting to piss me off now. Get to the point will you."

"I'll bet you forty quid that I can guess when, where, and who you broke your virginity with. If I'm right, you let me in for five minutes to talk. If I'm wrong, I'll give you forty quid, cash."

He eyes me suspiciously. "So let me get this straight. You guess who I popped my cherry with, and where, and if you're wrong you'll give me forty quid?"

"Yep. You've got nothing to lose apart from five minutes of your time."

Clearly Dave has nothing else in his diary and considers my bizarre proposition.

"Just so you're clear, there's fuck all worth stealing in here so if this is some ruse to rob me, you're wasting your time. And my carer is due any time so if you try any funny shit, he'll kick your arse."

"I just want to talk to you, nothing more."

"Alright then. I'll take your stupid bet."

"Tanya Phelps. Christmas 1985. On a judo mat in a storage room at the Sandy Lane Youth Club disco."

He doesn't react but his eyes fail to hide his surprise.

"How the fuck do you know that?" he eventually grunts.

"We had a bet, Dave. I won. Let me in and I'll answer your question."

He just stares at me for a few seconds. The temptation to pull the door shut must be at the forefront of his mind. But if I were in his shoes, metaphorically as he isn't wearing any, my curiosity would probably win out. Surely he wants to know how a complete stranger knows information he only ever shared with two people. Actually, he never shared it with me as such. I happened to be standing guard outside while he did the deed, for the entire six minute duration.

Just when I think he's about to pull the door shut, he cusses under his breath and spins around in his chair. A quick thrust of his stocky arms and he wheels away. I take it as the politest invite I'm likely to receive and step into a filthy hallway, closing the front door behind me.

What I smelt outside was fairly pleasant compared to the noxious stench beyond the door. The bare walls are a grimy shade of light blue and the laminated flooring not too dissimilar to the bottom of a heavily soiled litter tray.

I cross the hall and through to a square lounge. The curtains are partially drawn but there's enough light to determine I've just entered a pig sty. An unmade, metal-framed bed is wedged against one wall, with some sort of mechanical pulley contraption fixed to the ceiling above — it's a telling sight. Whatever accident or illness put Dave in the wheelchair, it appears to be permanent.

Besides the bed, there's a shabby armchair and a flatpack cabinet in the corner with a small TV sat on top. Beyond the path of Dave's wheelchair, the floor is covered with discarded clothes and general landfill. A half-empty vodka bottle and an overflowing ashtray take pride of place on a small table next to the armchair.

The whole place is as depressing as it is disgusting.

What the hell happened to my best friend?

18

Dave has positioned his wheelchair next to the bed and stares up at me like I'm the strangest of strangers.

"So?" he grunts.

The disturbing reality of the situation dominates my thoughts. What happened to the gym-obsessed Adonis I once knew? How did he end up in a wheelchair and why is he now a fat hobo living in squalor?

"Four minutes left," he says, lighting a cigarette.

Plan B now seems wholly inappropriate. Whatever happened to Dave, he clearly isn't in a sufficiently stable state of mind to accept I've returned from beyond the grave. God only knows what drove him to this pitiful existence, but I doubt hearing about the life he could have lived is likely to improve this one.

"I'm looking for a computer. A Commodore 64," I splutter.

"Good for you. Try eBay."

"Actually, I'm looking for a very specific Commodore 64. One I've been told is in your possession."

He takes a long draw on his cigarette before exhaling a plume of smoke towards the nicotine-stained ceiling.

"This is bullshit. Who the fuck are you?"

For Christs-sake Craig, don't tell him the truth.

"I'm…um…Jeremy. Jeremy Pelling."

"That supposed to mean something to me?"

"I'm Craig's cousin."

The spark of recognition that failed to ignite outside suddenly bursts into flame. The scowl on his face lifts in an instant.

"Shit. I thought there was something about you that seemed familiar. Why the fuck didn't you say that in the first place?"

"Dunno," I laugh nervously. "I wasn't sure you'd remember Craig."

"He was my best mate," he says wistfully. "But we've never met before have we? I don't remember Craig ever mentioning you."

"Um, we lived in Essex and my dad never got on with his brother, Craig's dad. I only met Craig a few times before…you know."

"Yeah, I know. Terrible what happened to him, poor bastard."

A sudden silence falls on the room, maybe as a mark of respect for the teenage version of me who died so young. It's unreal and unsettling. Dave eventually breaks the silence with a question that threatens to expose my bullshit.

"If you only met Craig a few times, why did he share the specific details of how l lost my virginity? Seems a bit random."

"Oh, well, he didn't actually tell me."

"Eh?"

"He kept a diary. I saw it, a few days ago when I visited his dad. The stuff about you losing your virginity was in the diary and I thought it was funny. That's why I remembered it."

"You're an odd one aren't you? Not the way I'd choose to introduce myself."

"Anyway, the computer?"

"What do you want if for?"

I could tell him the truth. We're all living in a parallel timeline and the Commodore 64 might be able to send me back in time so I can restore the past. Or I could lie.

"It's a bit of a long story. I've just got back in touch with Craig's dad, Colin, and I'm staying with him for a week or so. Anyway, we were chatting and he told me about a game Craig was working on before he…err, left. I thought it might be a nice touch to finish the game, maybe even convert it to work on a PC. Sort of like an online memorial to him."

"Nice idea, but seeing as the Commodore didn't have any internal memory for storing software, you don't actually need the computer, just whatever he saved the game on? Could have been a floppy disk or a cassette."

Bugger. His knowledge of retro computers has blown a hole in my concocted story.

"Yeah, right, of course. I sort of assumed that if I found the computer, the game might be stored with it."

"Afraid not mate. Mrs P just gave me the computer and the cassette recorder. To be honest, I didn't want the bloody thing as I already had a Commodore 128, but I guess the poor old girl thought I'd like something of Craig's, you know, to remember him. I took it home and just shoved it in the wardrobe."

"Right."

I dig my hands in my pockets and feel the wad of notes the old man gave me.

"Still, it would be quite something to show the computer to Colin."

"I doubt it. He was a miserable fucker. I don't think he showed much interest in anything Craig did."

Foiled again, and I've already exhausted my list of spurious reasons why I need the computer. This chase needs cutting.

"Do you actually still have the computer?"

"I think it's in the loft."

"You think?"

"Do I look like I spend a lot of time in the fucking loft?"

"Sorry, course not. But if it is, would you sell it to me?"

"Why are you so keen to get your hands on it?"

I ball my fists and consider the morality of punching a wheelchair-bound invalid.

"I collect vintage home computers and I thought it would be nice to include my late cousin's Commodore. That's it. Do you want to sell it or not?"

He stubs out his cigarette and immediately lights another one.

"There's quite a bit of sentimental value attached to it you know. It'd kill me to see it go, it really would."

Strange how only a moment ago he said he never wanted the bloody thing.

"I'll give you two hundred quid for it. Cash," I offer, leaving myself some room for negotiation.

"Two fifty," he fires back.

"Two twenty. Final offer."

"Deal."

It appears even sentimentality has a price.

"Great. If you point me in the direction of the loft hatch, I'll check it's up there. If it is, I'll give you the cash."

"The hatch is in the hall and there's a step ladder in the bathroom. The bath hoist keeps jamming so the carer left it in there."

"Okay. Thanks."

I leave Dave to plan how he'll spend his windfall and head back into the hallway. It doesn't require much investigation to establish where the bathroom is as the acrid stench of stale piss drifts from behind a partially open door. I nudge it open with my foot, step inside and grab the stepladder. I pull the bathroom door firmly shut behind me and breathe again.

The loft hatch is located in the middle of the hallway ceiling so I set the stepladder up directly below and tentatively climb the first few rungs. When I get close enough to reach the hatch, I nudge it with my hand and it lifts a few inches. No hinges. I move up another rung and place both palms on the hatch and press upwards so it topples into the loft. A cloud of stale, roasted air escapes through the opening and adds to the already unpleasant ambience of Dave's hallway. Undaunted, I climb the final two rungs and hoist myself into the black hole.

I position myself so I'm sat on the inner ledge of the hatch opening, my legs dangling into the hallway. Unsurprisingly, I can't see a damn thing. I pull my phone from my pocket and use the light of the screen to aid my search for a light switch. Two minutes of scrabbling around in the dark and I find it, fixed to a beam above my head. I flick the switch and pull my legs up, planting my feet either side of the hatch opening so I can stand. The forty-watt bulb provides enough luminescence to establish the loft floor is boarded, and that there isn't much up here.

Three sides of the loft are empty but there's a pile of bags, boxes, and suitcases neatly stacked into the eaves of the fourth wall; possibly forgotten remnants of the life Dave once had. I shuffle a few feet across the creaking boards and take a closer look. The front of the pile contains a stack of square boxes that look too small to house the computer. I move them one-by-one and rebuild the stack a few feet away. The oppressive heat prickles my skin and I can already feel sweat building across my forehead.

With the stack of boxes moved, I inspect the remaining pile of possessions. I pull several bags, more boxes, and a few suitcases from the pile, checking the content of each as I go. None of them contain what I'm looking for and my frustration mounts. I'm about to sift through another box when Dave calls up from the hallway.

"Found it?"

"Yeah, but I thought your loft would benefit from a little feng shui so I'm reorganising everything for the sheer hell of it."

"What?"

"No, I haven't found it."

Dave grumbles something and I watch the top of his head disappear from view beyond the stepladder. I'm too hot and bothered for niceties.

I return my attention to the last few remaining items: a suitcase, three boxes, and an opaque plastic storage crate that looks like it's full of towels and bed linen. I inspect the boxes but only find general household tat. The sweat continues to build and trickles down my face, dust sticking to my clammy skin. I yearn for a long shower more than I ever thought possible.

By the time I unclasp the catches on the suitcase, I've all but given up. Dave obviously sent me up here on a fishing expedition — I doubt he has the first clue where the bloody computer is. I flip the lid of the suitcase to find it full of women's shoes. Under any other circumstance I might be intrigued why Dave owns a suitcase full of stilettos and sling-backs, but my disappointment is too overwhelming to really care. I slam the lid shut and shove the case across the floor with my foot. This must be some sort of punishment. Fate dangling a carrot for me to chase, only to repeatedly pull it away when I get close.

As if to validate my theory that fate hates me, a droplet of dust-laden sweat runs into my right eye. It stings like hell and I try to blink it away but it feels like the inside of my eyelid is coated with sandpaper. I wipe it against my forearm but that only exasperates the problem. I find temporary respite by clenching my right eye shut. Now I'm hot, sweaty, angry and partially blind. This day just gets better and better.

In desperate need of something to wipe my eye with, I stumble over to the crate of linen in hope I'll find a towel or cloth that isn't encrusted with sweat and dust. I crouch down into the dark eaves, pull the plastic lid off and snatch a pillow case from the top. It's not ideal but absorbent enough to wipe the worst of the crud from my eye. I squeeze a few blinks out to confirm I can safely open my eye again. It's then I spot it — a thirteen amp plug, nestled between two fluffy pink towels.

It could be a plug for anything: a kettle, a hi-fi, a sandwich toaster. It seems an odd place to keep an electrical lead though. Intrigued, I lean over the crate and lift one of the towels away. The light is so poor I can't determine exactly what's beneath but it looks like a folded bed sheet. It might be cream or beige but it's difficult to tell. With my vision compromised I decide to investigate further with my hand. It touches the bed sheet but rather than the soft feel of fabric, the surface is hard, plasticky.

I snatch the other towel away to reveal more of the plastic material, and a silver sticker about an inch-and-a-half square. I move my head closer and squint at the faded black lettering. Nine letters tell me all I need to know — Commodore.

I can barely catch my breath. It could be the heat, or the dust, or the noxious cloud of filth rising up from Dave's living accommodation. It's more likely because I'm actually staring at the bottom of my Commodore 64. The machine that threw me back in time. The machine responsible for creating this broken future. Most importantly though, the machine that could unlock the door back to my previous life.

I delicately extract the rest of the linen, half-expecting fate to inflict another cruel twist. It would be my luck to unearth the bottom half of an empty carcase.

With the top part of the crate empty, and the entire bottom section of the computer exposed, I clasp both ends and gently lift. The weight feels about right. I twist it over and shuffle backwards into the light. Everything is where it should be and there's no obvious damage. I place it on top of a box and scurry back to the crate. I pull a few more towels away to reveal the cassette player and a tangled nest of cables. Clearly the computer was stored amongst all this linen to protect it. Whoever put it here will never know the true significance of that decision.

After a final inspection of the crate to check there's nothing else in there, my next challenge is to get the precious cargo out of the loft without damaging it. I nervously wrap the computer and the cassette player in towels and scour the loft for a suitable means to carry them down the stepladder. A bright pink holdall shoved inside one of the suitcases offers the best option. I place the towel cocoons into the holdall and lay the nest of wires on top before zipping it shut. I switch the light off, ignoring the mess I've left behind. It's not like Dave is going to check I've tidied up after myself.

I place the holdall on the edge of the loft opening and lower myself down onto the top rung of the stepladder. I carefully pull the holdall after me and drape the strap across my shoulder before reinstating the loft hatch. My mind conjures up an array of ways my precious cargo could be damaged so every movement is precise, considered. I finally work down the rungs, one step at a time with a double-check to ensure my footing is sound.

Only when I finally step on to the filthy laminate floor in the hallway do I dare breathe again. And with that final step, the enormity of what I've just accomplished hits me. A little over twenty-four hours ago I walked into a churchyard, weighed down with guilt and despondency. I had reluctantly accepted my new life and the shitstorm of crushing revelations it brought. The chance of finding the computer, of escaping this nightmare, too ridiculous to even consider.

But against all hope, against all the odds, the computer is now in my possession. Only time will tell if this is just fate inflicting another cruel hoax on me, or if this really is the miracle I prayed for.

19

I return the stepladder to the bathroom and head back into the lounge. Dave has extracted himself from the wheelchair and is sat in the armchair. The TV is on and he's staring blankly at the screen while sipping from the vodka bottle. I cough to attract his attention, although the smog of cigarette smoke is reason enough.

"Found it."

"Cash," he grunts.

I peel eleven twenty-pound notes from the wad and hold them towards him. He snatches the cash without moving his eyes from the TV.

"Nice doing business with you, Jezza."

For a second I wonder why he called me 'Jezza', before I realise it's an abbreviation of my fictitious name.

"Close the door on your way out," he adds.

Every part of me wants to follow Dave's advice and run back to the old man like Charlie Bucket with his golden ticket. Every part except my conscience. How can I leave my friend here like this? Whatever dragged his life down to this level, it was because of my meddling. I can't not say something.

"Do you mind if I ask you a question?"

"Not as though I can stop you."

"The wheelchair. Can I ask how it happened?"

He takes a glug of vodka and lights up yet another cigarette, all the time avoiding eye contact. I don't know if he's pondering the right way to answer my question or simply ignoring me in the hope I'll go away. Turns out to be the former.

"Why is that any of your business?"

"It's not. I just didn't recognise you as the kid Craig wrote about in his diary. What happened to him, that kid?"

He takes another glug of vodka and pulls a deep draw on his cigarette.

"Maxine Green," he spits.

"Sorry?"

"Maxine Green. That's what happened to that kid, or an older version of him, anyway."

"Who's Maxine Green?"

"Ex-girlfriend and the reason I'm stuck in a fucking wheelchair, in this hovel."

I move from his side and using my foot, I clear some space on the floor next to the TV. I sit down and lean against the wall. Dave looks ghostly from this angle, the light from the TV casting a grey hue and dark shadows across his pale face.

"Make yourself at home," he mumbles.

"Do you want to tell me what happened?"

"Not really."

"Okay."

Dave was never the sort to wear his heart on his sleeve. He was what you might call a man's man, and would gleefully mock if I ever expressed even a modicum of emotion. I doubt he'll pour his heart out to a complete stranger, even if that stranger happens to be the cousin of his former best friend. I need to try a different angle.

"Bit of a bitch was she, this Maxine?"

"The worst."

"Worse than Tanya Phelps?"

"You really did read Craig's diary," he snorts.

"Some of it. Tanya cheated on you a few weeks after than night at the disco, didn't she?"

"Shit man, that was just kids stuff. Maxine was a whole different ballgame."

"How so?"

Dave looks straight at me. He tilts his head a fraction, perhaps weighing me up.

"Anyone ever told you, you're a lot like Craig?"

"No, they haven't."

"Your features. The way you say certain things. It's a bit of a head fuck."

I feel uncomfortable. It feels like Dave can see inside my head, see my lies.

"We have the same grandparents. Must be something in the genes we share."

"Shared," he says flatly, correcting my use of current tense.

"Um, yeah. Shared."

I know I'm pushing my luck here and probably should have left when I had the chance. But I can't ignore the burning question about how Dave ended up like this.

"Anyway. Are you going to tell me why Maxine Green was such a bitch?"

"Skiing."

"Eh?"

He exhales a deep breath and scratches at his thick beard.

"Met her about five years ago. Usual shit. We dated, got engaged, moved in together."

"Okay."

"She'd been banging on about going skiing. She used to go every winter with her family and wanted us to go together. Never fucking skied in my life and didn't want to start. Maxine always got her own way though, so we booked a skiing holiday two years ago."

It doesn't take any huge leap of deduction to work out the rest, but I let Dave fill in the gaps.

"Fourth day I thought I had the hang of it, so she suggested we move off the nursery slopes. I remember standing at the top of this fucking huge slope and shitting myself. Couldn't let her see I was scared though, so I just went for it."

"What happened?"

"Man, it was so fucking fast. Too fast. I couldn't control myself, couldn't stop. I just stared down at my skis and tried to keep them pointing in the right direction. Didn't work though and I strayed from the piste. I remember looking up for a second and seeing a wall of rock about fifty yards ahead. I tried to turn but lost it and the world just kept spinning. Don't remember anything after that."

"Shit."

"Apparently I span out and hit the rocks at nearly thirty miles an hour. I was airlifted to hospital and came round two days later."

"I'm guessing that's the reason for the wheelchair."

He inadvertently glances across at it, his disdain obvious.

"I spent six weeks in some stinking French hospital before they moved me back to England. I had four operations and spent five months in hospital here."

"And Maxine?"

"The bitch got her brother to deliver a letter to me. Must have been about three days after they transferred me back to England. Said she couldn't face life living with a paraplegic, and she was sorry but we were finished. Can you fucking believe that? I was only in a wheelchair because I agreed to go on that bastard holiday with her."

"Christ. That's bad."

"That's not the half of it. By the time they let me out of hospital I'd lost my flat and my business. I used to be a graphic designer."

"I know. That's how I found your address."

"Social Services put me in this place. I thought I could rebuild the business, and my social worker even set up my Mac in the bedroom like a proper office."

"So why didn't you?"

Dave slowly lifts his right arm and holds it out in front of him. Even in the dim light I can clearly see his hand trembling.

"Nerve damage from the accident. I can cope with it for most things but can't use a mouse for shit. I tried for a few weeks but it was fucking hopeless."

I now know what drove Dave to this life. My curiosity has been sated, but I've given precious little thought to what happens next. I look down at the holdall next to me. Is the answer contained within the vivid pink canvas? Maybe there is a chance to restore Dave's previous life, the one where he married Suzy and therefore never stepped foot on that ski slope. Now, more than ever, I need to get the Commodore set up, and I need to know if I can go back.

The sound of the front door opening drags my attention back to the room.

A huge man steps into the lounge doorway, his bald head almost touching the top of the door frame. His light grey trousers and polo shirt are an ill fit for his imposing frame. The embroidered logo on his vast chest is stretched to the point where it's barely readable.

Dave turns and looks up at the giant. "Alright, Bartek."

"Yah, good. Who's your guest?" the giant named Bartek replies, his accent eastern European.

"He's just leaving," Dave replies.

I'm guessing Bartek is Dave's Social Services appointed carer rather than a casual guest. It makes sense as Dave must need a man of Bartek's size to help him in and out of the bath. His arrival is a convenient excuse for me to get out of here, my conscience absolved a little.

I clamber to my feet and grab the holdall. "Yeah, better be going. Good to meet you, Dave."

I take a few steps towards Bartek and offer a feeble smile. He begrudgingly steps aside and I dart past him into the hallway.

As I close the front door, a wave of relief washes over me. The fresh air is welcome, but the relief at leaving with the computer is palpable, verging on euphoric. I can scarcely believe I've actually done it. I allow myself a satisfied smile until the guilt about Dave's situation quickly quashes my elation. I grasp the holdall tightly, and walk back to the car.

As I turn the corner, I'm relieved to see the old man hasn't bailed on me, and his car is still parked up at the end of the road. I check my phone to see my task took well over an hour. I jog the remaining distance.

I clamber into the car and carefully place the holdall in the footwell.

"Well?" the old man asks impatiently.

I turn to him. "I got it, Dad. I can't quite believe it but I actually got it."

His face is a picture of genuine delight, and he then does something that takes me completely by surprise. He reaches across and clamps his hands around my cheeks.

"I knew you could do it, son. Well done."

I'm glad his hands are currently covering my cheeks because I feel them flush red. Twice now he's spontaneously shown physical affection towards me, and that's twice more than throughout the entirety of my previous life. Coupled with his positive words, it triggers a warm glow.

"Thanks, Dad, but it was your plan C that came good though," I reply with a broad grin.

"Doesn't matter. You were the one who went in there and came out with the goods. Smashing job."

He releases his grip on my face and starts the car, his excitement obvious. The guilt I felt about Dave drifts away as I bask in the old man's positivity. I feel like an eight-year-old who's just won the egg-and-spoon race at the school sports day. The sad irony is that the old man never attended any of my school sports days. What wouldn't I give to relive my life with the father sat next to me. I've seemingly not learnt my lesson about wishing for a different life.

We head back to Hale in good spirits, and at a less ponderous pace than the outbound journey.

As we pull into the cul-de-sac my thoughts turn to the reality of the next fifteen minutes. Assuming the old man's TV is archaic enough, I should be able to connect the computer to it. But what will happen when I finally switch it on? It could be excitement, trepidation, fear, or a mix of all three, but the question actually makes me feel a little queasy. What if my journey was a miraculous one-off, and the computer is now just a useless box of electronics? What do I do if I'm actually able to return to 1986? What if the computer doesn't work at all?

My nerves are already frayed by the time we walk in the front door.

"You fancy a cuppa or do you want to get on with setting that thing up?" he asks, pointing to the holdall.

"I think I'll just get on with it, Dad."

We head into the lounge and I pull the TV away from the wall so I can access the sockets at the back. I unzip the holdall and extract the nest of cables. I put them aside and lift the towel cocoons out, carefully unwrapping them on the floor.

"Anything I can do?" the old man asks.

"Start praying this thing still works."

I pick the computer up and place it on top of the bulky TV. I return to the nest of cables and extract the lead that runs from the computer to the TV. The correct sockets are present and I plug the leads in. Next, I need power for the computer.

I return to the floor, and tug at the thirteen-amp plug to pull the power cable from the tangled nest. It's at that exact moment a devastating realisation hits me — the power transformer isn't here. Without the chunky beige box there is no way to power the computer.

I grab the holdall and check every pocket, but I already know it's empty. I cast my mind back to Dave's loft and re-run the process of checking the storage crate. No, it definitely wasn't in there, I'm sure of it.

"Problem?" the old man asks.

"You could say that," I groan. "The power transformer is missing."

"What does it look like?"

"It's a beige-coloured block, about half the size of a house brick."

"Could it still be at Dave's place?"

"I dunno, I wasn't really looking for it. I know it definitely wasn't in the same place as the computer."

"And you definitely need it?"

"Yes," I snap.

I immediately regret taking my frustration out on the old man.

"Sorry. I didn't mean to snap."

It doesn't make sense that Dave would have stored the transformer in a different place from everything else I found in the crate. Notwithstanding the fact he probably wouldn't welcome another visit, I'd bet good money the transformer isn't in his loft. If Mum never gave the transformer to Dave when she handed over my computer, surely it must have stayed in my room. And if it stayed in my room, it must have been packed into one of the boxes now sat in the other room.

"You want the good news?" I ask. "Or the bad news?"

"Let's go with the good news."

"I think it might be in one of the boxes in the bedroom."

"The boxes we spent hours sifting through this morning?"

"Afraid so. That's the bad news."

"I think I'll make that cup of tea now."

We spend another two hours checking every one of the boxes we originally sorted through, and then all of the remaining boxes. One particular box set my pulse racing as I unearthed my old Ferguson portable TV. It did make sense that the transformer would bc stored in the same box as the TV but no luck. While I doubt using the original TV will have much bearing on whether the computer does what I hope, or not, at least I now have all the key components — minus the transformer.

The afternoon ends with the two of us sat on the bedroom floor, leant against the wall, defeated and deflated.

"Which plan are we on now?" the old man asks.

"D. Or it could be E."

"And that plan is?"

By the time we'd sifted through all of the boxes from my former bedroom, I'd already resigned myself to the fact we wouldn't find the transformer. We kept looking but I started thinking about what I'd do if our search proved fruitless.

"You can still buy Commodore transformers online but it's going to take a couple of days to arrive I'd imagine."

"Online? The Internet?" he asks.

"Don't worry, Dad. I'll do it when I get back to the flat. I don't think I could face Miriam again either."

"Good," he chuckles. "Tell you what, why don't we go and grab some dinner? There's a lovely pub a mile down the road. And I don't know about you, but I could murder a pint."

"That, all things considered, is a very sensible suggestion."

We pack everything away and safely store the computer, the portable TV and all the other components in a cupboard.

Barely ten minutes later, we're stood at the bar of The Wheatsheaf. We grab our pints and find a table in the beer garden. We only have to share the garden with a handful of other customers and the late afternoon sun is still sat high enough in the sky to warm the air. It's just about the perfect setting for a quiet pint.

A waitress arrives and takes our food order. We then sit in silence, supping our drinks and reflecting on the craziness of the last thirty-odd hours. Half-a-pint later, the old man poses a question.

"Have you thought about what you'll do, if you're able to go back again?"

"Not beyond the last ten minutes. I'm not planning to run through the streets this time."

"But you'll do everything else the same as before?"

"I guess so. I haven't had time to really consider anything. Besides, I didn't want to tempt fate and get ahead of myself."

"Right," he says quietly. "I was just wondering about our chat, the one we had in my shed."

"What about it?"

"I want you to promise me it still happens."

I think back to that conversation, and how nervous I was stood in the garden preparing to challenge my ogre of a father. It's not something I can honestly say I'm relishing.

"I don't want to be that man again, son. I wasted sixteen years of my life being angry and I need you to ensure I don't waste the rest of it," he adds.

Of all the lives I screwed up, one saving grace is the difference between the old man I left behind, and the man sat with me. For purely selfish reasons I'm happy to oblige, no matter how daunting it may be to revisit that shed.

"I promise, Dad."

"Good lad."

"Besides," I smile. "This is the first beer you've ever bought me. Can't have that again."

We laugh, and finish our drinks chatting idly about nothing in particular. Our food arrives and the conversation continues over steak and chips, and another pint. It's the tastiest, and most unhealthy meal I've had in nearly a year. Then, just as I assume the old man is about to offer me a lift home, he suggests leaving the car at the pub and having a few more pints.

"I'll pay for you to get a cab home," he offers. "I don't know how much longer I've got you for, so I'd like to make the most of whatever time we have."

I vowed to lay off alcohol for at least one day, but the look of expectation on his face melts my defences.

"Yeah, I'd like that, Dad"

"Excellent. It'll give me a chance to whip you at darts," he chuckles before heading back to the bar.

All too soon I'm sat in a cab on my way back to Farndale. A little drunk, a lot happy. No matter what happens to me in the future, the four hours I've just spent with the old man will remain a treasured memory. The alcohol helped to take the edge of any residual awkwardness and we talked openly, we laughed, and we drank, a lot. We played darts, and I lost. We played pool, and I lost. We even found some common ground in our choice of music on the jukebox. That common ground didn't quite extend as far as country and western music though — no amount of alcohol could fix that.

It's well after eleven o'clock by the time I clamber into bed. I set the alarm on my phone to go off at eight. My first priority in the morning is to locate a transformer for the Commodore. But for now, I'm happy to drift away in a drunken stupor, Slim Whitman's awful yodelling still ringing in my ears.

20

I'm *definitely* too old for this shit.

If it's true what they say, and hangovers increase in potency with age, the old man must be clinically dead this morning. I clamber out of bed and begin the now-familiar routine of making strong coffee and necking painkillers. I return to the bedroom and sit on the edge of the bed. With my trusty free wi-fi connection, and furnished with a debit card the old man generously lent me, I begin the search for a transformer.

I find plenty of websites that sell modern copies but I'm paranoid about it being original. I can only imagine the horror of plugging in a generic transformer and being greeted with the scent of burning circuitry. Thankfully, I find an online retailer who specialises in retro computer components and they have an original Commodore transformer in stock. I complete the order form, and pay extra for guaranteed overnight delivery.

I call the old man and give him the good news. Judging by his muted reaction I suspect he's also dealing with an epic hangover. At least he's still alive. I tell him I'll call tomorrow once the transformer has arrived. I don't think either of us is disappointed to end the conversation within a few minutes.

With my primary objective successfully completed before nine o'clock, I decide to escape my hangover and return to bed. I've got a whole ten hours to kill before I'm due at Lucy's house and a few extra hours sleep should ensure I arrive feeling vaguely human.

I manage three hours of fitful sleep, much of it spent tossing and turning as my mind swings back and forth like an emotional pendulum. Excited, fearful. Optimistic, nervous. Contented, unsettled. It feels like being back in 1990 when I was trying to find a decent job, away from Video City. On a few occasions, I got as far as being interviewed and then I'd endure days of anxiety, waiting for a letter to land on the mat. The content of those letters could only ever be binary; really good news or really bad news, nothing in between. My current situation doesn't feel too different.

By one o'clock I'm climbing the walls. I've eaten, I showered, I've watched TV, I've had my precautionary wank ahead of tonight. I'm full of nervous energy and need to direct it into something productive. I return to the couch and switch the TV on again.

Ten minutes into a mind-numbing property show and an advert for Morrison's Supermarket prods an unanswered question towards the front of my mind — the whereabouts of one Marcus Morrison. He is the last remaining piece of my 1986 jigsaw. Truth be told, I couldn't really give a shit where his life went after our altercation in the skate park, but boredom is motivation enough for me to try and find out.

I head back to the bedroom and grab my phone. I check all the major social media platforms to see if Marcus has an account, but find nothing conclusive. A Google search proves equally fruitless. Ten minutes into my online research and I'm already thwarted. Time for a little lateral thinking.

The one connection I still have with Marcus is the school we attended — Heathland Secondary School. I assume the reunion went ahead last year, and I'd bet my bottom dollar Marcus would have been there. Maybe I can get in contact with somebody who attended and see if they spoke to him, or know of his whereabouts. The question is, who?

I open the Facebook app on my phone and search for the most obvious candidate — Helen Robinson, the reunion organiser.

After almost a minute of scrolling past scores of women with the same name, a profile matches the Helen I'm looking for…

Helen Robinson
Works at St Joseph's Day Nursery, Farndale
Went to Heathland Secondary School

I jab the screen to open the profile. I'm greeted by a picture of Helen, gurning a duck-lipped selfie pose. I shudder, and quickly scroll past the picture to her news feed. It soon becomes clear Helen likes to post about every tedious moment of her day. There's a picture of her breakfast, of her morning latte, of the new air-freshener in her car. Does she really think her friends and family have any interest in this shit? Deluded woman.

On the plus side, Helen's propensity to share every part of her life with the world also extends to her contact details.

Furnished with her mobile phone number, I now have to determine my approach. I need to come up with a convincing reason why I'm interested in Marcus, and who I am. Helen probably knows the name of everyone from our year, so I can't pretend to be a former pupil. But if I never attended Heathland, in what capacity did I know Marcus, and why have I lost touch with him? A dull ache creeps up from the base of my skull, bringing with it some regret I've created this problem for no good reason.

I get up from the bed and stare out of the window as I try to concoct a plausible back story. I need to think of something that connects me and Marcus but has nothing to do with school. As we had so little in common and mixed in completely different circles, it's a very short shortlist of possibilities.

I remind my self this doesn't really matter in the grand scheme of things, and dial Helen's number. She picks up almost immediately.

"Hellooo," she shrieks.

"Erm, hello. Is that the Helen Robinson who organised the Heathland school reunion last year?"

"The very one."

"Great. I was hoping you might be able to help me. I'm trying to organise a reunion of my own, for kids who used to attend Sandy Lane Youth Club in the mid-80s."

"How lovely," she interrupts. "But I'm afraid my parents never let me go to youth club. They were concerned about some of the undesirables who frequented the place."

Dave, probably.

"I don't think I can help you," she adds.

"No, sorry. That's not why I was calling you. I'm trying to track down a few elusive people and I can't find them on Facebook. One of them definitely attended Heathland so I was wondering if he was at your reunion. If he was, I was hoping you might know how to get in touch with him?"

"Oh, I see," she chortles. "Who is it you're trying to find?"

"Marcus Morrison."

Silence.

"Hello? Helen?"

"Sorry. I'm still here," she says quietly.

"Did you hear what I said?"

"Yes. Yes I did."

"So, do you know where I might find Marcus?"

More silence.

"My apologies. I didn't catch your name," she eventually says.

"Craig."

"I hate to be the one to tell you Craig, but I'm afraid Marcus passed away, sometime in the early nineties."

The sudden tightness in my chest renders me speechless for a second. While I may not have cared about what happened to Marcus, I never imagined for one moment he would no longer be alive.

"God, that's awful," I croak. "Do you know what happened?"

Helen sighs, perhaps reluctant to be the bearer of not-so-glad tidings. Seconds pass before she finally decides to furnish me with more details.

"Most of what I know is just gossip from the reunion, but apparently he died of an AIDS-related illness. From what I gather, he left home just after we finished school and he ended up living in a squat, somewhere in London. Apparently he led quite a hedonistic lifestyle for a few years. Unfortunately, the 1980s wasn't the ideal time for a young gay man to be sowing his wild oats."

"No, guess it wasn't."

Neither of us knows how to fill the silence that follows. I stare out of the bedroom window at the cloudless blue sky — a lovely afternoon, in most respects.

"Sorry, Helen. I'm a bit shell-shocked. I'll leave it there. Thanks."

I end the call and sit back down on the bed.

It takes just a few seconds for my mind to pose the question. Was Marcus's premature death my fault?

I cast my mind back to our conversation in the skate park. He must have taken on-board something I said that morning. Did he confront his homophobic father and end up being kicked out of the family home? Did he decide to live in London so he could embrace his sexuality in a more liberal-minded environment?

I'll never know.

Beyond the shock and the guilt and the unanswered questions, frustration begins to mount. Why didn't I just leave this alone? Like a kid with a scabby knee, I had to keep picking at the wounds of my previous life. My mind will never heal as long as I keep poking around in things that should be left well alone. I'm such an idiot.

I slip my trainers on and storm out of the flat.

With the sun shining and my feet pounding the pavement at a brisk pace, I try to clear Marcus from my mind. I focus on nothing more than putting one foot in front of the other, much like I did on the treadmill during my early days at Broadhall. There is something inherently calming in the repetition and I wallow in the mindlessness of it. This is my therapy. My way to shut out the noise from an ever-growing list of questions that constantly loop in my head.

I wander aimlessly for over two hours, until my feet start to throb. I don't mind the pain. I quite like the feeling of aching limbs and tired muscles brought on by exercise. It's a different feeling from the random aches and pains my body used to endure every morning when I led a sedentary lifestyle. However, my body is telling me it's probably time to return to the flat.

By the time I get back, it's nearly four o'clock. Any remnants of my hangover are long gone but it's not so easy to shake the vision of a young Marcus lying on his death bed. It's so vivid I can see his face, gaunt and pale, and his body, emaciated. He looks scared. Terrified. I don't consciously recall creating this vision but it's there nonetheless. The work of my pernicious imagination, again.

The vision is so real I can only banish it by telling myself that maybe tomorrow, once the computer is working, I'll be able to go back. I'll relive that Sunday and ensure I never have a conversation with Marcus. He won't go to London and he'll never contract that hideous disease. He'll continue to be a complete twat though, but at least he won't be a dead twat.

I know, deep down, the chances of being able to return are slim, but I'd rather focus on that slim chance than dwell on Marcus's actual fate and the accompanying visions.

To keep my mind distracted, I put the TV on and scan through the channels. I settle on watching a game show and it proves to be an effective antidote. The idiocy of the contestants beggars belief and the show ends, not unsurprisingly, with the final contestant not knowing the currency of Poland is the zloty. It's a staple question of the pub quiz, for crying out loud. But no amount of shouting at the screen can help the fool and he fails to win the five-hundred-quid prize.

I scan the channels again, and find another game show, and another raft of fuckwits. Pamela from Bristol doesn't know there are one thousand metres in a kilometre, and Darren from Portsmouth is convinced a thesaurus is a type of dinosaur. I watch for another half-hour, and can't help but wonder how the contestant actually manage to find their way out of the house each morning, such is their stupidity. Where do they get these people?

The closing titles finally roll, prompting me to get on with preparations for my trip to Lucy's house.

I head into the bedroom and search for clean clothes. I should probably have done some washing by now, but I'll forgive myself on the grounds I've had a few more pressing matters to address in the last few days. I manage to find a clean pair of jeans and boxer shorts, and a black polo shirt.

With my attire sorted, I have a shave and then stand in the shower until the hot water runs cold. It's gone six o'clock by the time I return to the bathroom mirror. I take a minute to inspect my reflection, and my tussled hair. Back in my former life I used to have it cut short every four weeks, but it's now been over two months since it last saw a pair of scissors. I quite like it. It's messy but not untidy, almost like I've deliberately styled it that way. Another benefit to longer hair is that my receding hairline isn't so obvious.

I cover my body with deodorant and get dressed. A final inspection in the mirror and I'm good to go. Lucy's house is about half-an-hour away but I don't want to arrive in a sweaty mess so I give myself a forty-minute window for the walk.

With so much happening since we met up on Saturday night, I've barely had chance to think about Lucy. I use the two mile walk to think back to our first date, and contemplate what lies ahead this evening. It still feels surreal. We were friends for years but I never believed that our friendship could develop into something more. Yet here I am now, on my way to her house with possibly more than a snog on the cards.

For the next few hours I intend to forget about time-travel and troublesome computers.

Tonight I intend to make up for lost time.

21

Partridge Lane is situated in one of the oldest, and most tranquil parts of Farndale. Originally, the lane was once no more than a farm track so it's barely wide enough for two cars to pass and there's no pavement. Thankfully, very little traffic passes this way so I can walk down the centre of the lane towards number eleven without fear of being run over. Again.

I've only ever been to Lucy's house a handful of times, and not for a few years. But my memory serves me well as I stand in front of her quaint cottage, which looks unchanged from my last visit. The cottage once belonged to her grandfather and Lucy inherited it when he passed away. She'd never have been able to afford such a sought-after home on her RolpheTech wages.

I open the gate and make my way up a narrow path alongside the small front garden. To me, the garden looks overgrown, but I think Lucy has gone for that cottage-garden look by crowding the space with an abundance of wild plants with colourful flowers. One thing is for sure, everything would be dead within a week if it was under my care so I shouldn't judge.

I step up to a hardwood front door, gloss painted letterbox red. It's probably older than the home I used to own. I rap the brass knocker and shuffle nervously on the spot as I wait. A few seconds pass and the door opens.

"Hiya. Come on in," Lucy says enthusiastically.

I step inside the hall and she kisses me on the cheek. I remain motionless to avoid another clash of heads.

"You look amazing," I gush, suddenly feeling very under-dressed.

"Aw, thank you. Let's go through to the kitchen shall we?"

She turns and walks away. I pause for a moment to appreciate her svelte form, framed in a short summer dress. The delicate, light-blue fabric clings to her curves, leaving little to my imagination. I put my tongue back in and follow.

The kitchen, and indeed the entire ground floor of the cottage, are nothing like I remember. It would seem Lucy's business is doing well enough to fund some major renovations. Both the poky kitchen and dining room that used to occupy the rear of the building are gone. In their place is an open-plan room that stretches the full width of the cottage. A shaker-style kitchen with pale cream units occupies half the space, with a chunky, cherry wood dining table sat in the centre of the other half. A set of bi-fold doors are tucked away so the dining area is completely open to the garden beyond.

"This is so much better, Lucy," I mindlessly remark.

"Better?"

"Sorry. I mean…nice. It's so nice," I splutter.

Idiot.

"I had it done earlier this year. The place was a bomb-site for a month but it was worth it."

Seemingly happy to overlook my odd comment, she grabs a bottle of white wine from the fridge and places it on an island along with two glasses.

"Wine okay?"

"Perfect. Thanks."

She fills both glasses and carries them over to the dining table. I take that as invitation to sit and Lucy follows suit.

"I've prepped a sushi salad for dinner. Hope that's okay?"

"Sounds lovely."

I take a sip of wine, cold and tart. We sit and share awkward glances at one another, like teenagers at a school disco.

"Shall I put some music on?" Lucy asks. "What do you like?"

I'd guess she actually wants to fill the uncomfortable silence. The atmosphere feels a little strained. Maybe, in the cold, sober light of day, some of my revelations from Saturday evening are playing on her mind. I did throw her a few curve balls. I need to fill in a few of the gaps I left behind.

"I'm quite partial to a bit of James Blunt."

I hate James Blunt.

"That's amazing," she squeals. "I love James Blunt. I've got all his albums."

I knew that, of course. It was a great icebreaker but I've just condemned myself to at least three hours of James Blunt. Bollocks.

"Great," I reply with little conviction.

Lucy darts back into the kitchen and switches on a CD player. She returns to the table as the first track begins.

"What's your favourite album of his?" she asks.

Shit.

"Um, Back to Bedlam, I think."

It's the only one of Blunt's albums I know.

"Mine too. I'll never get bored of listening to it."

I already am.

"I can't believe it's been fourteen years since it came out. Seems like only yesterday," she adds.

She takes a sip of wine, seemingly deep in thought.

"Can I ask you a question, Craig?"

"Sure."

"This memory problem of yours. How come you can remember things like the name of songs and albums?"

A perfectly reasonable question. It's a real shame I haven't considered a perfectly reasonable answer.

"I wish I knew. Some things are there, others aren't. It's difficult to explain."

She nods slowly. I know her well enough to tell she's not convinced. I need to come up with a better explanation.

"Have you ever got so drunk you don't remember much, the next day?" I ask.

"Once or twice."

"And did you remember fragments of the evening, like flashbacks?"

"Yeah, I guess."

"So you know, for example, you were in a bar, but you might not remember which bar. Or you remember getting in a cab but can't recall the colour, or what the driver looked like."

"That's right."

"Well, that's what my memory is like. It hasn't been wiped clean like a computer hard drive. It's just been corrupted so I can't remember the specific details of my life."

She pauses for a moment to digest my almost plausible explanation.

"So, you won't have forgotten me by tomorrow lunchtime then?" she says with a smile.

I lean across the table and kiss her softly on the lips. I then withdraw but keep my face close to hers, our eyes locked.

"I'd say you're pretty unforgettable."

She gently strokes my cheek with the tips of her fingers and her smile widens.

"That's the right answer," she whispers before we kiss again, a little more passionately this time.

For the first time in my life, I'm grateful for the music of James Blunt. It proved to be the icebreaker I hoped, and after an hour of effortless chat and two bottles of wine, we finally get around to dinner.

Lucy heads over to the kitchen and dances between the fridge and two ceramic bowls on the work surface. After a few minutes, she brings the bowls over and places one of them in front of me. The sushi salad is beautifully prepared.

She takes a seat and passes me a bottle of what I assume is some sort of vinaigrette dressing. I give the bottle a shake over my salad and pass it back to Lucy. She proceeds to douse her salad with the dark liquid. I suddenly get a faint whiff of an odd smell, like a salmon on the turn. I put it down to something in the salad and we chat for a moment about our mutual appreciation of healthy food. I stab a generous forkful of salad and Lucy mirrors my action. Almost in sync, we both take our first mouthful of the lovingly prepared meal. Our eyes meet across the table and we hold one another's gaze as we chew our food.

I would love to say it was a tender, romantic moment. And it was, right up until the point where I register a taste akin to a tramp's perineum. I struggle not to gag as my eyes bulge and my nostrils flare. In any other circumstance, I'd have already projected the content of my mouth across the table, but even I know spitting raw fish at your host falls below acceptable standards of etiquette. I fight hard to swallow the filth.

Across the table, the chair is now empty. Lucy has plumped for a more direct solution, and is currently gagging over the kitchen sink.

I take a large gulp of wine and swill it around my mouth in an effort to remove the oily residue of whatever I poured on my salad. I'm no culinary expert, but I'm fairly certain it wasn't vinaigrette.

Lucy gingerly extracts her head from the kitchen sink and turns to face me.

"I'm…so…sorry."

It's a fleeting appearance. She spins back to the sink and dry retches, several times.

She tries again, and slowly turns around.

"Oh, god, Craig…what must you think of me?"

"I'm actually thinking you might want to consider a different brand of vinaigrette. What was that?"

"Extract of anchovy," she groans while trying to stifle a burp.

"Oh."

She shuffles across the kitchen, opens a cupboard, and pulls out a bottle. It's the same size and shape as the one on the table, and contains a similar dark fluid. Even the labels are the same colour.

"*This* is the vinaigrette," she says, holding the bottle aloft. "I blame the alcohol for impairing my senses."

She slams the bottle on the side and returns to the table, taking a large gulp of wine as she sits back down. I can't help but feel sorry for her.

"On the plus side, I'll definitely have no trouble remembering our first meal."

She struggles to fight back a smile.

"Cheese and pickle sandwich?" she asks.

"That will do nicely. I don't think I'll risk the pickle though."

"Fair point," she chuckles. "One cheese sandwich coming up."

Lucy heads over to the kitchen and returns five minutes later with our substitute dinner. As cheese sandwiches go, it's a particularly nice one.

With food consumed, I offer to do the washing up while Lucy empties our bowls into the bin, her face puckered like she's extracting the contents of a heavily-soiled nappy. As I wash up, Lucy dries, and we settle in to a comfortable routine almost as if we're an old married couple. We chat idly about nothing in particular, and sip more wine while James Blunt wails away in the background. It strikes me this is just the type of domestic bliss I never experienced with Megan. Doing things together, no matter how menial, and simply enjoying each other's company. It feels like the most natural thing in the world.

Once the kitchen is spic-and-span, we retire to the cosy lounge at the front of the cottage, a fourth bottle of wine and our glasses in hand. It's a small room but beautifully decorated in warm pastel shades. The main focal point is an open fireplace with an ornate art-deco style mirror hung above. It feels like the perfect room to spend cold winter evenings, snuggled up in front of a roaring log fire.

Lucy sits down on one of the two soft leather couches, and pats the space next to her. I don't need asking twice. We talk a little more, and kiss a lot. Inevitably, things become more heated and our kissing is accompanied by some full-on groping. Just as things approach boiling point, Lucy breaks from my clutches and informs me she needs to visit the bathroom. It's no great surprise considering how much wine we've necked. She flashes me a smile and disappears upstairs.

I stretch out on the couch and bathe in a self-contented glow. Sat in silence, it doesn't take long for my mind to start analysing the situation. For all the horrors of the last eleven months, or indeed my life before, have I ever felt this content? No, I don't think I have. My mind drifts towards my previous life and imagines what it could have been if I'd lived with Lucy rather than Megan. Would I have still felt so resentful, so unfulfilled, so unloved? I doubt it.

In hindsight I don't think it matters what might have been. The only reason I'm sat here now is because I'm no longer a fat oaf. Why would somebody as attractive as Lucy have ever given me a second glance? What could I have possibly offered her? No, it's delusional to think I had any chance with Lucy in my former life. But I'm here now, with Lucy, and maybe this is my silver lining.

As I conclude my deliberation, the lounge door wafts silently open. Lucy is stood in the doorway — her smile is still present, her dress isn't.

22

I scramble to sit upright so I can get a proper view of her white nightshirt, unbuttoned to her navel, the hem barely reaching the top of her thighs. My hanging tongue reappears.

She takes three slow, seductive steps into the room. "I was wondering if you'd like to see the improvements I made upstairs?"

Is that a euphemism? Is she asking me to inspect her tits? Regardless, I nod and slowly get up from the couch.

Lucy holds out her hand and I clasp it in mine. She turns and leads me from the lounge, up the stairs and into her bedroom. The curtains are already closed but sufficient light leaks through to afford me an encouraging view of Lucy's scantily-clad body. I have precious little interest in the interior design.

She stands in front of me and places her palms on my chest. With a gentle nudge, she pushes me backwards onto the bed and clambers on beside me. I'm about to pull her towards me but she suddenly grabs my wrist and holds it hanging in the air.

"Tell me I'm not about to do something I live to regret," she says, her expression expectant.

I free my wrist and shuffle onto my side.

"Why would you think that?"

"Experience," she replies.

It's a valid point, and I wonder if this version of Lucy is as unlucky in love as her counterpart from my previous life. She only ever had three relationships in all the time I knew her. I never wanted to know the details but none of them ended well, the last one in particular. I met him once; a smarmy tosser called Julian. They dated for about eight months and he was controlling, overbearing. He appeared to delight in undermining her confidence, and she became increasingly withdrawn as their relationship developed.

I want to reassure Lucy I'm nothing like Julian. I want her to know she's my soul mate. Sadly, I can't profess to either.

"I could live a hundred lives and I doubt I'd ever meet somebody like you, Lucy."

"But you don't think this is too soon? I don't want you to think I do this sort of thing all the time."

"What? Lull unsuspecting men into your home and poison them?"

She playfully punches my arm. "No, *this,*" she says as she waves her arms theatrically.

"Ah, you mean *this*?" I parrot. "No, I don't think you do this all the time. But seriously, if you want to go back downstairs I honestly wouldn't have a problem with it. Some things are worth waiting for."

My reply is greeted with a slight shake of her head and a snigger.

"How do you always manage to say exactly what I want to hear?" she says gently. "This is crazy, and I know we've only known each other a few days but it just feels…so right. I can't find the words to explain it, but it's like I've known you forever."

She leans forward so our faces are only a few inches apart. "Please tell me my instincts about you are right. This isn't just a one-night stand is it?"

It's a closed question with only one realistic answer. Surely if I was intending to have my wicked way and disappear into the night, I wouldn't admit to it. But that's Lucy. Her optimism, or maybe naivety, has always been part of her charm. She prefers to seek out the good in people — even losers like me.

"No, Lucy. It's not. I can honestly say I'm not that type of man. Never have been. Never will be."

Seemingly happy to accept I'm worthy of her trust, she begins to slowly unbutton her nightshirt. I'm torn between watching her, or tearing off my own clothes. Before I can decide, Lucy gets off the bed, and slowly peels herself out of the nightshirt. Once removed, she holds it out at arm's length before letting it fall to the floor. She stands motionless a few feet away, clearly at ease with her nudity.

I know it's rude to stare but the sight of her naked body is mesmerising. After years of seeing it wrapped in an unflattering RolpheTech uniform, it feels like I'm privy to the first unveiling of a long-lost work of art. If I wasn't rendered speechless, I may have even gasped.

At this point, any other man would be all over Lucy like a rash. I, on the other hand, can barely move. I'm no doctor, but I think I might be experiencing symptoms of mild shock. My friend for all those years is currently stood in front of me, naked as the day she was born. If this was the Lucy from my past, there would be a mutual awkwardness between us. I now have to carry that awkwardness on my own, and for some reason I'm finding it debilitating. How can two people who've been friends for so long, not feel just a little apprehensive about crossing this line? This is not heavy petting on the couch, I'm about to have sex with my friend. Actual intercourse. Full-on penis in vagina intercourse, with Lucy.

The theory was great, but the practice is something else. My head spins to the point where I'm not even sure

I can go through with this. It's all I can do to lie on the bed with a vacant expression plastered across my face.

"You okay?" Lucy asks, clearly confused by my inertia. "You look white as a sheet."

"Ugh?"

She frowns and moves across to the bed, taking a seat on the edge.

"You're not a virgin are you?" she asks, with obvious incredulity.

"What? No…I'm, um…"

"Unsure about your sexuality?"

"No. It's just…"

"My body repulses you?"

"Christ, no. You're stunning."

"What is it then? It doesn't do much for a girl's confidence when a guy stares at her like he's just seen his mother getting out of the shower."

I've really surpassed myself this time. I've managed to offend Lucy without actually saying anything. And I've tarnished what should have been a beautiful, intimate moment. I don't know what to say, how to explain how surreal this is for me.

"Sorry," I murmur.

Pitiful.

Lucy gets up from the bed and snatches her nightshirt from the floor. I have no more than a few seconds to salvage this. This is not her fault. I need to get past my hang ups or risk destroying the only good thing in this life.

"Lucy, wait."

I scramble from the bed and grab her wrist.

"What?" she snaps.

"It's not you, it's me."

"Seriously? I'll give you two out of ten for originality," she snorts.

"Sorry, that wasn't meant to come out that way. Please, just give me a second to explain."

This is no time for subtlety. I can't hold anything back if I'm to convince Lucy I'm not a sex-shy weirdo.

"Look, the truth is I really like you, Lucy. I mean, I *really* like you, a lot," I profess. "I know it sounds a bit lame, but I was suddenly a bit overwhelmed."

I take her other wrist and pull her closer to me. She doesn't resist.

"I've never such a strong connection to anyone before, and if I'm honest, it just freaked me out for a moment. That's all."

Her frown fades and her opal-green eyes widen just a fraction. I've got a fairly good idea of what's going on behind those eyes.

"Really? There's nothing else?" she eventually asks.

"Really, there's nothing else," I reply. "You're just a bit too good to be true. You're funny, intelligent, beautiful…"

The edges of her lips curl upward and her dimples deepen.

"Keep those compliments coming," she whispers as she pulls me into a kiss.

If I still had any qualms about enjoying a sexual liaison with my good friend, Lucy takes the initiative and quickly dispels them. Somehow, I have managed to turn the situation around simply by telling the truth. I then learn it's surprisingly hard to reel off a list of superlatives while a naked woman is slowly unbuttoning your jeans.

"You're lovable," I add.

She grabs the hem of my polo shirt and lifts it up. I put my arms out in front of me, and a second later the shirt is lying on the floor.

"Enchanting..."

"More," she purrs, while planting delicate kisses on my naked chest.

"Thoughtful…"

She traces the tip of her tongue across my stomach, slowly moving south.

"Witty…"

Her tongue flicks over a now-prominent part of my anatomy.

"Jeeesssus!"

Despite my precautionary wank earlier, I daren't leave Lucy down there for more than a minute. I encourage her to stand back up while I extract my feet from the denim tangled around my ankles. We fall onto the bed together, and I take my turn to show Lucy the full extent of my sexual repertoire.

Back when we used to visit the pub after a day at RolpheTech, Lucy, and the some of the other female staff would gaggle together and discuss their love lives. I would sometimes stand nearby, and it was near-impossible not to overhear snippets of those conversations. I discovered that Tina, a part time sales assistant, enjoyed spanking. I learnt that Jill, a weekend supervisor, was partial to watching hardcore porn. And I was shocked to discover Elaine, our fifty-something stockroom manager, occasionally participated in swinging.

As luck would have it, I also gained some insight into Lucy's preferences, modest as they were. It would be amiss of me not to take advantage of that insider knowledge. So I do, and with no further thought on the matter, Lucy transitions seamlessly from being my friend to my lover.

What ensues in the next fifty-one minutes is an awful lot of impassioned screaming, scratching, swearing, and sweating. It is, without doubt, the best fifty-one minutes of my life. We are just like those two Tetris pieces coming together, the perfect fit, almost as if we'd danced the dance a hundred times before.

Glorious. Incredible. Perfect.

Indeed, it was so wonderful, neither of us thinks twice about indulging in a second round. By the time we collapse into one another's arms in a breathless finale, little of Tuesday remains. Even less of my energy reserves remain.

As I lay there, with Lucy's head tucked under my chin and my arm around her, I conclude I have never been happier. Despite all the grief, the guilt, the despair, despite everything I've been through, I am happy — and I think I'm in love. It's a bittersweet irony that I'd never have experienced this moment if I hadn't so monumentally fucked up my life. Lucy would now be living in Brighton and I'd still be married to Megan, unhappily. Maybe I'd still be looking for a job, and certainly the old man would still be a miserable bastard.

I don't push my thoughts any further in that direction. Better to wallow in this moment and forget everything else for now.

"What are you thinking about?" Lucy asks.

"Honestly?"

"Yes, honestly."

"I was thinking about that cheese sandwich. It was really tasty."

She gently slaps my chest and smiles up at me.

"Seriously," she chides.

I exhale a deep, contented breath. "I was thinking about how perfect this evening has been. If you overlook the food poisoning, oh, and my cold feet earlier."

"Almost perfect then," Lucy sniggers.

"I think I can safely say the last couple of hours more than made up for the less-than-perfect parts."

"Agreed."

She plants a kiss on my chest and nestles her head back under my chin. I pull her tighter to me, like she's the last woman on earth and I daren't let her go.

I close my eyes and let every muscle relax, to the point where it feels like I'm floating. The silence in the room only adds to my bliss. I can barely hear Lucy breathing but I can feel her chest slowly rise and fall against mine. Minutes pass and her breathing slows. I wonder if she's fallen asleep but I don't want to disturb her. I close my mind and within minutes I follow her.

23

On my return from that weekend in 1986, I woke up in a hospital bed — back in my fat body, confused and in pain. It was the worst start to the worst day of my life. Today could not be more different. Today, I wake up to the sound of birdsong, the smell of freshly brewed coffee and Lucy's smile.

"Morning sleepyhead."

Lucy is kneeling next to me on the bed, wearing her white nightshirt.

"Sleep well?"

I blink a few times to ensure I'm not dreaming, and return her smile.

"Yeah, like a baby. You?"

"Best night's sleep I've had in years. Coffee?"

She turns, plucks a mug from the bedside table and hands it to me.

I sit up and take the mug. "Thanks."

"I didn't put sugar in but I can go get some if you take it?"

"No, it's fine like this thanks, hot and strong."

Lucy grabs her coffee and positions herself so we're lying next to each other, mugs in hand, resting on chests. Silence returns but it doesn't feel strained. We lie for a while, sipping coffee and simply enjoying the moment. Lucy speaks first.

"What have you got planned for the day?" she asks.

"Quite a lot for a change. I'm expecting a delivery and then I've got a few IT issues to resolve. You?"

"Got a meeting with my accountant at nine."

"What is the time?"

"Just gone seven-thirty."

"Right," I casually reply. "I'm guessing you haven't had a shower yet?"

"Not yet. Why?"

"I was wondering if I could offer my scrubbing services, you know, to save you some time?"

We turn to face one another.

"And you think your service will actually save time?" Lucy asks with a wry smile.

"Maybe. Probably not though."

"Let's go and find out."

Coffee mugs are hurriedly slammed onto the bedside table as we make a frantic dash for the bathroom.

Turns out my service actually prolonged Lucy's shower by a good twenty minutes. It's gone eight o'clock when we return to the bedroom, both of us glowing from the hot shower, and the shenanigans that accompanied it.

In the thirty seconds it takes me to get dressed, Lucy is still deciding on what underwear to put on. I offer to wash the coffee mugs and leave her to it. Maybe it's a hang up from my previous life, but I'm wary of women getting ready for work in the morning.

I skip down the stairs and into the kitchen, suddenly aware I'm whistling. I rarely whistle, and certainly not in the mornings. This is a new development. I smile to myself and pour another coffee. I sit down at the dining table and soak up the silence. Three of the four wine bottles we emptied are still present on the table. Despite our alcohol intake last night, I don't appear to have a hangover. In fact, I feel remarkably chipper.

I finish my coffee and wash the mugs. I'm in the process of drying them when Lucy walks in.

"Ooh, you're domesticated too. Wonderful," she laughs.

"Thanks, and while we're throwing gender-stereotypes around, I'm impressed you got ready in less than ten minutes."

"Touché, Mr Wilson."

It still feels weird hearing that name.

"Where did you park?" she asks.

"Err, I didn't. I walked here."

Lucy doesn't question why I walked and offers me a lift home.

We leave the cottage and walk thirty yards down the lane to where Lucy's red Audi is parked — Lucy's almost new, very expensive red Audi.

"Nice car," I purr.

"Thanks. Business has been really good in the last year, so I thought I'd treat myself."

As we get in the car, I'm tempted to question Lucy about her business. I decide against it on the grounds I don't want to come across as some sort of gold-digger. She fires up the engine and switches the stereo on. More James Blunt, only louder this time. I'm pinned back in my seat and close to being deafened as the car accelerates up the lane, Lucy grinning like a lunatic at the wheel. Nobody's perfect I guess.

Within five minutes of our departure, Lucy's manic driving is abruptly halted by the rush-hour traffic as we skirt the edge of town. We crawl along, the car never shifting beyond third gear. By the time we get within a few streets of my flat, it's already eight-forty. Lucy doesn't show any signs of impatience or concern for keeping her appointment as she happily sings along to yet another James Blunt track. I don't share her patience though, and when a fat bloke slowly waddles across a zebra crossing in front of us, I can't help but vent.

"Come on you fat bastard. Move your big arse," I mutter.

Lucy stops mid-chorus, silences the stereo and turns to me. "Are you usually so judgemental about people you don't know?"

At first I think she might be joking, but her furrowed brow suggests I've touched a nerve.

"Eh?"

"You don't know that guy. He could be an artist, a poet, a musician, or a painter. He might be a doctor, or a charity volunteer. He might be a wonderful man with a wife who adores him and kids he dotes on. Just because he's a bit overweight, doesn't make him any less worthy of respect."

It seems I've not so much touched a nerve, more hit it with a hammer.

"Sorry, I didn't mean anything by it."

I feel my cheeks redden. I have been well and truly told off.

"For the record, I was once overweight, as a teenager. I got bullied relentlessly for it so I'm a bit touchy about the subject. One thing I learnt from that experience is to judge people by their actions not by their physical appearance. And what makes you think you're any better than that guy?"

"Well, nothing I suppose. But aesthetically…"

"What?"

Don't say another word Craig. Don't dig yourself into a deeper hole.

"I can't imagine he has women queueing around the block for a date. I mean, you wouldn't date him, would you? Honestly?"

"Honestly? I'm offended you think I'm so shallow I judge people purely on their physical appearance."

I warned you.

Lucy swings the car into a bus stop.

"I need to get to the office. You can walk from here."

"Look, sorry, Lucy. I didn't mean to offend you, honestly. You're right, and I don't have any right to judge anyone."

She stares straight ahead and doesn't reply. I lean across to give her a kiss but she turns her head away.

"I'll call you later," I sigh.

"Call me when you've sorted out that attitude. Not before."

I get out of the car and it screeches away barely a second after I close the door.

Well-played Craig. Nicely done.

I look to the heavens and shake my head.

It's only a three-minute walk to the flat; nowhere near enough time for a full analysis of my stupidity. I'm still chiding myself as I walk through the front door. While Lucy never told me about her weight problems as a teenager, I should certainly have known not to be so judgemental. Only eleven months ago I was that fat bloke. Now I feel like one of those sneering pricks who stands around in a gym, throwing contemptuous looks at anyone without a six-pack. It was because of such idiots I decided to stop visiting the gym in my previous life. Actually, that was just one of the excuses I used, but the point remains valid. I've experienced that prejudice and I should have known better.

I make myself a coffee and slump down on the couch. With no idea when the transformer is due to be delivered, I've potentially got enough time to reproach myself, and think of a way to placate Lucy. I catch a faint hint of her vanilla-scented perfume, captured on the fabric of my polo shirt. It only serves to heighten my sense of regret.

However, my sulking about the incident in the car is masking a much bigger issue. When the transformer arrives, it might bring with it the chance to go back, to return to 1986. My current guilt could prove to be totally moot if that's the case. The circumstances that brought Lucy and me together will be deleted from history.

It's a troubling thought.

I think back to the moment I found the Commodore 64 in Dave's loft. The excitement, the relief, the prospect of undoing all the damage I've done. Up until last night, I would have given anything for that opportunity. But now? I have the chance of happiness with Lucy. No wife, no history, no baggage. We have a clean slate on which we can create a new future together. Do I seriously want to delete that? The utter certainty I want to go back has just dropped by some margin.

This, of course, is all hypothetical. I've let my imagination live out decisions that may never need to be made. I have the computer but that is all. In all likelihood, when I turn it on it will be just a run-of-the-mill Commodore 64. That's even if it still works. I'm still a long way from even having to contemplate going back. As is stands, I don't have any decisions to make. One step at a time.

I down the last mouthful of coffee and get up to make another one. Just as I reach the kitchen area, the intercom buzzes. I have a visitor it would seem, hopefully carrying a box containing the transformer.

I dart into the hallway and lift the intercom handset.

"Hello."

"Parcel," grunts a voice.

"Okay. I'm coming down."

I scurry down the stairs and open the door to an impatient-looking courier.

"Sign here," he mumbles as he hands me a device like a mobile phone.

I scribble my name on the screen and he hands me a nondescript box. He's already heading back down the path before I can offer my thanks.

It's then I spot something which immediately pours cold water on my excitement — a pea-green Citroen 2CV.

"For fucks sake," I mutter under my breath.

"Morning, Craig."

A man appears at the end of the path, a wide smile on his milky white face and a leather document pouch tucked under his arm.

"Morning, Stephen."

Crap. My case officer from Broadhall. What does he want?

"Can I come up for a chat?"

As much as I don't want to, I have little choice but to let him in. I plod back up the stairs with Stephen at my heels. He tries to engage me in small talk but I have no interest and offer only single-syllable replies. As we enter the flat I drop the parcel on the floor in the hallway and Stephen follows me into the lounge. Without invitation, he takes a seat on the couch. I sit on the arm, as far away from him as possible.

"So, how are you doing?" he asks.

"Good. Everything is really good."

"Glad to hear it, but you were supposed to call me on Monday. What happened?"

Fuck. In all the excitement of locating the computer, I totally forgot I was supposed to call Stephen with an update.

"I'm really sorry. I meant to call but it just slipped my mind."

"Right. I don't want to come across as a jobsworth, but it is imperative you stick to the agreed release program."

"Fair enough. It won't happen again."

"Let's hope not."

Just as I hope he's ticked whatever boxes he needs to tick, he unzips the document pouch and pulls out a buff-coloured folder.

"Shall we have a coffee while I bring your assessment paperwork up-to-date?"

I reluctantly get up and trudge over to the kitchen. I switch the kettle on and grab another mug from the cupboard. While I wait for the kettle to boil, I take a few steps towards the lounge area.

"Will this take long, Stephen?"

"Why? Got somewhere to be?"

"Kind of. I've got a computer booked at the library. I'm researching potential careers."

From previous experience, I know this is the sort of positive nonsense Stephen likes to hear.

"Excellent. I'll get through this as quickly as I can. Promise."

I'm about to return to coffee making duties when my phone vibrates on the small table in front of the couch. I take a few steps towards it as Stephen leans forward to examine the phone. I get within four feet when my heart drops to my stomach. The caller's name is emblazoned across the screen — DAD.

I glance at Stephen to see if he's noticed. As I do, he turns his head and stares back at me. His expression suggests he has. Before I can do anything, he snatches the phone from the table and accepts the call.

Shit. Shit. Shit.

"Hello. Craig's phone," he chimes in his Scottish accent.

A few seconds pass before he speaks again.

"No. He's busy at the moment. Can I take a message?"

I look on in horror. Helpless.

"Sure, I'll tell him. Who shall I say called?"

No Dad, please don't say it.

"Right. Colin Pelling, his dad. Got it."

He hangs up and places the phone back on the table.

"That was your dad. Apparently the furniture for your bedroom is being delivered at four o'clock this afternoon."

As agile as my mind is at resolving problems, I can't think of any plausible explanation for the call Stephen just took. I'm screwed.

"You had no right to answer my phone," I bark.

"I wouldn't have answered your phone if I hadn't seen the call was from your dad. As you apparently have no recollection of your life before you were admitted to Broadhall, I was curious how you managed to contact a man you couldn't even remember ten days ago."

He stares at me, waiting for a reaction or an explanation.

"And considering you were released because we thought you'd got past this obsession with Craig Pelling, I'd say I was right to take that call, wouldn't you?"

My beautiful day that started so perfectly, has turned into a complete and unimaginable car crash.

"Clearly you don't have anything to say so I'll ask the questions and you just answer."

I nod.

"For the moment let's overlook the fact you're referring to him as Dad, and he's taking delivery of furniture for you. Can you explain why you're in contact with Craig Pelling's father at all?"

This is bad. This is really bad. Of course I can't explain, least not in a way he would believe.

With nothing to offer, I shrug my shoulders.

"This is serious, Craig. I knew it was a bad idea to locate you in Farndale."

He pulls out a form from the buff-coloured folder and clicks his pen. Seconds pass as he furiously scribbles notes on the form.

"What are you doing?" I gulp.

He doesn't answer immediately and completes his notes. Long seconds pass before he looks up at me.

"In my professional opinion we got this wrong. Either you were released too soon or we put you in the wrong place. Either way, we need to get you re-assessed as soon as possible."

"What?"

"I'm sorry, but I think we need to recall you to Broadhall."

24

I stand, frozen. This cannot be happening. What the fuck have I done to anger the Gods so much they'd inflict this on me?

Stephen gets up from the couch and moves towards the door, as if blocking my exit.

"Listen, Craig," he says, his voice calm. "It's not as bad as it sounds. Hopefully this is just a blip and we can get you back on track within a week or so. There's no need to worry."

A blip? A week? They kept me in that place for eleven fucking months last time. Now Stephen has evidence I've been in contact with the old man, Craig Pelling's old man, there is every chance my return visit to Broadhall could be permanent. I can't take that risk.

"I'm not going back, Stephen. If you need to reassess me, you can do it here."

"It doesn't work like that. We need to ensure you're in a safe environment, for your protection as much as anything."

"I'm perfectly safe here, thanks. I'm not going back, no way. You can't make me."

He sighs and folds his arms.

"Try and look at it from my point of view. This fixation with the Pelling kid is the reason you were admitted to Broadhall in the first place. Now, I don't know what you're up to with his father but it's not something I can ignore. You convinced us this whole delusion about Craig Pelling had been put to bed, but clearly it's still in your head and we need to establish why."

We reach an impasse as Stephen quietly ponders his next move. He's not alone in that.

"You've got two options here, Craig. You can come with me now and we can deal with this together, quietly and calmly."

"Not interested."

"Or if you're not willing to do that," he continues, ignoring my protestation. "I'll have no option but to call in support. If it comes to it, we can forcibly return you to Broadhall. Please don't take that option."

Stephen has revealed his hand. He wants me back at Broadhall one way or another. Now it's time to play my hand.

"Okay, Stephen" I relent. "Looks like I don't have a choice."

He visibly breathes a sigh of relief. "Good man. Shall we get going then?"

"Sure. Can I take my phone?"

"Um, if you like."

I step across to the table, pick up the phone and drop it into my pocket. I turn back and take a few steps towards Stephen with my hand held out, inviting a handshake.

"Sorry about the dramatics, Stephen. No hard feelings?"

He takes my hand and I inwardly cringe at his feeble handshake.

"No hard feelings, Craig. As long as we get you sorted, I'm happy."

"Good. Do you mind if he comes with us?"

I nod towards the kitchen and Stephen instinctively turns to see who I'm referring to. Obviously there's nobody there but it buys me an invaluable second.

With his sweaty hand still locked in a handshake with mine, and his attention elsewhere, I step backwards and yank at his arm. He stumbles forward just as I turn and stretch my right leg out. As I hoped, he trips over my outstretched leg and sprawls headfirst across the laminate floor. It's not the most sophisticated of moves but it does do the job.

As tempting as it is, I dismiss the idea of offering a witty departing quip and dart through the door. I grab the parcel from the hallway floor and slam the front door shut behind me.

I'm conscious I've only bought myself a few seconds breathing space. I need to get clean away from here, and quickly, before Stephen calls in reinforcements. I don't know what protocols are enacted when a patient is unwilling to return for treatment, but I doubt they'll sit on their hands and do nothing. There have been too many high profile cases of mental health patients harming members of the public for them not to take my abscondence seriously.

Technically, I'm now a fugitive.

Unequivocally, my new life is now fucked.

With the precious parcel tucked under my arm, I sprint through random streets with no route in mind. My objective, such as it is, is solely to put as much distance between myself and Stephen as possible. As my trainers slap the pavement, an overwhelming sense of deja-vu descends upon me. This is not the first time I've run through the streets of Farndale with no destination in mind. I can only hope for a better ending this time.

Five minutes of sprinting and my lungs are on fire. I jog to a stop and take a seat on a bench at a bus stop to catch my breath. Between paranoid glances up and down the road, I try desperately to get my thoughts in order.

This is not good. This is not good at all. I've actually made some real progress in the last ten days but if I'm sent back to Broadhall it will have all been for nothing. There is no way they'd let me see the old man, my fledgling relationship with Lucy would be over, and any prospect of testing the Commodore 64 would be snuffed out.

One missed phone call has developed into one catastrophic situation. I need a plan and I need one now.

I pull my phone from my pocket and frantically jab at the screen. Six rings before the old man picks up.

"Dad, it's me. Listen carefully. I'm in trouble and I need you to do something for me."

"Now? I was about to weed the borders," he groans.

"Sod the borders. They want to send me back to Broadhall."

"Oh, that's not good."

"No, it bloody isn't. I need you to grab some things and meet me at the skate park on the estate. You remember where it is?"

"I think so. Yes."

"Good. I need you to bring the computer, the portable TV and the pile of cables we put in the cupboard. You got that?"

"Computer, TV, cables. Got it."

"And Dad, don't hang around. I've got an awful feeling you might receive a visit from the police pretty soon."

"The police? Why are they involved."

"I can't explain now. Just get those things together and get over to the skate park as quickly as you can."

"Alright, son. I'm on it."

I end the call and get up from the bench. The skate park is almost two miles away but it's the only place I could think of that's likely to be quiet on a Wednesday morning. I can't imagine the Farndale police department have instigated a full-scale manhunt just yet, but with so much at risk I don't want to take any chances. I bow my head and walk briskly towards the estate, keeping to the back roads and public footpaths wherever possible.

The walk gives me the chance to consider the full implications of this morning's events. There is no getting away from the fact Stephen wants me back at Broadhall. And not for one moment do I believe it will only be for a week or so. Unlike the judicial system where you're innocent until proven guilty, at Broadhall the opposite is true. Unless they're convinced I am of sound mind, and pose no threat to society, my stay will be indefinite. The fact I'm taking calls from the father of a dead teenager, who I once claimed to be, does not strengthen my case.

But while going back to Broadhall is not an option, there aren't too many others on the table. In fact, there's only one glimmer of hope — the Commodore 64. All I can do is get it switched on and hope, pray even, that it offers me a way out of this mess. It's a far-fetched, ludicrous hope at best, but it's all I have. If I discover it's now nothing more than a bog-standard computer from the 1980s, it's game over.

Twenty minutes later, I turn the corner from MacDonald Drive and the skate park is directly ahead of me.

When I had my altercation with Marcus, the park was less than a year old and in pristine condition. Now it looks more like a backdrop to a low-budget rap video. The chainlink fencing that once encircled the park is no more, and every concrete surface is daubed with crude graffiti.

I make my way up the grass embankment, now overgrown with long grass and weeds. Of the three benches that once sat on top, only one remains. I plod over to it and sit down, crouching forward with one eye on the perimeter road. With all the kids in school and most of the estate residents at work, it's eerily quiet. Much like my current mood, the sky is grey and foreboding. It wouldn't surprise me in the least if it started pissing down, such is my misfortune in the last hour.

The vibrating of my phone catches me by surprise. A text message, and only two people have my number.

Sat here feeling stupid. I really over-reacted and hope u can accept my humble apology. Buy u a drink later 2 say sorry? L xxxx

In all the arguments I had with Megan over the years, I can't recall her ever accepting blame, let alone apologising. If I didn't already think Lucy was the perfect woman, this text seals it.

I smile to myself, but just for a moment. The reality of my situation quickly snuffs-out the brief moment of joy. I don't know how to reply. By the time she finishes work I could be over three decades away, or locked up in Broadhall — the latter being far more likely. I start, and quickly delete four messages before I finally send something.

No need to say sorry. I'm an idiot and you were right. Will call you late afternoon about meeting for that drink. xxxx

It only postpones the inevitable, but what choice do I have?

A reply quickly arrives.

Bless u. And what you said last night, about really liking me, the feeling is mutual u know. L xxxx

In any other circumstance, those words would have me dancing in the street. Now, they just provoke more regret, more frustration, and more annoyance at how unfair this all is. I reply with five smiley faces and four kisses. Lame, but what else can I say?

A car horn blares from behind me.

I spin around and breathe a sigh of relief at seeing the old man's car. I scoot down the embankment and jump in.

"Thanks for this, Dad."

"It's okay, although I'd like to know what's going on. Who was that Scottish chap who answered your phone this morning?"

"Stephen. My case officer from Broadhall."

It takes a few seconds for the old man to connect the dots.

"Oh, crikey. I gave him my name."

"Yes, you did. And now he thinks I'm trying to rekindle my life as Craig Pelling."

"That's not good."

"No, Dad, it's not good. He wants me to go back to Broadhall. Actually, he was quite insistent about it, up until he flew across my lounge floor and I ran off."

"Are they looking for you?"

"No idea, but I have to assume they are, hence the urgency. I can't go back there, Dad."

"What was he doing at your flat, anyway?"

"I was supposed to call him and check in on Monday. I forgot."

"Well, that was a bit silly," he sighs. "This could have all been avoided."

"You probably don't remember, Dad, but after our visit to Dave's place, we spent much of Monday evening in the pub."

"Ohh, yes. We did, didn't we. Sorry."

He slowly shakes his head and peers out of the window towards the skate park.

"This is a right pickle. What are you going to do, son?"

"I've got one option. I need to get the computer set up. Did you bring everything?"

"All boxed up in the boot."

"Good. Now we just need to work out where we can set it up. Any ideas?"

"Assuming my place isn't a sensible option, we could book a hotel room?"

"Too early. Most don't allow check-in until the afternoon."

We sit in silence while we try to think of a suitable venue. I draw a blank but the old man suddenly starts the car.

"You thought of somewhere?"

"There's a large tool shed at the vicarage. It's got a workbench and power."

"What about Father David?"

"He won't be around till this lunchtime. He makes his school visits on a Wednesday morning."

I give the old man a thumbs up and slouch back in my seat.

In less than twenty minutes we should know whether my future lies in the past, or in Broadhall.

25

The old man appears to have been taken by the spirit of Lewis Hamilton, the car's feeble, one-litre engine screaming as we tear through Farndale towards the church.

"Dad, if you're trying to appear inconspicuous, you're doing a bloody awful job."

"Sorry, son, I'll slow it down a tad. I don't get much excitement in my life these days."

"I'm glad you find this exciting. Not the word I'd use to describe it."

He eases off the accelerator and we pootle along at a pace less likely to attract passing police cars.

"Are you not excited then son, about going back?"

"If I were a gambling man, I'd wager a fair sum it won't be an option."

"Really? You don't think you'll be able to go back?"

There's something in the tone of his voice. The slightest intonation of optimism.

"Your question almost suggests you don't want me to go back."

"No, don't be silly, course I do."

"But?"

"Nothing."

"Dad?"

He doesn't answer and points out of the window at the church spire, sitting above the rooftops maybe half-a-mile away.

"Nearly there, son."

We cover the half-mile in less than a minute, with the old man steadfastly ignoring my question. We pull into the church car park and rendezvous at the boot. The old man takes the box containing the computer, while I struggle with the less-than-portable TV and the transformer box. We make our way through a gate into the vicarage garden, just as the clouds release a misty drizzle.

I follow the old man beyond a hedge and up a path past a vegetable plot and greenhouse. We pass another hedge to find a robust-looking shed, about fifteen-feet square with a small window designed to let in light rather than offer a view. He places the computer box on the floor and withdraws a bunch of keys from his jacket pocket. My heightened heart rate isn't eased as the old man takes an age to find the correct key.

Finally, he opens the door, picks up the box and steps inside the shed. I follow him in and kick the door shut behind me.

The inside of the shed is a far cry from the potting shed in the garden of our former home. The internal walls are boarded and painted white, and the floorboards are covered by heavy-duty lino. It appears the church spared no expense kitting it out with an expanse of fitted storage units along one wall, and a sturdy workbench opposite. Dozens of hand tools are bracketed to the wall above, with a row of plastic containers sat on a long shelf. The place is tidier, and more organised than a chef's kitchen.

As I place the TV on the workbench, two fluorescent tubes above my head flicker into life, banishing the gloominess beyond the window.

"Shall we do this then, son?"

I return a nod and a nervous smile.

I unpack the transformer, hoping to God they sent the right one. With some relief, I extract the beige block from the packaging and place it on the workbench. I sit the Commodore 64 in front of the TV, and pull all the cables from their tangled ball in the box. Slowly, methodically, I connect everything together, the fear I might still be missing a vital component haunting the entire procedure.

Finished, I triple-check every connection and stand back. My nerves are now shredded and I have to make a conscious effort to keep my breathing in check.

"Right. That's everything connected."

"What now?"

"We turn it on."

This is it. My entire future will be determined by what happens once I've pressed all of the four switches: two for the TV, one for the transformer, and finally, the power switch on the Commodore 64. Four switches, less than six seconds to activate them all. I feel queasy.

I move back to the bench and hit the power switch on the wall socket, the one housing the plug for the TV. If the TV was damaged in the move from my teenage bedroom, this is over before it's begun. I take a step to the side and press the power button on the TV set.

Two of the longest seconds of my life pass before I hear the quiet hiss of electricity coursing through the ancient circuitry. The reassuring smell of burning dust fills my nostrils before the screen finally splutters into life. I have never been so pleased to see a screen full of static. But just as my panicked breathing eases a little, my pocket vibrates. Someone is calling me.

"Who's that?" the old man asks.

As I don't possess x-ray vision, I shoot him a frown, and struggle to pull the phone from my pocket of my damp jeans. It's not Lucy, and aside the man currently stood next to me, nobody else has my number.

"Dunno, but it's not a number I recognise."

"You going to answer it then?"

"No."

It buzzes four more times before the caller gives up. It could be a cold-caller for all I know, and for once, I'm happy to make that assumption. I regain my focus and return to the task in hand. Like a diver stood at the top of a ten-metre board, I take three deep breaths and prepare to switch the transformer on.

My phone buzzes again. A message. Who the hell is hassling me? I pull my phone out again and read the message.

Craig, call me back within the next 5 mins. I've informed the police you've absconded. You can't hide from this. Stephen.

"Fuck."

"What is it, son?"

"Stephen. I'm guessing he's been nosing around the flat and found the paperwork for my phone, and my number."

"Just ignore him. He'll give up if you don't answer his calls, surely?"

"But he says he's contacted the police."

"So what? There's no way they'll be able to work out where you are."

"Oh shit."

"What?"

I fumble with the phone and it falls to the floor, disappearing under the workbench. I scrabble around frantically before I'm able to grasp the phone and turn it off.

"They can trace these bloody things," I yell. "I don't know how it works, or if they can determine my location from the message I just read, but we have to assume it's a possibility. They're on to me, Dad."

"Calm down," the old man chuckles. "I think you're being a bit premature. There's no need to panic."

"With respect Dad, your knowledge of modern technology does nothing to ease my panic."

He steps forward and places a reassuring hand on my shoulder.

"Do you remember that old police drama on TV, The Bill?" he asks.

"What? Err, yeah, think so."

"I'm assuming it was a fairly accurate representation of police procedure and what they used to track mobile phones. Judging by that, it isn't a five minute job. First Stephen has to physically visit the police station to report your disappearance. That will probably involve an hour or two of questions and paperwork. Then they have to submit a request to a specialist department, and they have to get around to actually tracking the message. And that's assuming they even consider you a viable threat to the public, which I doubt they will. I'd estimate we've got at least three or four hours before we need to worry, if at all."

"Yeah, of course, you're right. Sorry, this is a bit stressful."

"It's alright. Take a deep breath and let's get this done."

Calmed slightly by the old man's words, I lean across the workbench and hit the power switch for the transformer. There is nothing to indicate if it works or not, and the real test will be when I hit the power switch on the computer.

I move across to the computer and rest my finger on the switch, offering a silent prayer. If the transformer is faulty, or the computer took a knock during its journey to Dave's house, any of the sensitive circuits could burn out within seconds. There would be no comeback from that, least not one I could practically implement before Stephen tracks me down.

I close my eyes and hit the switch.

There's no crackling, no hissing, and no scent of burning circuitry. I cautiously open my eyes and stare down at the tiny red LED light, shining brightly above the keyboard.

"Does it work?"

"Don't know yet. It hasn't exploded, and everything appears normal so far, but I won't know until I tune the TV in."

I glance across to the line of buttons that determine which channel is selected. Of the eight buttons, the second one is pressed in, hence the static on the screen. I cast my mind back to the day I sat in my teenage bedroom, before this whole episode began. I'm sure the fifth button was tuned to the computer.

I raise my hand and press the button.

26

The static disappears, replaced with a vibrant blue screen. It works. I cannot believe my trusty Commodore 64 actually still works. My eyes scan the pale blue text on the screen...

**** COMMODORE 64 BASIC V2 ****
64K RAM SYSTEM 38911 BASIC BYTES FREE

The sense of relief is like nothing I have ever experienced before. I could almost cry as I turn to face the old man.

"It's working, Dad. It's only bloody working."

"Thank Christ for that," he beams.

I turn back to the screen, and the moment of truth. It takes a split second to realise it's not the truth I'd been wishing for.

It's not the text I see on the screen that causes my heart to slump, more the text I can't see. Unlike when I first reactivated the computer, there is no line of text about a path corruption error. Nor is there anything about a date or a duration. There is just one line of unfamiliar text…

PATH RESTORED. RE-SET? Y/N

What the fuck does that mean?

I take a second to shake the frustration from my head. This is not the worst outcome — at least there is some reference to the path. I've got something to work with and that in itself is a damn sight more encouraging than a generic screen with no sign of the computer's previous mischief. Whatever unimaginable trickery this plastic box once held, it's clearly still present. It's not quite what I hoped for, but a lot better than I feared.

"What is it, son?"

"It seems to be still running the program that sent me back to 1986, but it's now giving me an option I didn't see before."

The old man shuffles up and stands beside me, leaning forward and squinting at the text on the screen.

"What's a path?"

I give him a quick explanation of the game I was working on, and how a character I created was able to go back in time and change the path of his life.

"That's what I did. I restored my path by going back to that weekend so I could revert a few decisions. If I hadn't been hit by that van, I guess I'd have woken up to a new version of my life, updated to reflect the changes I made to my path."

"Not sure I get it."

"You're a good example. You are different now because I altered the path when we had that chat in your shed. If I hadn't altered the path by having that chat, you'd still be a miserable old bastard."

"Right. Thanks for that example, son."

"You're welcome."

"But it says re-set, not restore. What's the difference?"

That is one question I'm unable to answer.

"You know as much as I do now, Dad. I can only guess."

"And that guess would be?"

"Restore implies going back to a previous point, like on a PC. If you get a virus or a bug, you can restore the PC to a point before the problem occurred. All your data and settings are saved. But a re-set, I think, completely re-sets the PC back to the factory settings, like a new machine. Everything is deleted apart from the core operating system."

We stand for a moment in silence, both trying to get our heads around the implications of those five letters and a hyphen. The old man is the first to offer a theory.

"Do you think a re-set would send you right back to the beginning, before anything happened?"

"You mean back to the point before I went back in time?"

"Yes. That's the way I read it. Make sense?"

It does, but that still leaves another question to be answered.

"But what if I hit the 'no' option?"

He shrugs his shoulders, understandably. While selecting 'yes' might re-set everything back to the day when I first turned the computer on as a fat, middle-aged man, what happens if I select 'no'? Will it allow me the option to restore the path like before, so I can go back to that weekend in 1986 and ensure I don't place my teenage self in front of a van? That would be the ideal solution as opposed to simply going back to my drab life. But what if it simply ends the program and the computer returns to its normal operation? That would be catastrophic.

I don't know what to do.

"I think you're right about choosing the 'yes' option, Dad, but that would mean returning to the life I had before."

"That's what you wanted wasn't it?"

It's a question I've been avoiding asking myself.

"If you'd asked me three days ago, I was absolutely certain I wanted to go back, no matter what. But if you'd asked me at eight o'clock this morning, I might have answered differently. If I could relive that weekend again I'd have already hit the button. But going back to my previous life, which was a mess, I'm not so sure. And there's the added complication of Stephen and his desire to send me back to Broadhall. I really don't know what to do."

"I think we need to talk this through, son. Act in haste, repent at leisure, as they say."

He walks over to the wall of storage units and opens up a cupboard. He pulls out two foldaway canvas chairs and sets them up in the middle of the floor.

"Sit down, son."

I do as instructed and the old man settles into his chair opposite me. The irony of all ironies — the two of us, once again in a shed, about to have a chat that will have a huge bearing on my future.

"Ignoring this Stephen fellow for a moment, what's changed in the last three days for you to consider staying here?" he asks.

"For starters, there's you," I sigh.

He breaks eye contact as his head drops a little.

"Monday evening in the pub, and everything before and after," I add. "That's the dad I always wanted in my life, but it won't be the dad I'll be going back to."

He fiddles with a loose thread on the sleeve of his jacket. I can only imagine how difficult this subject must be for him.

"I appreciate your honesty, son," he says in a low voice. "But you do realise there is no version of me that's a bad man? There might be a version of me that hasn't seen the light. That day in the shed, I saw the light."

"What are you saying? I go back and tell you, err…him, that he's not my father?"

He winces at my question.

"No," he says quietly. "I wouldn't want to put anyone through that."

"Why not? It worked before."

"You think I never loved you when you were growing up? You think it didn't break my heart when you said you knew, that I wasn't your biological father? Well, I did love you, and your mum, more than anything. And I know I never showed it, but what you said that afternoon in the shed, those words tore right through me."

"Sorry. I didn't realise."

"I'm not blaming you son, I deserved it. My problem was I couldn't let the love rise above my resentment and my anger. I was a stupid man, but a stupid man who loved you both, despite my behaviour. The man you're going back to, he does love you, he just hasn't seen the light yet."

"But you only changed after I threatened to tell Mum I knew."

"You scared the hell out of me, and that's all that changed. You made me realise what I had, and what I risked losing. You can't force somebody to love you, son, it has to be there in the first place. I changed because I wanted to, had to, not because you threatened me."

We both take a moment to quietly reflect on that revelation. I can scarcely believe how candid this version of my father is, and it takes some getting used to. I try to steer the conversation back to more practical matters.

"So what would you say to him then, to get him to change his ways?"

He looks up to the ceiling for a moment, considering my question, I assume.

"Gilbert Fripp," he eventually says.

"Who?"

"Gilbert Fripp, my old schoolmaster. Remember that name. I'll never forget it, that's for damn sure."

"Why?"

"He was a bully. A vindictive, cruel, spiteful man who took pleasure in making my life a misery. He took a cane to my backside more times than I care to remember, for even the most innocuous of reasons. I've never hated anyone as much as I hated Fripp. I had nightmares about the man for years after I left school."

"He sounds horrendous, but why would saying his name prompt a sudden change of attitude in your counterpart?"

"If you compare him to Fripp, he'll understand the true measure of his behaviour. If anyone, even now, said I reminded them of Gilbert Fripp, I'd change my ways in a heartbeat. I'd rather be dead than suffer the knowledge I was continuing that man's legacy."

I nod, as the old man tries to send his memories of Gilbert Fripp back to the recesses of his mind.

"What else has changed then?" he puffs, apparently keen to change the subject. "Surely it can't just be me?"

My turn to look to the ceiling.

"A girl."

"Really? You've only been back in Farndale five minutes."

"It's somebody I knew from my previous life. I worked with her for years and we sort of re-connected, although she doesn't know that, obviously."

"And I'm guessing you've developed feelings for her?"

"I already had feelings for her, just didn't realise it. She's perfect, Dad, and we could have the perfect life here."

"You're going to have to fill in the blanks here, son. Why can't you be with this girl if you go back?"

"Because I'm married to someone else."

"Ahh, yes, my daughter-in-law. Megan isn't it?"

I throw him a quizzical look.

"Your notes. You mentioned her a few times. Something about working in a video store. That's how you met, right?"

"I won't bore you with the details but we married for the wrong reasons. Twenty-five years in a loveless marriage. And for ten of those years, I worked alongside the woman I should have been with."

He shakes his head and tuts under his breath.

"Ever heard of a divorce? People do it all the time I'm led to believe."

"Well, yeah, but I was different back then. I don't think Lucy would have given me a second glance, even if I'd been single."

"Different how?"

"I was a fat, hapless oaf. I think she's only dating me now because I look and act differently."

"Good Lord, you really are an idiot sometimes, son."

"What?"

"This whole mess, it was because you went back in time to change things, right?"

"Yeah."

"You didn't have to go back in time to change the course of your life. You could have confronted my counterpart about the DNA test as soon as you knew. And you could have told this Lucy girl how you really felt about her at any point in the years you worked together. But you did neither. Why is that?"

"Um, I dunno. Fear I suppose. It might have destroyed my friendship with Lucy if I'd said anything. And as poor as our relationship was, I guess it was better than not having a father at all. I thought that if I told you about the DNA test, the secret would be out in the open and our family would fall apart."

"So you assumed the worst would happen in both cases? I know, for sure, I would have changed my ways if you'd confronted me. And the fact you're already serious about the girl suggests there must have been something she saw in you beyond how you look. Besides, if she's that shallow, why would you want to date her in the first place?"

"You're the second person to use the word shallow, this morning."

"Who was the first?"

"Lucy. I made a stupid comment which may have suggested she was shallow. She flipped."

"Like I say, you're an idiot sometimes, son."

He gets up and nudges the chair closer to mine before re-taking his seat.

"Listen, Craig. You wanted to make your life better, I get that. You had this ridiculous opportunity to go back and change all these things that happened in your past, but the one thing that didn't change was you. If you go back to your previous life, you'll still have ample opportunity to talk to me, to your wife, and to this girl of yours. It's never too late."

"You make it sound so easy."

"I never said that. I'm guessing it was hard for you to confront me in the shed that afternoon?"

"Bloody hard, but I only had forty-eight hours to do it. Without that time constraint I doubt it would have happened. I only had one chance."

"And that, son, is where you're going wrong in life. None of us know if today is our last chance. Surely you've learnt that much from all this? You just need to change your mindset and take your chances the moment they arrive. Live for the moment, grasp the nettle."

I am an idiot, but not so much of one I don't know good advice when I hear it.

"And besides," he continues. "Don't you want to see your mum again?"

Of course I do, more than anything. I'm also acutely aware that Megan, Marcus, and twelve innocent coach passengers, are currently residing in a cemetery because of my interference in the past. Then there's Dave. What life did I create for my best friend? I turned him into a paraplegic drunk. I put him in a wheelchair, in a hovel. I took away his future.

I don't have a decision to make. Not really. I have to go back.

It then crosses my mind there will be two women disappointed with my decision when I fail to show up as expected. I can imagine Lucy waiting anxiously for my call later; staring at her watch every five minutes. She'll assume the worst, that I was simply playing her last night. She'll feel foolish, angry, maybe even a little heartbroken. And I can see Brenda tutting repeatedly, and calling me every name under the sun when I don't turn up for work tomorrow.

It's pointless concern for both women. Once I hit the button on the keyboard, our time together over the last ten days will be deleted. Lucy will be just my ex-colleague once more, and Brenda will be somebody I never even met.

Shame. I really like Brenda. I really love Lucy. Maybe it's slightly more than a shame.

But however much it pains me, I don't have a choice. Nor do I have a choice about saying goodbye to the man sat next to me. The man I'm proud to call my dad.

As I contemplate how hard that goodbye is going to be, the shed door swings open.

27

We both twist in our chairs to face the figure stood in the shed doorway. The old man reacts first.

"Father David," he splurts. "What are you doing here?"

The vicar steps into the shed and closes the door behind him. The cheerful, friendly expression he was wearing when I last saw him is no longer present.

"I could ask you the same question, Colin. And who is your guest? He looks familiar."

"Err, this is Craig, my estranged son."

The perturbed look on Father David's face isn't beyond comprehension. He's just walked into his tool shed to find two men sat in deckchairs, with a retro computer set up in front of them. I'm glad I'm not the one who has to explain it to him.

"We were…just, erm," the old man splutters.

"Frankly Colin, my primary concern is not what you two are doing in here. What I want to know is why there's a police car in the car park, and why two officers are currently searching the church grounds?"

The old man looks at me. I look back.

"Shit," we remark in unison.

For an old man with a once-dodgy hip, he moves at remarkable speed. He's up and out of his chair in a second, darting across the shed to the door. He pokes his head out, looks left and right, and then ducks back in.

"Father David, you really need to look at what's happening in the vegetable plot."

Intrigued, the vicar moves towards the doorway as the old man steps back. Once Father David is stood outside, peering down the garden towards the vegetable plot, the old man slams the door shut. A frantic fumbling ensues as he locates the key and locks the door. Realising he's been duped, or possibly underwhelmed by rows of turnips, the vicar starts pummelling the door with his fist.

"Colin, open this door. Now."

"Forgive me Father, for I have sinned," the old man shouts back.

"Damn you, Colin. Open this door," Father David retaliates.

Just for a second it feels like I'm sat in the middle of a Monty Python sketch. The old man quickly brings me back to reality.

"Son, you really need to hit that button. His yelling is going to attract those policemen pretty quickly. That door is solid but it won't stop three of them."

I jump up from the chair, dash across the floor and stand over the computer. The old man decides to ignore the vicar for a moment and joins me.

"So much for your theory on mobile tracking, Dad."

"Maybe, but they might have picked my car up on a camera, or they possibly spoke to Miriam next door. She knows I work here and wouldn't have thought twice about doing her civic duty."

"Guess that's one mystery we'll never solve."

"I don't think it really matters now, son. Well, it won't when you hit that button."

I shuffle awkwardly on the spot for a moment. I've never been one for heartfelt goodbyes. I'm suddenly slapped with a reminder of the old man's earlier advice. I won't get this chance again.

"Thank you, Dad, for everything. I couldn't have done this without you."

"The pleasure was all mine, son. You've made an old man very happy, and very proud."

More fists thump at the shed door, followed by a series of kicks. It appears Father David has uniformed reinforcements.

I throw my arms round the old man. "Love you, Dad," I whisper.

"Love you too," he croaks.

We break apart just as the wood around the door handle begins to splinter.

"Hit it, son. Now."

I take a deep breath and do as I'm told.

The TV screen fades to a vibrant shade of red, yellow text across the centre…

Re-setting Path - Please Wait…

I turn to face the door, my vision already tinged red. Dad casually takes a seat in one of the canvas chairs, his attention on the door. I can imagine the vicar and two policemen on the other side, taking turns to kick, barge and thump.

It only takes three more attempts before the lock finally gives way and the door crashes open. A policeman stumbles in and stops to survey the scene. The other policeman and Father David stand in the doorway, faces confused.

I turn back to Dad, now looking up at me. I can only see his face, my peripheral vision clouded red.

"See you on the other side, son."

I think he might have given me a thumbs up. I can't be sure because a second later, my body starts to pulse and the red canvas engulfs my entire vision.

The pulsing slowly increases towards a crescendo as the red canvas fades into a calming white. For the third, and I hope, the final time, my body is pulled across time. My only concern is where in time this journey will end. Too late now.

The kaleidoscope of indeterminate shapes return and I feel myself falling. I don't focus on the shapes though. I see faces in my minds eye: Mum, Megan, Dave, and finally Lucy. Her face is tear-stained, sad, and my mind dwells on that image. The colourful shapes continue to zip past but they're a mere backdrop to Lucy's face.

It's the last face I see.

It's the last anything I see as everything becomes dark. Everything becomes silent.

Everything then becomes nothing.

28

I think it was a Saturday in 2004 when Dave married Suzy, and we sensibly decided to hold the stag night the Saturday prior. However, Dave was staying at our house the night before the wedding, and we went out for a few beers to toast his last night as a free man.

We rolled in around 3.00am, some eight hours before Dave was due to walk down the aisle.

I remember sitting in the church feeling horrendous. Not so much because of the hangover, more the lack of sleep. At some point during the reading of the vows, I must have nodded off. I don't consciously remember falling asleep but I do remember Megan's elbow in my ribs. I awoke with a start, momentarily confused, unsure where I was and feeling groggy.

I have just gained consciousness in a very similar fashion, although I'm fairly sure I wasn't asleep this time, or elbowed in the ribs. I am sure I'm sat on a chair, and it's quiet.

I squeeze my eyes shut and blink several times. The mist clears to reveal text on a blue screen. The screen belongs to a portable TV which is sat on a desk, behind a Commodore 64. I sniff the air and catch the faint smell of a certain brand of fabric conditioner. For a moment I do nothing other than sit motionless, reflecting on the events that have returned me to this chair.

It couldn't have been more than a minute that separated my inexplicable journey and an undetermined period of detention back at Broadhall. If it were not for the old man's quick thinking in locking Father David outside the shed, I wouldn't have had that precious minute. The finest of margins between success and failure, between hope and despair.

I inhale a deep breath and slowly exhale, partly to clear my head but mainly to ease the adrenalin still present in my bloodstream. The sense of relief is still palpable. I can only hope that relief isn't short lived because although I'm know *where* I am, I'm not yet entirely sure *when* I am.

I do know I'm not naked though, which is a huge relief. Nor am I suffering the crippling headache I awoke to after my previous journeys through time. I don't know why this journey was different. Maybe it's because this is just a re-set back to how things should be. I can only guess.

I lean forward and inspect the text on the screen. As I do, I'm suddenly aware of my bloated stomach in the way. I look down at it, and my chunky thighs. I'm a fat man again. I let out a groan and turn my attention back to the text on the screen.

The word, READY, and a blinking cursor — exactly what I'd expect to see on a run-of-the-mill Commodore 64. No mention of paths: corrupted, restored, or otherwise. I feel something in my pocket digging into my vast gut. I sit back, shove my hand into my pocket and pull out an iPhone. I unlock the screen and check the date — Thursday 14th July 2016. The exact date I began my eleven-month journey. It's a revelation that summons mixed emotions. A part of me hoped I'd be sent back to 1986, or at least back to the moment I left this bedroom. Still, at least I no longer have to worry about Stephen, or the prospect of being sent back to Broadhall. Stephen Ferguson will never see my name on a case file.

Although I'll never be able to tell him, the old man's theory about the re-setting of the path was correct. It appears I'm back where I started. I am Craig Pelling again. Fat, unemployed, unhappily married. But I'm not quite the same Craig Pelling who was plucked from this chair eleven months ago. Like the teenage kid who was struck by a van in 1986, that version of Craig Pelling is dead, metaphorically.

I clamber to my feet and receive a sharp reminder of what it's like to carry six stone of excess blubber. That's the first item on my to-do list, albeit a long-term task. I take a few seconds to adjust to my ponderous body. It definitely has to go.

I wander over to the window to get some air and try and clear the residue grogginess. The old man's garden is a sorry sight. I may be a new man but my horticultural skills almost certainly haven't improved sufficiently enough to rescue the garden. Minutes pass as I take deep lungfuls of air. A dog starts barking a few doors down, but there's no reaction in my head, no anxiety. Maybe it's a consolation prize from my time at Broadhall, or maybe I just have more important things to concern myself with.

I close the window and return my attention to the to-do list. I sit on the edge of my teenage bed and open the notes app on my phone.

For the next fifteen minutes I work on my plan of action. Who I need to talk to, what I need to say. Buoyed by the old man's advice, I'm determined to grasp the nettle and confront every problem I had when I left this room for 1986; the problems still waiting for me beyond the door. They may be the same but I'm not. I don't need a return visit to the past in order to change my future. I can, and I will do that today.

The first item on my list is the one I'm relishing the most. I get up from the bed and leave my teenage bedroom.

I lumber down the stairs, the fog of cigarette smoke no longer a feature in my parent's home. The door to the lounge is closed and I stand for a moment, clutching the handle. It's going to be a challenge to keep my emotions in check but as far as my parents are concerned, I've been upstairs for less than an hour. As much as I might want to, I can't steam in there like I've just returned from a six-month tour of duty.

I open the door and step into the sitting room.

Both parents are still sat in their wingback chairs. The old man peers at me over the top of his ever-present newspaper but quickly returns his attention to the page. Mum, dreamily gazing out of the window, turns and looks up at me.

"Everything sorted, sweetheart?"

As much as I want to dash across the room and scoop my dear old mum into my arms, I don't. Instead, I slowly pad over to her, plant a kiss on her forehead and kneel down next to her chair. It's no mean feat, lowering my bulky frame onto knees that creak in complaint.

"Nearly there, Mum," I smile.

I reach across and take her hands in mine. She looks at me, wide-eyed and curious, but doesn't resist.

"I was thinking Mum, how would you like to go out for lunch on Sunday, maybe go for a drive in the country afterwards? My treat."

Her face lights up. "That would be lovely. Thank you, sweetheart."

"Brilliant. I'll book us a table, somewhere nice."

I lean across and kiss her on the cheek, lingering long enough to inhale the familiar and comforting scent of her perfume. She gives my hands a squeeze as I get back to my feet.

I take a few steps back, and look down on her as she returns her attention to life beyond the window. It's a sight that fills me with shame. Is this really the life I let her live? Married to a tyrant and blessed with a son who was rarely arsed to call, or just pop round for a cup of tea once or twice a week. As ecstatic as I may be about seeing my mum again, I now know what darkness lies behind those eyes. I also know I haven't brought much light to her life in recent years.

I wonder if she considered taking her own life when my grandparents died, as they did twenty-two years ago. Maybe it was just my presence in her life that stopped her falling over the edge. I saved her, or maybe I condemned her to this. What happened to the bubbly mother who served toasted crumpets and homemade Battenburg? I wonder how much of that woman is still in there, and how much I can salvage. I don't know, but I do know I'm going to try my damnedest to help her enjoy her twilight years.

One parent down, one more challenging parent to go.

I step across the room and stand a few feet in front of the old man.

"Dad, you mind if we go outside and have a quick chat?"

He lowers his newspaper and stares up at me, his blue eyes cold and his expression stony. It's scarcely believable this is the same man I was hugging half-an-hour ago. I swallow down hard as I try to keep my inherent fear of this old man in check.

"You can ask me a dozen times, my answer won't change," he snaps. "I'm not lending you any money, boy,"

He lifts the paper back to his face. Conversation over.

"I don't want your money, Dad. I need to talk to you about something. It's important."

The paper is forcibly returned to his lap, his frustration obvious.

"Not interested. Shouldn't you be at the job centre or something, rather than bothering me?"

It would be so easy to just walk away at this point. Maybe he's beyond redemption and I just have to accept he'll never change. I look over at Mum and recall the words of the old man's counterpart. For Mum's sake as much as mine, I have to confront him. I go with a different tact.

"Dad, either you get up and talk to me outside, or I'll pick you up and carry you out there. Your choice."

"Ha," he scoffs. "I'd like to see you bloody-well try, boy."

I take two steps forward and lean over him. "I'd like to see you bloody-well stop me, old man."

I keep my expression dead-pan. I don't want him to see any sign of weakness or doubt. I want him to believe I'll carry out my threat.

He mumbles something under his breath and folds his paper away. Perhaps it's a sign of defiance, or a petty attempt to retain some control, but he moves at a deliberately slow pace as he clambers to his feet. If he's going to comply, it will be on his terms it seems.

"You better not be wasting my time, boy."

I lead him slowly through the kitchen and out the back door into the garden. He painfully lowers himself into a chair, positioned next to a small bistro table on the patio, and I take a seat opposite. The old man stares blankly at the table, avoiding eye contact. Or maybe it's because he's unable to look at the sad garden beyond my shoulder. It must be a constant reminder of his deteriorating mobility.

"Right. Get on with it, boy," he barks impatiently.

"Saturday afternoon," I calmly declare.

"What?"

"Saturday afternoon. Any plans?"

"What business is it of yours?"

"Alright, let me put it another way," I say confidently. "On Saturday afternoon we're going down to the pub, and we're going to sit there and drink until we're able to leave as father and son."

"Are you drunk now?" he spits.

"Nope. Stone cold sober."

"I've got better things to do than sit and listen to your whinging all afternoon."

"I won't be whinging. It's just a chance for us to clear the air, get a few things straight between us."

He shakes his head and his perma-frown deepens.

"Have you been reading women's magazines? I have no interest in supping ale while you get all touchy-feely. Grow up, boy."

I was hoping not to use this card but our current conversation is going nowhere.

"Okay. Maybe we could discuss Gilbert Fripp instead? See if we can work out how his tutelage left such a lasting impression on you."

His head snaps back like he's just caught wind of a foul smell.

"What did you say, boy?"

"You heard me. Gilbert Fripp."

"Who told you about Fripp?" he rumbles, his voice low.

"Nobody. I just did a little research to try and understand why you're such a fucking tyrant. From what I understand, this Fripp character was quite the tyrant too. What was he? Your mentor?"

The muscles in his sallow cheeks begin to twitch. If he was capable of storming away from the table, I'm pretty sure he'd already be slamming the back door shut at this point. I've no idea what's going through his mind, but it isn't coming out of his mouth.

"So, Saturday afternoon?" I casually add. "I'll come round about two o'clock?"

He ignores my offer again. "Why did you mention Fripp?" he eventually asks, his voice surprisingly level.

"My research suggests he was a universally despised individual. Cruel, spiteful, vindictive. Sound about right?"

He nods but doesn't expand on my summation.

"Remind you of anyone?"

From nowhere, he thumps his clenched fist onto the table. I appear to have pushed him a little too far.

"Don't ever compare me to that bastard," he yells. "I never beat you with a cane. I never locked you in a cupboard for hours. I never dedicated my life to making yours a misery."

"Well, you're innocent on two of those three charges."

"What the hell is that supposed to mean?"

"Making my life a misery," I snap back. "You think I derived happiness from being ignored by my own dad? Do you think your complete apathy to my wellbeing didn't make me miserable?"

"I did my best," he retorts.

"Fuck off, Dad. You did nothing like your best and you know it."

He grimaces, as if my words physically stung. After my venting, a heavy silence hangs over the table, both of us plotting where we go next. I decide to keep up the pressure and push him into a corner. I throw him a question I would never have dared ask before.

"Simple question, Dad. Do you love me?"

Despite his body being riddled with arthritis, he squirms in his chair like a fidgety toddler.

"Well?"

He would rather stare at his sad garden than look me in the eye, but eventually he mumbles a reply.

"Course I do," he whispers.

It's a breakthrough moment. It's something to work with.

"Good. And despite the fact you don't deserve it, I do love you."

His eyes dart around the table as he scratches his head. This is a man used to conflict, to control. Now he's a man in unchartered territory, way beyond his comfort zone.

"Make it half-two," he mumbles.

"Eh?"

"Saturday. The pub. Come round about half-two. I'll be ready."

"Alright. Half-two it is."

"You're buying the first round, mind," he adds.

The deep lines on his craggy face make it hard to tell, but I think there might be a vague hint of a smile in there somewhere.

"Deal, as long as you promise not to play Slim Whitman on the jukebox."

He snorts a laugh and immediately tries to hide it by forcing his perma-frown back in place. Too late though. I saw a glimpse of the old man who helped me return to 2016. He's in there somewhere, I just need to coax him out.

I decide not to push my luck and get up from my seat. The old man gratefully follows suit.

"Thanks for the chat, Dad."

I offer him my hand. Probably too soon for a hug.

He reaches across and takes my hand. "It's okay, boy."

"Please don't call me boy. I'm forty-six years of age."

"Right, yes."

We break our handshake and return to the sitting room. No further words are exchanged between us. Nothing else needs to be said, for now.

I give Mum a kiss and a long hug. Probably a hug too tight for such a short visit, but a hug that is long overdue. I tell her I love her and give the old man a parting nod, which he returns.

I close the front door behind me and exhale a long breath. The first box on my to-do list can now be checked.

Time to move on to the next.

29

If you leave a car sat stationary almost a year, you're likely to return and find the battery flat. That thought crosses my mind as I waddle across the road to where my crappy red Mazda is parked. It's going to take a little getting used to — the fact that while I've been away for over eleven months, I've only been in my parents' house for a couple of hours. That fact is born-out when I clamber into the Mazda and it spits into life on the first turn of the ignition key.

I exit their road with all the caution of a learner driver, keenly aware my driving skills are a little rusty through lack of use. If I didn't have so much to do for the remainder of the day, I'd be tempted to walk.

After a slow drive, and having twice stalled the car, I reach the outskirts of the town centre and pull into a short-stay car park. I have four tasks to complete and none of them require a visit to the new shopping centre or its expensive multi-story car park.

I park the Mazda and make my way towards the centre of the town. I don't have a specific destination in mind. I'm actually on the lookout for a specific type of establishment. After half-a-mile of laboured walking, I find three of them, all clustered together in the same road. I don't know the difference between the three but one of them has a name I vaguely recognise so I decide to offer them my custom.

I push open a frosted glass door and survey the scene. Three pasty-faced, middle-aged men are sat on stools, staring up at a row of screens that extend along one wall. They pay me no attention as I shuffle past them towards a counter at the rear. There's one man sat at the counter, protected from customers by a thick sheet of glass, much like a bank teller. He looks bored with his job, bored with his life.

I approach him. “Hi. Wonder if you can help me?” I ask.

He lazily turns his head from a digital screen and appears to size me up. I’m sure he can tell I’m a newbie at this.

“Go on,” he sighs.

“I’d like to place a bet.”

He eyes me with contempt, much like a waiter would if you walked into a restaurant and just asked for ‘food’.

“A bet on what exactly?”

“Erm, one of those three-in-one bets, you know, where all three things have to happen to win.”

“It’s called a treble accumulator.”

“Right, yes. One of those, please.”

He shakes his head and picks up a pen.

“What’s the first bet?”

“Donald Trump to win the US presidential election.”

I know for sure that Trump will win the US election three months and twenty-six days from now.

“Right,” he snorts while scribbling on a notepad. “Next one?”

“Sam Allardyce to be the next England manager.”

Despite his reign lasting just one game, I know Allardyce will be appointed England manager in eight days’ time.

“This is a joke, right?”

“No.”

“Okay, your loss mate. Last bet?”

“Angelina Jolie to file for divorce from Brad Pitt within the next three months.”

I rarely take much notice of celebrity news but in just over two months time, news of Miss Jolie's divorce petition will, for some inexplicable reason, be big news.

"You do realise all three of these have to happen for you to win?"

"Yes, I'm aware of that."

"As long as you know. How much do you want to stake?"

"Three hundred quid."

The man starts laughing. I give him the benefit of the doubt and assume it's shock at my apparent recklessness.

"Are you absolutely sure about this, mate?"

"Yes," I snap back. "Do you want to take the bet or not?"

"Alright, calm down. I'll go and check the odds for you. Give me a few minutes."

He gets up from his chair and disappears through a door, still shaking his head and chuckling away. He won't be chuckling when I return in four months time for my winnings. I'm not a gambling man, but it would be amiss of me not to take this opportunity. Maybe if I'd known I'd find myself back where I started, and my final days in 2017 hadn't been quite so crazy, I might have memorised the lottery numbers or researched football results. Still, I'm hopeful a number of my financial problems will be solved simply as a result of watching the news in my room at Broadhall.

The man returns and taps the keyboard below his digital screen.

"The combined odds on a treble accumulator would be 2100 to 1. So, in the event all three bets come in, you'll win about £630,000 with a £300 stake."

I try not to let my excitement show, while also considering if I should invest more of my meagre funds. It quickly dawns on me that I'm actually unemployed and it's going to be months before this bet pays out. Besides, a shade over six hundred grand is more than enough for me to implement my plans for the future.

I hand over my debit card and the man processes my payment before returning a betting slip, and a smirk.

"Good luck."

"Thanks. See you in November," I smile back.

I tuck the slip and my debit card into my wallet. As I turn to leave, one of the three middle-aged patrons clambers off his stool, swears several times and storms out of the betting shop. Clearly he's not a happy man and his demeanour reminds me of someone. I turn back to the man behind the counter.

"Can I make the same bet please?" I ask.

"You wanna bet another three hundred quid on the same treble accumulator?"

"No, just twenty-five quid this time."

The man shakes his head and takes my debit card again. He returns it with another slip and I leave the betting shop. Another box ticked.

I make my way further into the town centre and my next destination. I pass an office building with reflective, smoked-glass windows. For the first time in a long while, I get to see the full horror of my fat body reflected back at me. I pause for a moment and stare at the chubby man. I always used to avoid mirrors, preferring to hide from the reality of how I looked. Not now though, because I know this really isn't me. I know the slim, toned man who I always wanted to be is not so far away. I'm going to keep looking at mirrors until that man looks back at me.

I take a final glance at my fat doppelgänger and continue on my way.

Five minutes later I'm stood outside the MISSO charity shop. I push open the door and make straight for the spherical woman behind the counter.

"Yes, my love? What can I do for you?" Brenda chimes in her thick west country accent.

"Hi. I was wondering how I go about volunteering to work here?"

Brenda eyes me suspiciously. "You're a man."

"Well spotted."

"We don't get many men volunteering here. You are aware we're a miscarriage charity?"

"Yes, I know. My wife suffered a miscarriage. It was a long time ago now, but I've just been made redundant and I thought I could do something worthwhile while I look for another job."

"Oh, I'm sorry to hear that. Do you have any experience of working in a shop?"

"You could say that," I chuckle. "Up until yesterday I was the manager of an electrical store, over on the retail estate."

"Ohh, that's marvellous," she grins. "It'll make a change to have somebody around the place who actually knows what they're doing."

"Well, I'm keen to help," I reply with a smile.

"You need to complete an application form, but I'm sure we can find a space for a fellow with your experience."

Brenda ducks down below the counter to locate an application form. Seconds pass as cupboard doors are opened and slammed shut. Red-faced from her excursion, she resurfaces and slaps an application form on the desk.

"There we go, my love. Fill that in and drop it back to me. I'm Brenda, shop manager."

I offer my hand to Brenda and she reaches across the counter. As she stretches, her flabby arm knocks over a mug, spilling cold tea over the counter.

"Oh, fuckety-bugger," she yells.

Fortunately, my application form absorbs most of the liquid.

"Sorry about that, my love," Brenda says, as she dangles the sodden form by the corner. "I'll get you another one."

She ducks back below the counter in search of another form while I try to suppress my laughter. I don't know how long I'll be able to work here but I do know my life will be better for having Brenda in it.

"Here you go," she grins as she presents me with a dry form.

"Thanks, Brenda."

"You're welcome…what's your name?"

"Craig. Craig Pelling."

"Well, Craig Pelling, I look forward to getting that back, and hopefully working with you."

She carefully reaches across the counter and I take her hand in an uneventful handshake.

"And sorry about my language," Brenda adds. "I don't usually swear like that."

"Right," I reply with a wry smile. "I'm sure you don't."

I say goodbye to Brenda and leave the shop with my application form safely folded in my pocket. Another box ticked.

My third task requires a visit to a place I've frequented before, albeit for a relatively brief period. After a five-minute walk I'm stood in the reception area of the aptly named, Winning Losers Gym. I used to hate this place with a passion. I hated the smell, the sounds, and the fact I had to pay good money to endure an hour of hell twice a week. I hated the slim, fit people who pounded the treadmills, curled weights, and contorted shapes with apparent ease.

But now I realise what I hated more than anything — my naivety.

The one thing I learnt from my time at Broadhall is that there's no secret to losing weight. In fact, it's just number crunching, and the one thing my mind is good at is crunching numbers. I learnt that an average man will burn around 2500 calories a day. Consume more calories than that and you'll put weight on. Conversely, if you eat slightly less and exercise more, it's not hard to drop 1000 calories below that daily threshold. My epiphany came when I read that one pound of fat equates to roughly 3500 calories. So, if I had a deficit of 1000 calories a day, I'd lose at least a couple of pounds every week. And so I did, and suddenly it all made sense.

The problem with my previous experience at Winning Losers Gym is that I had no short-term goals, nor did I understand the numbers. I wanted to lose five or six stone, and I wanted to lose it quickly. Unrealistic and naive. All I really had to do was enter the gym four times a week and burn 400 calories each time. If I'd done that, and made a few changes to my eating habits, I'd have eventually achieved my goal. But when you stand on the scales and see you've only lost three pounds from the eighty-odd you want to lose, it's de-motivating. I gave up and blamed everyone and everything, except myself.

But this time I know different.

A cheerful personal trainer called Gary processes my membership and I decline the offer of a free induction. This time I know what I have to do — there will be no excuses, nor will there be any bacon rolls for a while. I leave the gym with a plastic membership card and a steely determination.

My final destination on this leg of my quest is a fifteen minute walk away. I could probably go back to the car and drive there, but I've got a couple of hours to kill until I have a more pressing matter to deal with once I return home. Besides, the walk there and back will burn a few hundred calories from my daily target.

I stroll away from the town centre towards the retail park on the edge of the town.

30

Next to the drab concrete facade, the fluorescent yellow posters really stand out and are clearly visible as I approach the RolpheTech store. I guess that's the point. While the promise of closing-down sale bargains might appear attractive to passing consumers, I think the posters are a cruel taunt to the people on the other side of the glass. I doubt most customers will give the staff any thought though. As long as they're walking away with a half-price toaster, who cares if the poor soul who served them will be without a job next week?

I enter the store and take a moment to drink in the atmosphere. It's busy with customers and the queues at the tills are longer than I've ever seen them. Vultures picking over the bones of a decaying carcass. It's the only difference between the drab store I walked away from yesterday, well, eleven months ago. But what is truly sad is that I've seen what this place could be like with some investment. I've seen the refurbished version, busy with customers on an average day. I've seen what the future could have held for this store if it wasn't for Marcus Morrison and the greed of the directors.

Sadly, there's not much I can do to change the future of the store itself. But I can make a difference to the staff. To do that, I need to find my old colleague, Geoff Waddock. I make my way towards the most likely place I'll find him, and true to form he's sat on his arse behind the customer services desk.

"Afternoon, Geoff."

"Oh, it's Lord Lucan," he grumbles. "What happened to you yesterday?"

"Long story. Very long actually, but I was escorted off the premises by Marcus before I had a chance to talk to you all."

"Right, so I'm guessing you're joining the rest of us on the dole queue?"

"Afraid so, but I wanted to give you something before you left."

He stares up at me with his default expression; a frown tinged with cynicism and weariness.

"I like you Craig, but if it involves hugging and a tearful goodbye, I'm not interested."

"No," I snigger. "Something to help with your retirement fund. Something that should deliver a better return than your shares."

I pull my wallet out and retrieve one of the betting slips, ensuring I offer Geoff the one with the twenty-five quid wager.

"Here."

He takes the slip and examines it before returning a confused look.

"What's this?"

"It's a bet I made on your behalf. If it comes in, that slip will be worth over fifty grand."

He returns his attention to the slip and reads it again.

"You're kidding me, right," he snorts. "There's more chance of me being the US President than Trump. And as for the other two bets, you're deluded, my friend."

"I thought you might say that, so here's a sweetener. If that slip proves worthless, I'll give you what it would have paid out myself."

"What? Have you lost the plot?"

"Nope, never been saner, and that's official. And if you tell the other staff to make the same bet, I'll give them all double their stake money back if they lose. They can have that in writing if they want."

"I'd get a second opinion if I were you. These bets are crazy, and trust me, bankruptcy is no fun."

"Well, we'll find out in November. Anyway, keep that slip safe and promise me you'll share my offer with the other staff. The Allardyce bet comes in next week so tell them not to hang around."

"Alright, it's your funeral."

Not this time, Geoff.

I shake his hand and we agree to meet up for a beer soon. Likely one of those tenuous plans that neither party will ever instigate. Still, I've done my bit and hopefully Geoff keeps his promise.

Now, there's just one other person I want to see while I'm here.

"Oh, before I go, is Lucy around?"

"No, mate. She phoned in sick. I think she took the news about the store closing quite badly, especially as you ducked telling her."

"Right, thanks for the heads up."

It looks like I've got some serious bridge building to perform later.

I say goodbye to Geoff and make my way towards the doors. Just as I pass the queue of vultures at the tills, a figure steps out from behind a display, blocking my exit.

"Pelling," Marcus barks. "What the hell are you doing here? I thought I told you to stay away."

"Marcus," I smile. "Good to see you alive and kicking again."

"What?"

"Nothing. I'm just leaving so don't go stressing yourself."

"Good," he spits. "But as you're here, you'll be pleased to know I got my bonus this morning. Hefty it was too, after I saved the company thousands of pounds by not paying out your redundancy."

That all-too-familiar smirk returns to his plastic face. I guess he's expecting me to run off with my tail between my legs. It comes as a surprise when I step forward and look him straight in the eye.

"Funny, I was only thinking about you this morning, Marcus."

"What?"

"I was thinking about school, and us growing up on the estate together. You must remember the estate? The skate park, your house in Orchard Gardens?"

"If there's a point to this, Pelling, get on with it."

"Your dad. I only met him once when I dropped off a game you ordered me to lend you, but he left quite an impression."

His smirk dissolves the moment I mention his father.

"He was a narrow-minded, spiteful, obnoxious prick too, wasn't he?"

A crease develops across his pristine forehead and his mouth twitches. For once, he seems unable to find any words.

"You're a chip off the old block, Marcus," I taunt. "I'm sure he's very proud of you."

There's no comeback. Marcus adopts a stunned silence as I shoot him a parting smile. I have no room in my new life for negativity, or for worrying about irrelevant arseholes like Marcus Morrison. I leave RolpheTech for the very last time, my head held high.

The walk back to the car is a challenge for a body so used to being sedentary. I manage it with a combination of resolve and satisfaction. So much accomplished in such a short space of time, but I know I've got bigger mountains to conquer before my head hits the pillow tonight.

I drive home knowing one of those mountains will be on my horizon pretty soon.

As I clamber out of the Mazda, I take a moment to reacquaint myself with the road on which I live. Of course, nothing has changed since I drove away almost five hours ago. Nothing except me, and it's a very different man who unlocks the front door to my marital home.

It feels strange as I wander through the house, a bit like that feeling you get when returning home after a fortnight's holiday. I haven't been on a holiday and I've been away for a lot longer than a fortnight, but the feeling is definitely the same. It is, however, a reassuring comfort to make a coffee and slump down in my favourite armchair. I take a sip of coffee and pull my phone from my pocket. A few jabs at the screen and four rings before a familiar voice answers.

"Alright, mate."

"Alright, Dave."

"What's up?"

Men rarely call one another for an idle chat. There's always a purpose and it's an unwritten rule that once we've established we're both 'alright', we get straight to the point.

"Fancy a beer tomorrow night?" I ask.

"Yeah, sure. Usual place?"

"Yep. Seven-thirty?"

"Yep. Seeya then."

"Cool. How's Suzy?" I ask.

Enquiring about the well-being of a mate's wife is not part of the accepted conversation protocols.

"Same old, same old. Why?"

"No reason, just asking."

"Fucking weirdo. Seeya tomorrow."

Dave hangs up. I smile, with relief more than anything else. Dave's less-than-perfect marriage is still intact, as is his spinal cord. I suspect I won't be going for beers quite as frequently as I once did, so tomorrow will be a final blow-out, and a chance for me to bring Dave up-to-speed on today's events. I doubt he'll really care that much but I'll tell him anyway. I may even ask if he fancies a skiing trip. Or maybe not.

I finish my coffee and revert back to my to-do list. Only two boxes remain unchecked. I dial another number and my call is answered almost immediately.

"I was wondering if you were going to ring."

"Hi Lucy. Sorry, I should have rung earlier but I've been trying to sort a few things out."

"I gathered as much. Marcus took great pleasure in telling us you'd been put on gardening leave."

"Yes, well, at least I'll never have to see his smug face again."

"Guess not," she says flatly.

The line falls silent. I suspect Lucy is still sore with me after the conversation we had on Tuesday. The very conversation in which I told her to go to Brighton. It's clear my bridge building can't be achieved in a phone call.

"I was wondering if I could pop by and see you later?"

"Why?"

"I wanted to have a chat with you about something?"

"I think you said everything you had to say on Tuesday didn't you?"

Yes, she's clearly still pissed with me. I can't say I blame her.

"No I didn't. Look, Lucy, give me half-an-hour tonight and I'll explain why I said what I did."

"Fine," she sighs. "Come by at eight."

"Thanks. I'll see you then. Looking forward to it."

"Whatever."

A stinging end to the call but at least she agreed to see me. I'm going to have my work cut out, that's for sure.

As I tuck my phone back in my pocket, another of my unchecked boxes unlocks the front door. I hear footsteps clack into the kitchen. The fridge door opens, and a few seconds later slams shut. She says something I don't quite catch, but probably includes a few expletives. Was I supposed to get something in for dinner? I prepare my excuses. I probably won't tell her about the time travel, or my being institutionalised for eleven months, worthy excuses as they are.

Megan clacks into the lounge and stands with her hands on her hips, face like thunder.

"For fucks sake Craig," she snaps. "All you had to do was get something in for dinner. Was that too much to squeeze into your busy day?"

"Evening wifey. I've missed you."

And actually, I have.

31

"What?" Megan snaps.

"I said I've missed you."

"Have you been drinking?"

"Nope, not a drop."

I get up from my armchair, pad across the lounge and put my arms around my wife. I feel her body stiffen for a second before she half-heartedly returns my embrace. She probably doesn't want to hug me but her surprise at my rare display of spontaneous affection stifles any objection.

"I'm sorry," I whisper as I pull her tighter to me.

She breaks from my embrace and stares up at me.

"Sorry? What have you done?"

"Can we sit down for a moment and I'll tell you."

"Fine," she sighs. "But keep it brief. I'm going out in a couple of hours."

We perch on opposite ends of the couch as I try to think of the best way to start this conversation. It's a conversation I should have had with Megan years ago, but sat here now, I quickly realise why I've avoided it. The words don't come easy.

"Are you…happy," I splutter. "Honestly?"

Her eyes narrow as she considers my question.

"Why do you ask?"

One of her most infuriating traits is to answer a question by posing one of her own.

"Please, Megan, just tell me. Are you happy?"

A moment of silence and a deep sigh provide a clue to her answer.

"No, not really," she replies, unsurprisingly.

"How long have you been unhappy?"

"I never said I was unhappy, just not happy. And, I don't know, for a while I guess."

Not happy or unhappy. Semantics really. It all boils down to the same thing.

"But someone else is making you happy, aren't they?"

Despite the instant flush of guilt on her face, I guess it's just instinctive to go with a defensive approach, and she does.

"Don't be ridiculous," she snaps. "I don't know what you're talking about."

I shuffle across the couch so we're not talking across a void.

"Megan, I'm not angry, and I'm not looking to lay blame anywhere. If you have found someone else, I understand. Actually, I'd be happy for you. All I ask is for you to be honest with me. We can't go on like this, can we?"

This is where our conversation could go one of two ways. We either descend into a petty argument or Megan comes clean and we move past it. She decides to split the difference.

"Look, I'm not admitting to anything," she mumbles. "But you're right, we can't go on like this."

"Maybe you're not willing to admit anything, but I am. I admit I've been a lousy husband. I admit that we probably got married for the wrong reasons, and I admit that I don't love you as much as you deserve to be loved."

She leans forward and presses the tips of her fingers into her temples. As much as we both know our marriage is broken, sharing the truth still bites. An uneasy silence allows us both to take stock for a few seconds.

Megan eventually turns to face me. "Ditto," she says in a low voice.

For the first time in a long time, we are in agreement on something.

"So what do you propose we do about it?" she asks.

"Depends. If you could look into a crystal ball, would you still want us to be here, like we are, in five years time?"

She doesn't hesitate in shaking her head.

"Me neither. I think we both know there is only one way forward."

Now it all comes down to one of us being brave enough to mention that seven letter word. One word to signify the end of our twenty-five year marriage.

"We've reached the end, haven't we?" I murmur.

"Guess so."

There is no joy, no elation. We've shared three decades of our lives, almost two thirds of the time we've been alive. And no matter how rocky our marriage may have been, the inevitable collapse is not something to celebrate. Despite both of us knowing we're making the right decision, it's impossible not to feel some regret, some lament.

I don't really know what to say now. What is there to say? My pragmatic mind decides to deal with the practicalities rather than the emotions.

"I…err…think I should probably move out then. I can move in with Mum and Dad."

"No, there's no need," she says softly. "I'll move into the spare room. I wouldn't condemn my worst enemy to a house-share with your father."

We both find a smile from somewhere.

"Thank you. I'll contact an estate agent tomorrow and get the house on the market. Assuming that's what you want?"

"Actually, no, it isn't."

"Oh, what then?"

"I'd prefer to buy you out, if you're okay with that?"

"How will you get the money together?"

"I'll re-mortgage. I earn enough, and Mum and Dad will help if I need it."

"Right. Sounds like you've already given it some thought."

"To be honest, Craig, I thought about it last night, when you suggested re-mortgaging to raise funds for your new business venture. I was going to say something then, but, guess I just didn't have the bottle."

That would explain why she was so vehemently against the idea of us re-mortgaging together. To think, if she had made this offer last night, I might not have gone to my parents earlier to beg for money. And I might not have bothered clearing out my bedroom, and the trip back to 1986 might never have happened. One moment. One decision.

"So you're happy to pay me half the value of the house? No need for lawyers?" I ask.

"Yes, of course, it's only fair. And no need for lawyers, definitely not."

And with the practicalities sorted, that is that. Years of avoiding it but a conversation barely ten minutes from start to end. I can't help but feel annoyed with myself for wasting so many years, and I suspect Megan feels the same.

I get up from the couch and Megan follows my lead.

"Can I ask you a question?" she says.

"Sure."

"Why now? We've bumbled along like this for years and you suddenly decide to do something about it. I'm not questioning your motives, just curious I suppose. You have to admit it's a bit out of the blue."

"The reason? My parents."

"I'm not with you."

"I went round to see them earlier."

"And?"

"You know what their relationship is like. Do you think either of them is happy?"

"I'd say they're the opposite of happy."

"Precisely. But neither of them has made any effort to address their problems. Maybe their marriage is beyond fixing, who knows. What I do know is that I don't want to wake up in thirty years time and discover we've become my parents."

"Right. Fair point."

"And I'm guessing you don't want that either?"

She grimaces and shakes her head.

"So, for better or for worse, this is the right decision. I think we both know that."

We stand, facing one another, both trying to find words that might do justice to the finality of the moment. There aren't any, not really. Megan steps forward, places her hand on my arm and plants a kiss on my cheek.

"Thank you," she says softly.

"For what?"

"For making this as painless at it could possibly be. Not many husbands would have been so…reasonable."

"I just want you to be happy, Megan."

And I genuinely mean that. Without me, Megan might one day live that life I envisaged for her while I lay on my bed at Broadhall. She could marry the right man and together they could adopt a couple of kids.

Maybe that big house with a farmhouse-style kitchen isn't beyond the realms of possibility. I hope it's not.

As for my own future, that's still very much in the balance.

Megan flashes a weak smile and clacks out of the room. I slump back into my armchair and let the relief wash over me. I've imagined the conversation we just had hundreds of times. Not once did I imagine we would behave like adults and calmly discuss our problems, let alone reach an amicable agreement. All those years of hiding away from the problems in our marriage, wasted. I might feel relieved but it comes served with a side order of annoyance.

With little appetite, I head into the kitchen and force down a bowl of cereal. Keen to keep the peace with Megan, I wash up my bowl before I head upstairs for a shower.

Getting undressed in the bathroom is not a pleasurable experience. For the first time in a long while, I get to see all seventeen stone of my naked bulk. I step into the shower and, with my body occupying so much space, it feels claustrophobic. I resentfully lather up my flabby folds and pine for the feel of my slim body, my taut skin and toned muscles. It actually feels like I'm washing a small car but serves as a motivator to get my slim body back again.

Megan does her best to keep out of my way but we pass on the landing and swap uncomfortable smiles. She's already moved her toiletries into the spare bedroom. I don't know how long we can live like this, but for now we'll both have to deal with the awkwardness.

I get dressed, and rather than endure the strange atmosphere in the house, I decide I'll leave early and take a slow walk to Lucy's. Beyond the fact it's still pleasant outside, I may need to partake of some alcohol to put a tick in my final box of the day.

I leave the house and begin my slow saunter to Partridge Lane.

Inevitably, it doesn't take long for my mind to drift towards the subject of my impending divorce. It still doesn't quite seem real — I'm going to be divorced soon. My twenty-five year marriage will be over. Finished. Terminated. I know plenty of people who've been through a divorce but I never imagined I'd one day join their ranks. It's always been Craig and Megan. It's always been *us* and *we*. But very soon, and for the first time in our adult lives, it will become *I* and *me*. I know we're doing the right thing but you can't just turn a relationship off, like a tap. It's going to keep dripping away for a while, I suspect.

I push my thoughts towards the practical aspects. I don't know how long it takes for a re-mortgage to go through but I'd imagine it'll take at least a few weeks for Megan to sort out her finances and to complete all the legal paperwork. It's just a guess but that would take me to mid-August, and about three months before my bet pays out. It looks like I will have to rent somewhere in the short term. It might be dead money but it's a drop in the ocean compared to my impending windfall. I'll live with it.

With my thoughts elsewhere I pay little attention to my journey, and before I know it, I'm plodding down Partridge Lane towards Lucy's cottage. Only now does it strike me that maybe I should have invested some of my attention in deciding what I'm going to say to Lucy. Too late now but maybe that's no bad thing. Perhaps for once in my life I might be better off letting my heart lead my head.

I'll soon discover if that's a good call, or not.

32

Lucy's garden and front door look no different to how they looked yesterday, or how they'll look in eleven months time for that matter. I skirt up the path and rap the knocker, feeling more nervous than I did yesterday when I was greeted by a woman who I hoped to have sex with. I don't think there will be much sex on the agenda this evening. Actually, putting the presumption aside, I'm not sure I even want to have sex with Lucy in my current form.

Lucy opens the door and grunts a half-hearted greeting before she turns to walk away. Not the welcome I was hoping for. I follow her into her poky kitchen at the back of the house. It's a far cry from the stunning, open-plan kitchen I sat in yesterday.

"Coffee, or wine?"

"Wine, please."

She pulls a glass from a cupboard that looks like it was installed during Thatcher's tenure. There's already a half-full glass on the side, next to an open bottle of Pinot Grigio. She fills the glass and hands it to me before plucking her own up.

"Cheers," she says, with little enthusiasm.

I raise my glass a few inches, and take a mouthful of the tepid wine. I watch Lucy as she mirrors my actions. Her look this evening is the polar opposite of last night's. No skimpy summer dress, just jeans and a light-grey sweatshirt. Her auburn hair is tied into a loose ponytail and I don't think she's applied any makeup. She still looks every bit as beautiful though.

She doesn't waste any time in getting to the point.

"I don't want to appear rude, Craig, but I've got a lot to do this evening. What is it you wanted to chat about?"

It's clear from the boxes and piles of newspaper scattered around the kitchen that Lucy has already started packing for her move. Maybe I've left it too late. Now I'm stood here, I feel significantly less confident, especially in this body.

"Um, sure. About Brighton."

"What about it?"

"You're definitely going?"

"I've already accepted an offer for the house, and as you can see, packing is underway."

"Right."

I take another large gulp of wine, hoping to bolster my ailing confidence.

"And you definitely think it's the right thing to do?"

She opens a cupboard and starts pulling out random items of kitchenware.

"Who knows, but there's not much worth staying in Farndale for."

Say it Craig. Just say it.

"There's me."

She snatches a Pyrex jug and lays it on the pile of newspapers. Plenty of aggressive wrapping but not much in the way of a reply.

"Did you hear what I said, Lucy?"

"I heard you."

"And?"

She lets out a sigh and deposits the newspaper-cocooned jug into a box.

She turns to face me. "No offence, but I'm not sure my friendship with a colleague, sorry, *former* colleague, is reason enough to stay."

No amount of Pinot Grigio is going to help me here. I only have one last card to play before I admit defeat.

"Even if that former colleague really cares about you?"

Lucy starts to chuckle away to herself. It quickly develops into a belly laugh.

"Oh, Craig," she says between peals of laughter. "You're priceless. You *care* about me? Like a pet hamster? How quaint."

Not the reaction I expected. I don't know what to say, and I certainly don't know how I'm supposed to react.

"Sorry, this was a mistake. I'll leave you to your packing."

The laughter stops in a heartbeat, and her face takes on a red hue. I'm guessing I chose the wrong reaction.

"Fuck you, Craig," she snaps. "How dare you turn up here, screw with my head and then run away."

"Look, Lucy. Can we just pretend this never happened? I'm sorry if I offended or upset you."

Her face is now crimson. "Which one are you apologising for? Upsetting me or offending me?"

"Eh? Um, both."

"You don't know if I'm offended or upset?" she says, her voice dripping with indignation.

I stare at the floor. I don't know how to answer her without upsetting her further. Or offending her. Or both. Who fucking knows? Clearly I don't.

"See, that's your problem, isn't it?" she snipes. "Craig Pelling — the man who can't see the obvious."

What is obvious, even to an idiot like me, is that Lucy is close to tears. If I had to commit, I'd wager she's upset.

"Okay, before I do or say anything else that either offends or upsets you, can you clarify what you mean by that?"

A plump tear rolls down her cheek.

"Tuesday," she sniffles. "I asked you if you thought I was doing the right thing, moving to Brighton."

Oh, shit.

"And you said it was."

"Yeah, but I only said that because I knew you were going to be made redundant."

"You're a bloody idiot."

Why do people keep calling me an idiot?

"What? Why?"

"Do you really think I gave a damn about my job?"

"Err, I don't know."

"I wanted you to tell me to stay. I wanted you to beg me to stay."

"Ohh."

"But you didn't. You let me walk out of that office with the impression you couldn't have cared less."

"Sorry."

"Do you have any idea how much that hurt?"

"A lot, I guess."

"Yes, a lot. And do you know why?"

A void develops in my head, and a penny teeters on an edge, ready to drop through that void. It doesn't, and I stand with my mouth agape while I wait for an answer to come.

Lucy jumps on my indecision. "You see my point? You don't know why, do you?"

Seconds pass and the penny wobbles but steadfastly refuses to drop.

"Um, err…"

Lucy throws her arms in the air. "Un-fucking-believable."

Clink.

"Are you saying," I gulp, "what I think you're saying?"

"Yes, you stupid, stupid man. I'm in love with you, okay? How the hell could you not see that?"

A few quids worth of pennies drop through the void.

"Christ. Really?"

"Yes. Really."

I feel like I should don a dunce's cap and stand in the corner for a while.

"I honestly didn't know, Lucy."

"Well now you do. And if you don't mind, I've got packing to get on with."

She returns her attention back to the pile of newspaper.

"But…"

"But nothing, Craig," she interjects. "Clearly it's not mutual."

How could I have been so monumentally stupid? All that time, and not only did I ignore my own feelings for Lucy, I totally failed to recognise how she felt about me. I *am* an idiot. A twenty-four karat idiot.

"It is mutual, Lucy. Totally. I…I love you too."

She stops wrapping and stares up at the ceiling.

"Well, that's just great," she sighs. "You love me, I love you. You're married, and I'm going to live in Brighton. How's that for a happy ending, folks?"

"I'm..not married," I stammer. "Least I won't be soon. We're getting divorced."

She turns and faces me. "What?"

"I talked to Megan and we've decided to get a divorce."

"Really? You never said anything. When did this happen?"

"About two hours ago."

"Oh. Should I offer congratulations or commiserations?"

"Both, I suppose. But it's what I want."

It feels like an appropriate moment to reflect, and we both take a silent moment to gulp down the content of our wine glasses.

"I didn't imagine it would be like this," Lucy says as she refills our glasses.

"What do you mean?"

"I imagined some romantic scene where you confess your undying love for me. You know, all hearts and flowers, soft light and violins."

"You've actually thought about it?"

"Course I have. I didn't imagine we'd be stood in my kitchen, me looking like shit while knee-deep in newspaper and boxes."

"You don't," I chuckle. "Look like shit, I mean. You look the absolute opposite of shit."

"Gee, you really know how to woo a girl don't you? I'm sure there was a compliment in there somewhere."

"Sorry, I'm just not very good at all this."

"You don't say," she sniggers, but her smile quickly fades.

We both know there is still a sizable elephant sat in the corner of the kitchen — Brighton. While I'm clearly not blessed with the ability to recognise or articulate emotions, I can at least try to address the practicalities of our situation.

"So, Brighton?"

"Yes, Brighton," Lucy replies.

"Can I ask, do you really want to go?"

"I never really wanted to go, if I'm honest."

"So, stay then."

"You know the reasons why it's more complicated than that."

I probably *did* know the reasons. However, what with the eleven months' detour I took between Tuesday's conversation and now, they've kind of slipped my mind.

"Shall we just recap the issues, just so I'm clear?"

"You don't remember?"

"I may have been a little distracted when you told me."

"Fine," she groans while rolling her eyes. "My sister has bought the house next door to her hotel. There's a detached annexe building in the garden of that house which I'm going to buy. My sister will use that money to pay for the renovations on the main house. Got it?"

"Okay, understood."

"So, if I don't sell this place and buy the annexe, she won't have the money to do those renovations."

"Right."

"And I'll be dropping her right in it."

"Can't she get a bank loan?"

"That's the real bitch. The bank will lend her the money, but only once the house is renovated and she's doubled the hotel's occupancy."

"Really?"

"Yep. It's a crazy catch-twenty-two situation, so you see why she needs my money."

"How much does she need."

"Ninety grand."

"So let me get this right. She needs ninety grand for a few months in order to renovate the house, and then she can get a bank loan once those renovations are complete?"

"In a nutshell, yes."

"And what about the job offer that came with the annexe?"

"I think maybe that was just a token offer; a sweetener to convince me to move down there. Claire is more than capable of running the place, with or without my assistance."

"So it's just your money she really wants?"

"When you put it like that, I guess it is."

Perhaps the Gods have finished shitting on me, and are now smiling down.

"I'll lend her the money."

"Really? Where will you get that sort of money from?"

"Megan wants to buy my share of the house, so I'll have at least ninety grand in the bank in a few weeks time."

"I can't ask you to do that, Craig."

Now is your chance Craig. Prove to her how much you want this.

I step towards Lucy and take her hands in mine. Strange really, I've already gone a lot further than hand-holding with Lucy, but for this version, it's the first time I've ever shown her any physical affection.

"I'd give away my last penny if it meant there was a chance of us having a future together."

She stands motionless, almost dazed by my confession. "Do you actually mean that?" she squeaks.

"More than I've ever meant anything."

Lucy suddenly darts forwards and throws her arms around me, all seventeen stone of me. I try not to flinch. How can this beautiful creature not be repulsed by my flabby body? She eventually releases her hold on me and we stand, facing one another.

“I don’t wish to ruin the moment, Lucy, but there’s one minor issue I need to resolve. If I lend your sister the money, it sort of removes my funds for renting somewhere to live.”

“I think I can help you with that,” she replies with a grin.

“How so?”

“Perhaps in a week or two, we might be able to find a space for you upstairs. You know, once the dust has settled.”

“You sure?”

“Totally. I think we’ve wasted enough time, don’t you?” she whispers, just before she leans in and kisses me gently.

Our first kiss. Well, sort of.

“But I too have a minor issue to resolve,” she adds as our lips part.

“What’s that?”

“A small thing called a job.”

Suddenly a picture of Lucy, stood behind a desk at Senior Connections, drifts into my mind.

“You could work for yourself. Start your own business. That’s what I’m planning to do.”

“Funny you should say that. I’ve been kicking this idea around for a few years but, and you’re going to think I’m a soppy cow, I didn’t want to leave RolpheTech because I got to see you every day. Now, seeing as that’s no longer a problem…”

“Go for it. Whatever it is, I know you’ll be a success.”

It’s not just rhetoric, I know for sure it will be a success.

We seal the deal with another kiss; a long lingering kiss, a decade in the making.

"Can I abandon the packing now then?" she asks.

"Absolutely."

"Thank fuck for that. It's tedious."

We laugh, and kiss again.

"And does this mean…"

"Yes it does."

"You sure?"

"Positive."

"Craig and Lucy," she purrs. "A couple. Boyfriend and girlfriend. I like that."

"Me too."

SEVEN MONTHS LATER...

33

"Next please," the young sales assistant calls out.

Miles away, my head snaps up, and I'm beckoned forward with a smile. I place a pair of jeans on the counter.

"Have you got these in a thirty-two-inch waist?"

"I'll ask one of my colleagues to take a look. Give me a moment."

She disappears and I return to my daydreaming. Two slender arms appear from nowhere and encircle my waist from behind.

"How's it going?" a voice whispers in my ear.

"Nearly there. Just need another pair of jeans."

"Good. If you don't mind, I'm going to go and look at some shoes. Shall I meet you downstairs in the coffee shop?"

I twist around and plant a kiss on Lucy's forehead.

"Sure. See you in three days."

She looks up at me with those opal-green eyes and strokes my cheek.

"Maybe just the two days," she giggles. "Love you."

She spins around and I watch her as she skips off to the shoe department. Bless her for not putting me through that nightmare.

"One pair of jeans. Thirty-two-inch waist," the shop assistant says.

I turn back to her and hand over my debit card. I don't know the price, nor do I really care. She drops the jeans into a carrier bag and I add it to my burgeoning collection. Clothes shopping, done and dusted.

I vowed I wouldn't replace my wardrobe until I reached the same weight I was the day I walked out of

Broadhall. It's been a slog, trying to juggle my hectic life with visits to the gym and eating the right things at the right time, but I've done it. Just as well, as my previous clothes now hang off my slender frame. Still, it's a great motivator to put on a pair of baggy jeans and reach the last hole at the right end of my belt.

I gather up my bags and head out of the department store.

I avoid the escalator and make my way down the stairs to the ground floor of the shopping centre. It's mid-afternoon on a Thursday so the coffee shop is quiet. I order an Americano and slump down on a couch next to the window. I sit and listen to the piped music, thinking of nothing and gazing mindlessly at the drones beyond the glass, buzzing between the shops.

"Craig," a voice shouts from behind the counter.

I make my way over, grab my cup and return to the couch. I don't know how long Lucy will be, but I'm happy just to sit here and sip coffee in relative peace. I still don't enjoy shopping — it still tests my patience.

I stretch my legs out and enjoy this rare moment of doing nothing. For the last seven months my life has been frenetic. Actually, my life has been pretty crazy for the last eighteen months if you include my eleven month sabbatical in the future, some of which is still yet to happen. Oh, and that weekend in 1986. How could I forget?

What I really yearn for now is normality. Not mundane, just something close to normal.

On the domestic front, Lucy and I are getting there. I moved into the cottage three weeks after our heart-to-heart, and having lived with Megan for so long, it took a while to adjust to Lucy's way of doing things. Maybe it was tougher for her as she wasn't used to sharing her home with another adult. She is pretty independent and for a while I felt like a spare part. I don't mean that in a negative way, it's actually quite nice not having to think about meals or constantly repair wardrobe doors. And while Megan hated cooking, Lucy has a real passion for it and the kitchen is very much her domain. However, when I first moved in I did surreptitiously conduct a thorough search of her kitchen cupboards. I didn't find any extract of anchovy but better to be safe than sorry.

The toughest challenge in living with Lucy was not adapting to Lucy herself, it was adapting to life with her teenage daughter. Grace is fourteen, going on twenty-one. She's smart, quick-witted, and like her mother, fiercely independent. My initial attempts to connect with her through the medium of music were quickly thwarted when she made it clear my taste in music is beyond lame. Seeing as I know nothing about fashion, makeup, or teenage boys, her three favourite things, I had to seek other common ground. Thankfully, I discovered that we do share a similar sense of humour. I'm still lame, but at least I'm funny with it, and Grace now seems happy to accept me as part of the furniture.

Although I eventually integrated myself into life at the cottage, I did still feel a bit like a lodger. So, when my bet finally paid out in November, one of the first cheques I wrote was to Lucy, as payment for a half-share in our home. It is now our cottage, and she's already invested some of her windfall by putting a deposit down with a builder to remodel the kitchen and dining room. I've already sat in it, despite the fact work doesn't actually start until next month. She'll be delighted with the finished product, I'm sure.

And true to her word, Lucy's sister returned my loan within three weeks of completing the work on her hotel.

So now I own half a cottage and I've still got over four hundred grand in the bank. Whatever worries I might have in the future, I doubt they'll be of the financial kind.

Speaking of finances, this month marks the official launch of Pelling IT Solutions. As soon as Claire repaid my loan, I belatedly signed up for the franchise I'd been struggling to finance before. And having undergone a three-month induction which involved being trained and tested until my brain ached, I am now qualified to offer tech support to local businesses. I've already got a couple of clients on board, and while it's early days, I'm genuinely excited at the prospect of running my own business.

The offices of Pelling IT Solutions are situated in a building on Victoria Road. Conveniently, my new business is located in an office right next door to Senior Connections — Lucy's new venture. She's worked tirelessly to get it up-and-running and despite a few early setbacks, it's now starting to turn a reasonable profit. I'm pretty confident she'll replicate the success of the venture she was running in that fractured timeline I deleted.

While my personal and professional lives have been demanding, I have made a conscious effort to spend more time with my parents. They eventually moved into their retirement flat and their quality of life has significantly improved. Mum has joined several of the community groups they run, and she seems to have found a new lease of life. The old man is still the old man, although he has definitely mellowed. Every now and again I see a flash of the father I left behind when I re-set my timeline. The original version is still a work in progress but we're in a much better place than we were seven months ago.

The only setback with my parents came when I told them about my decision to divorce Megan. Mum in particular was disappointed, but perhaps not surprised. Considering the loyalty she's shown my father over the years, I guess I should have expected her less-than-enthusiastic reaction. The old man was slightly more philosophical, especially when he tasted Lucy's Beef Wellington the first time they visited the cottage for lunch. I hope in time they both grow to love Lucy just as much as I do.

The divorce my parents objected to was, in itself, relatively straightforward. I would say it was painless, but in reality it was never going to be. While there was no acrimony, and no lawyers, there were certainly a few tears shed by both of us. The irony is that once you remove all the negativity that festers when you live with someone for so long, what you're left with is two people who simply know each other inside-out. And with all those marital hang ups removed, it's a natural progression into friendship, and that's what I have with Megan now.

In the interests of transparency, it wasn't long after we had our chat in the lounge that Megan admitted she had indeed been seeing a guy from work. For about five months as it turned out. I'd be lying if I said her revelation didn't hurt a little, but I appreciated the honesty. On the plus side, her confession cleared the way for me and Lucy to go public. I decided to tell Megan first and if she was surprised, she certainly didn't show it. It wasn't what I was expecting, but our chat ended with hugs and good wishes, and a fair dollop of relief on both our parts I suspect. Megan eventually rented out our former marital home and moved in with her lover, who is actually now her fiance. It's good to know I didn't totally put her off marriage.

On the whole my life is now where I always hoped it would be. I enjoy a fulfilling relationship with a woman I truly love. I'm fit and healthy. I work for myself and control my own destiny. I live in a lovely house, and I no longer have any financial woes.

All perfect, you'd think.

But while I managed to shed several stones of flab, I continue to carry around a sackful of regrets. I couldn't do anything to help my grandparents, nor could I rescue Aunt Judy from the horrors of her past. Then there's Malcolm and his premature death at the hands of his Thai wife, Mali Surat. By re-setting my timeline, I took away their futures — I fixed the code and then deleted it.

Perhaps their futures were fated? Maybe what happened to them was pure bad luck?

When I wake up in the mornings, I sometimes stare out of the bedroom window at the trees and open fields beyond our garden. I have to pinch myself because I feel like the luckiest guy in the world. I then look across at the woman I now share my bed and my life with, and I know for sure I'm the luckiest guy in the world. But no matter how lucky I might feel, I know luck played no part.

Nor did luck play any part in what happened to my grandparents, Aunt Judy, or Malcolm.

I've thought about everything that happened to me and the people in my life, and I know for sure our lives weren't changed because of luck or fate. Nor were our lives ultimately changed because of the decisions I made. Life is too complex, too unfathomable.

When I was a kid, my grandparents gave me a game for Christmas. It was called Domino Rally and the basic premise of the game was to line up scores of plastic dominoes on their edges. You'd then nudge the first domino and it would tumble into the next one, setting off a chain reaction. Life is like Domino Rally. Once you nudge that first domino, all you can do is sit back and see if it pans out as you hoped.

If I've learnt anything from the last eighteen months, it's that sometimes the dominos fall perfectly, and sometimes they don't. Either way, there isn't anything you can do about it once you nudge that first domino. The only thing you can do is set them up as best you can, and have the courage to nudge that domino in the first place. If it doesn't work, you just have to try again, or concede you're shit at Domino Rally and go play something else.

The same could be said about the decisions we make in life. Sometimes they work out, sometimes they don't. You can dwell on those decisions or you can move on. After my inexplicable journey, I now know that nothing good ever comes from avoiding a tough decision or dwelling on the outcome.

No matter what Professor Lance Gilgrip might have once thought, none of us have corrupted paths, just corrupted attitudes.

A tap on the window drags me back from my reflection. Lucy is stood the other side, clutching a carrier bag in each hand and grinning ear-to-ear. I suspect shares in Jimmy Choo have just spiked. I neck the remnants of my Americano, gather my own collection of carrier bags and join her outside.

"Sorry," Lucy says. "I got a bit carried away."

"Don't worry. I was just reminding myself how nice it is to sit on my arse and do nothing."

She looks up at me and scrunches her face. "You know the trouble with sitting on your arse?"

"No. Do tell."

"I can't see it."

"I'll let you have a look when we get home."

"Promise?"

"Promise."

We make our way up to the tenth floor of the car park and I pull a key fob from my pocket. A press of a button and the lights on the Audi blink on. We deposit our bags into the poor excuse for a boot, open the doors and collapse onto the leather upholstery. I do love our new car but I sort of miss my pug-ugly Mazda. It was like a perennial friend; always there, always reliable. Not the sort of friend you'd go on the pull with, but a friend nonetheless.

I turn the engine on and the stereo illuminates in soft blue light. Lucy reaches across and stabs at the buttons to find a station playing music. We scan past newsreaders, traffic announcers, and a hyperactive DJ. Then, just as she's about to stab another button, I recognise the start of a song I haven't heard in a while.

"Leave it on that station, honey."

The opening verse to Rockwell's 'Somebody's Watching Me' rings out from the car speakers. I can't help at chuckle at the serendipity — it's the same track that was playing on the radio when I drove to RolpheTech for my first meeting with Marcus. That moment feels an absolute lifetime ago.

"What's so funny?" Lucy asks.

"This song. It reminds me of somebody."

"Who?"

"Oh, just somebody I used to know. He's not around anymore — he went travelling, never came back."

"Does this somebody have a name?"

I can't tell her I'm referring to myself. I pluck a name from nowhere.

"My uncle. Uncle Bungle."

Before You Go...

If you enjoyed reading this book and have a few minutes spare, I would be eternally grateful if you could leave a review on Amazon. If you're feeling particularly generous, a mention on Facebook or a Tweet would be equally appreciated. I know it's a pain but for indie authors like me, it's the only way we can compete with the big publishing houses.

For more information about me and to sign up for updates on new releases, visit my website...

www.keithapearson.co.uk

Printed in Great Britain
by Amazon

39986658R00184